Resounding p ... **JORDAN DANE**

"A fabulous new voice."
New York Times **bestselling author Cindy Gerard**

"Her novels are twenty-first-century *noir* with guts and heart and a wicked sense of humor."
Jonathan Maberry, multiple Bram Stoker Award-winning author of *Patient Zero*

"Dane's smooth style, believable characters, and intense pacing will remind readers of Lisa Jackson, Lisa Gardner, and Tami Hoag. . . . Her tight plotting and male characters are exceptional, bad guys and good."
Publishers Weekly

"Jordan Dane will make you think twice before you ever walk alone in the dark again."
Robin Burcell, award-winning author of *The Bone Chamber*

"Thrills and chills that blend beautifully with human pathos and emotions. A wonderful author who sets you up on a roller coaster, rising, falling, twisting."
New York Times **bestselling author Heather Graham**

"Jordan Dane will wring your emotions dry as she takes you on a wild ride . . ."
USA Today **bestselling author Merline Lovelace**

"Non-stop action, hold-your-breath suspense, terrific characters . . . what more could you ask? I cannot wait to have the next Jordan Dane in my hot little hands."
Mariah Stewart

By Jordan Dane

RECKONING FOR THE DEAD
THE ECHO OF VIOLENCE
THE WRONG SIDE OF DEAD
EVIL WITHOUT A FACE
NO ONE LIVES FOREVER
NO ONE LEFT TO TELL
NO ONE HEARD HER SCREAM

JORDAN DANE

Reckoning for the Dead

A SWEET JUSTICE NOVEL

HARPER

An Imprint of HarperCollinsPublishers

This is a work of fiction. Names, characters, places, and incidents are products of the author's imagination or are used fictitiously and are not to be construed as real. Any resemblance to actual events, locales, organizations, or persons, living or dead, is entirely coincidental.

HARPER

An Imprint of HarperCollins*Publishers*
10 East 53rd Street
New York, New York 10022-5299

Copyright © 2011 by Cosas Finas, LLC
ISBN 978-0-06-196969-0

First Harper mass market printing: October 2011

Printed in the United States of America

Visit Harper paperbacks on the World Wide Web at
www.harpercollins.com

10 9 8 7 6 5 4 3 2 1

To my uncles and aunts—
Loren, Beth, Larry, Joyce, and Lorena.
Laughter is like taking a vacation
without returning home ten pounds heavier.

ACKNOWLEDGMENTS

In this fourth book of the Sweet Justice series, I was influenced by the escalating violence along the United States/Mexican border. And after researching how the drug cartels work through the gangs on the U.S. side, I had to write a story to shed light on that. Covert operative Alexa Marlowe goes off the grid when her former lover and boss, Garrett Wheeler, goes missing under mysterious circumstances and is suddenly replaced by someone she doesn't trust. And when surprising DNA evidence surfaces on an old cold-case murder in Wisconsin, Jessie Beckett learns more about her already frightening past as her relationship with Seth Harper deepens. Will Jessie let Seth into her life enough to help her through the ordeal? I love writing about strong women and the men who love them. As a writer, it's my job to throw roadblocks in their way even though I feel bad when I do so. The characters in this series have become very dear friends. And I feel blessed to have them be a part of me.

And speaking of blessed, I'm fortunate to have friends and family who bring joy to my life. My dear husband constantly surprises me with the many ways he supports my work. And my parents have always nurtured each of their children in unique ways. I'm truly blessed to have them. And my weapons wizard, Joe Collins, is a real-life hero that I'm lucky to have as a friend.

Special thanks to my amazing editor, Lucia Macro. Your collaboration is remarkable. As always, you bring everything together and make it fun. And thanks to all the staff at Avon Books who played a part in this project, with special recognition to my agent, Meredith Bernstein. I'm so happy to have you in my life.

And finally I want to express my profound gratitude to my readers. I love hearing from you through my Web site at *www.JordanDane.com*. Except for the many voices I hear in my head, writing is a solitary activity, but finishing a book is only part of the equation. The most important part is for you to read the book and take a journey with me. You complete my creative circle, and I'm especially grateful for all of you who have been following this series and enjoying my books. The passion I feel for writing is made richer by your continued and cherished support.

Reckoning for the Dead

CHAPTER 1

El Paso, Texas
Nearly midnight

After he'd sent a text message on his cell phone, twelve-year-old Ruben de los Santos did as he'd been ordered to do. He followed the man from a safe distance as he left the cantina, heading for his car. The parking lot was down two blocks and around a corner if the man stuck to the well-lit streets. If he knew of the shortcut, he would use the alley.

That was what Ruben prayed he would do.

When the stranger looked over his shoulder, Ruben ducked into the shadows of a doorway and waited until it was safe to move. With his heart racing, he counted to five before he emerged from the shadows. By the time he did, the man was gone.

"Ay, Dios mio," the boy muttered, with his eyes alert.

Ruben looked down the lit street and saw no sign of the man, but when he turned toward the alley, he caught a glimpse of movement. It had to be him.

He ducked into the alley and stepped up his pace to catch the man. When he got to the end of the alleyway, he stopped and held his breath. Slowly he inched closer to the corner and peered into the darkness.

That was when a hand grabbed his shirt collar and pulled him off his feet.

"Please . . . don't hurt me," he begged.

Ruben covered his face with his hands and raised his voice higher, sounding more like the boy he was.

"Why are you following me, kid?"

The tall, muscular man kept ahold of him. His body was cast in nothing more than a bluish haze. Ruben couldn't see his face. And although the boy felt the heat of the man's breath on his cheek, he tried not to be afraid.

Ruben de los Santos wasn't alone.

"You will see soon enough, *señor.*" The boy forced a smile with courage he didn't feel.

The big man released his grip on Ruben and pulled away. He reached for his weapon, but it was too late. Members of Ruben's gang emerged from the shadows like ghosts rising from the grave. The stranger was surrounded.

"Who are you? And what do you want?" the man demanded. He aimed his weapon into the crowd, shifting his barrel from face to face. He was outnumbered and outgunned.

"Lower your weapon, *pendejo*. You will not be asked a second time." Arturo, one of the older boys, stepped forward and held his gun sideways, aiming between the man's eyes. Ruben held his breath, unable to take his eyes off the two men. If one of them fired, many would die. And Ruben had no doubt he would get caught in the cross fire.

The standoff continued, neither man backing down, until the one Ruben had trailed into the alley finally lowered his weapon. The boy let out a ragged breath and made a quick sign of the cross, but it wasn't over.

After they'd taken the man's weapon, every gang member of *Los Chupacabras* beat and kicked the stranger until he dropped to the asphalt.

After he was down, lying unconscious and bleeding on the ground, Ruben searched his pockets for his wallet. He pulled out the few hundred dollars he had in cash and gave it to Arturo, the boy in charge. And Ruben got a look at the man's driver's license and saw his name and where he lived.

"I'll need that." Arturo held out his hand. "Cash is ours, but his ID goes with me."

One of the other boys pulled a van into the alley. They loaded the wounded man into the back and carried out the rest of their orders. The man was to be taken across the Mexican border and delivered to someone linked to the Pérez cartel in Juárez. Ruben's gang in El Paso had powerful connections on the other side of the border, men who supplied them with drugs to sell. And in return, *Los Chupacabras* carried out execution-style killings, acted as drug mules, and bartered for weapons with their brother organization. That was why Ruben had taken the risk to follow an armed man into the alley.

He had passed his initiation. And the unconscious man in the back of the van had been his ticket in, but what the American from New York City had done to piss off the cartel and earn him a one-way trip across the border, Ruben didn't know.

And didn't care.

Outside Ciudad Juárez, Mexico
Three hours later

Ramon Guerrero's footsteps echoed as he walked the shadowy corridors of the rancho, guided by the meager light from flickering torches. The old hacienda belonged to his family, handed down through the generations. Although it had no electricity, and its only source of water was an old well on the property, it served its purpose by sheltering him and his men. It had been a good location to hide the many hostages who were held for ransom as a funding source for his drug operation. And being remote, the ranch enabled him to carry out the unsavory side of cartel business without anyone's knowing what went on behind its adobe walls.

An armed guard stood at the end of the long passage. The man had been slouched in a chair but now stood at attention as Guerrero approached.

In his native tongue, he asked the guard, "Has he admitted anything of value?"

The man only shook his head.

"Then it is my turn. Unlock the door," he ordered. The guard did as he was told.

A dark silhouette of a man was backlit by moonlight from the only barred window, with eerie shadows, cast from a single torch, undulating against the wall. The hostage had been stripped of his clothes. Completely naked, hanging from a metal bar, his body sagged from its own weight. Ropes cut into his wrists, and blood had run down his arms. Deep contusions were visible on his taut belly and rib cage, an aftermath of the beatings he had endured before and after he'd been delivered to the hacienda.

In the corner of the cell was a wooden bucket. Guerrero picked it up and threw dirty water at his prisoner.

"Ah." The man groaned and tried lifting his head, without much success.

"My name is Ramon," the drug lord said in English. "Your fate is in my hands."

"Go to . . . h-hell."

Guerrero grimaced at the prisoner's lack of respect.

"You will make it there well before me. I can assure you."

When Guerrero got close, he held his breath. The stench of blood and other distasteful smells made it hard to breathe. He grabbed the man's dark hair and yanked his head back. The prisoner's face was battered and bleeding. And one eye was swollen shut. Guerrero had allowed his men first crack at the hostage.

The man had brought unwanted interest. He'd been asking too many questions across the U.S. border in El Paso, calling attention to Guerrero's Juárez operation. After receiving reliable intel from a number of sources, Guerrero figured he had an edge to exploit that could expand his reach. He gave the order to take the man alive and deliver him, and any identification he had on him, to the rancho's gate. Perhaps the hostage would be Guerrero's way of gaining more power within the cartel.

Like many, Guerrero had ambitions. The hostage had crossed his path for a reason. His appearance could not merely be chalked up to good fortune. He preferred to think of the opportunity as his fate, his much-deserved due.

"I am surprised you took such a risk. Did you not think we would find out what you were doing in Texas? Did you think being across the border would protect you?" Guerrero walked around the naked man, taking in every old scar that marred his body. One scar in particular had caught his eye. No doubt, the man had seen his share of fights, but the prominent burn scar on his back had betrayed him. And, given what Guerrero already knew, he had enough to get what he wanted without the man's cooperation. It was one thing to have the man's ID but quite another to truly know who he was and what he did for a living.

"Surely someone of"—he paused for effect— "your stature would have others to take such risk."

The hostage flinched only for a second, but Guerrero was certain he'd seen a reaction.

"I don't know . . . w-what you're t-talking about."

"That doesn't matter. Not anymore." He leaned closer, and whispered, "You see, I know who you are . . . who you really are. And that will be enough to get me what I want."

"You don't know shit, Raymond."

"The name is Ramon." He gritted his teeth at the man's insolence. "And if you wanted your real identity to remain a secret, you should have removed that scar from your back."

The hostage glared at him but didn't say a word. Even beaten as he was, he mustered enough contempt to provoke Guerrero.

"Why are you pissing on my turf?" he pressed. "What did you hope to gain?"

The man did not hesitate. "I'm looking for a man . . . to kill him."

Guerrero stared at the hostage in disbelief at his gall before he burst into laughter. The sound echoed off the walls of the cell—a foreign noise in a place where screams were more common.

"And how is that going for you?" Without waiting for an answer, he shook his head, and said, "You Americans have such arrogance, but we shall see how long that lasts."

Under his belt at the small of his back, Guerrero pulled out a black hood and covered his prisoner's head. The hostage jerked and fought it, but he didn't say anything. The American didn't have the good sense to cower. He held his head up, and the black cloth moved with every breath of his defiance. When Guerrero pictured the smug look on his face under the hood, he balled his fists to make his point about who was in charge.

In the stifling heat, he punched the hostage in the gut. *Once. Twice.* The prisoner clenched his stomach muscles and took the blows without uttering a sound, withstanding the abuse in silence.

"We shall s-see"—Ramon panted—"h-how strong . . . you are."

It took all his willpower to lower his hands. He stopped the beating only because he had a call to make. "Th-there are far worse . . . things to endure."

When he had first communicated his part in the capture of such an influential American, his cartel boss had sent word promptly. He had ordered him to make a journey to a rendezvous point, bringing the prisoner with him. Guerrero would make a gift of the American and, hopefully, reap rewards for his efforts.

Gasping and winded, he walked across the cell and spoke to the guard on the other side of the door. In minutes, his man returned and, between the bars, handed him a loaded syringe. With a smirk on his face, Guerrero shoved the hostage's head to one side and injected the needle into his neck. The man struggled, making a futile attempt to fight back. As his prisoner fought the drug, Guerrero hit speed dial on his cell phone and contacted the man he hoped would be very grateful . . . and generous.

As he listened to the phone ring in his ear—waiting to report he'd confirmed ID and give the details of how he would transport the prisoner—Guerrero wasn't done tormenting his hostage. Before the man drifted into a merciful oblivion, he leaned closer and whispered in his ear.

"Your name is Garrett Wheeler." He spat on the man's bare chest. "And I know who you work for, *cabrón*."

"I'm picking up a cell-phone signal from inside the walls of the residence outside Juárez. No ID on the caller, but I can track the GPS signal. If the guy with the cell moves, I'll know it." The handler for the mission had made contact with the man who had ultimate control over the op. From an encrypted international phone, he spoke to him now, nothing more than a voice on the other end of the line.

"Did we get a visual? Do they have the hostage inside?"

"Yes. We got a visual confirmation from team two."

After the hostage had been taken by a group of young thugs known as *Los Chupacabras* in El Paso, surveillance tracked the movement of the van the gang had used to cross the border into Mexico. Once they left U.S. soil, the handler rotated surveillance teams, so they wouldn't lose their target.

"Your order, sir?" the handler asked.

"Make contact with team one in Juárez. Tell them you have a signal you're following. It's their backup plan, in case something goes wrong on their end. If that GPS signal moves, I want eyes on it. Keep me informed."

"Copy that."

Short and sweet, the man taking the lead on the operation gave his orders and ended the call. The handler's part in the mission had ramped up. He made his call to team one and followed orders.

New York City
Before dawn

Dressed in gray slacks and black cashmere sweater, Alexa Marlowe stared out her apartment window, located on the third floor of a brownstone on the Upper East Side. For the last week, she'd been restless, and sleep hadn't come easy. In her line of work, that was a hazard of the trade, but she had another reason to worry. And after getting a call from Tanya Spencer yesterday, arranging for an early-morning meet at Alexa's place, she wondered if the Sentinels' analyst had been losing sleep for the same reason.

When she heard the soft knock on her door, she rushed to answer it.

"Good morning, Tanya." She forced a smile. "Please . . . come in."

"Thanks for accommodating my crazy schedule."

Even before dawn, the woman was impeccably dressed, in a navy Burberry blazer and a pencil skirt. Her black skin looked radiant, with only a hint of the flawless makeup she wore. And her Southern drawl could melt butter. That voice had calmed Alexa on many covert-ops missions when she had needed analytical support . . . and a friend.

"Sorry to get you up this early, but I thought we should talk somewhere away from headquarters. And your place was on my way to work."

"No trouble. Can I get you coffee?" Alexa asked.

"Yes, please."

Alexa already had a pot made and served Tanya a cup before they sat in the living room.

Being a covert agent, Alexa viewed the world differently from most people. She looked for ulterior motives and conspiracies under every rock. It was how her brain worked, out of necessity. Her survival sometimes depended on it. And since Tanya Spencer had a similar background—

having worked many years with the privately funded Sentinels and served as Garrett Wheeler's right hand for the last decade—Alexa figured the woman's cryptic words meant she was only playing it safe.

"So tell me what's on your mind, Tanya?"

"I'm not sure if I should be saying this, but . . ." the woman began. " . . . I haven't heard from Garrett in almost ten days. And that's not like him." When Alexa didn't act surprised, Tanya said, "What's going on? Do you know anything about this?"

"No, I don't." Alexa shook her head and heaved a sigh. "But I've noticed the same thing. I thought it was me. After I broke it off with him, our relationship changed. It had to, but I haven't heard from him either. And that's got me losing sleep."

Tanya was one of the few people within the Sentinels who knew about Alexa's personal relationship with her boss, Garrett. She considered the woman a trusted friend.

"Isn't anyone else concerned about this?" Alexa narrowed her eyes. "He's head of our organization. What's he been working on?"

Tanya had been Garrett's senior analyst and advisor for the last ten years. She usually kept close tabs on him. And he trusted her with every aspect of what he did. They were a team.

"That's just it. I don't know." The woman shook her head and put down her coffee. "And it's got me worried sick. He's never done this, Alexa. He's always involved me with anything he touched. That's why I wanted to talk here, at your place. Something's been going on, and I've been cut out of the loop. The people Garrett answers to, they have to know something, but they're not clueing me in."

"So who's in charge with Garrett gone? I've never seen him work with anyone in particular who could step into his shoes."

"Yeah, I haven't either, not with the secrecy above his level. But this can't go on forever. If Garrett is AWOL, someone's got to assume his duties."

"You have any idea who?"

Tanya only shook her head. She was normally unflappable, but seeing the grimace on her face told Alexa all she needed to know about how concerned the woman was.

"We'd have to be careful looking into this. We could blow his op and put him in danger if we barge in without knowing what's going on."

"Does that mean you and Jessie will be looking into this?" Tanya asked. "I've tried tracking Garrett, but I've got nothing. Maybe if we trace other movements within the organization, we'll have better luck."

Tanya was right. If Garrett was involved in a covert op that excluded his top analyst and his most trusted agent, it had to be really big. But that also meant the Sentinels' resources would be dedicated to the operation. And if Alexa could handpick someone to dig through the veiled secrecy of the Sentinels—an organization of international vigilantes who operated off the global grid to dole out their brand of justice—she would have Tanya Spencer at the top of her list. The woman had connections in and out of the organization. And with her internal-systems knowledge, she could slip through virtual back doors without anyone's noticing.

"I'm meeting Jessie later for breakfast. She's pretty new to how things work within the Sentinels, but we'll see." Alexa sat back on her sofa and crossed her arms. "If we do this, we'd need your help."

Tanya nodded, and said, "Count on it."

Alexa knew that what she was planning on doing—using the organization's resources to trace a covert operation involving her boss and former lover—would not be a sensible thing to do. It could turn into a career ender, at best. Or a death sentence, at worst. And to involve her new partner, Jessie, would not be wise either—especially for Beckett's sake.

Relying on her gut instinct, she'd have to make that call when she talked to Jessie. If she read anything in her that raised a red flag, she'd let it slide and go it alone with Tanya. But one way or another, she'd take the risk for Garrett—because he would do the same for her.

New York's Lower East Side

The ringing of a phone early in the morning was never a good thing.

Jessie Beckett pulled the bedcovers off her face and fumbled for the light switch. And after she flicked on her lamp, she squinted at the alarm clock on her nightstand.

"Six twenty? Who the hell—" She winced and grabbed the cell phone off her nightstand and flipped it open without looking at the caller's number. "You better have a damned good reason for breaking into my beauty sleep."

The sun had barely made an appearance. And that meant she didn't give a rip about winning Miss Congeniality.

"Jessie? It's Sam."

She recognized the voice of her best friend. Samantha Cooper was a vice cop in Chicago. And she had better sense than to call her at this hour if it wasn't important.

"Sam? What's up? Is Seth all right?"

Her worry barometer worked double time when it came to Seth Harper, a guy who had nestled into her heart and made a home. The whacked-out computer genius had a habit of getting into trouble, and not only because he knew her. The boy had a serious way of attracting it on his own. And with his recent recruitment into the Sentinels for his mad skills with a keyboard—the same organization Jessie worked for—Seth had more than doubled his gift for luring trouble.

"No, Seth is fine, I guess. I haven't seen him lately, but I was calling you about . . . something else."

"Oh?"

Her friend cleared her throat and stalled. And that wasn't like her.

"Spit it out, Sammie."

"Chicago PD received a bulletin from a police chief in La Pointe, Wisconsin."

"Where the hell is that?"

"It's at the northern tip of Wisconsin. On Madeline Island in Lake Superior, to be exact. I looked it up on a map."

"Thanks for the geography lesson." Jessie ran a hand through her dark hair. "Explain why I should care about this?"

Sam cleared her throat again. Definitely stalling.

"You should care because the police there are working an old cold case. A pretty gruesome murder that happened over twenty years ago."

"Twenty years. We were both kids back then. Why are you calling me about this, Sam?"

Jessie didn't like where this was headed. Twenty years ago, she was a kid in the hands of notorious pedophile, Danny Ray Millstone. At least, that was what she believed. She had been too young to really know the truth about how she ended up with him—or maybe she'd blocked it out. And insult to injury, after she was rescued by Detective Max Jenkins of the Chicago PD, no one from her family stepped up to claim her. Not even the national media coverage afterward shed light on what had happened to her. That aspect of her past had remained a black hole. And she'd given up trying to find where she'd come from.

Looking into the details of her childhood nightmare had always been too painful.

"Yeah, well, back then DNA wasn't used to solve crimes like it is now," Sam said. "But an old case caught the eye of this local police chief. And he sent in evidence he had stored in archives to the state crime lab. When the lab ran its findings against the CODIS and NCIC databases, the chief told me he got a hit on DNA evidence—and his first new lead in over twenty years."

Jessie's mind worked double time, thinking how a DNA test would link to her. The FBI maintained both the Combined DNA Index System and the National Crime Information Center. The first held DNA profiles in a database, while the other was a repository for specific criminal records on known fugitives, missing persons, stolen property, and other details. Such database information was available to state and federal law-enforcement types and was meant to be shared across jurisdictions. Since she'd been a missing person as a child, her gut twisted with the implications of where Sam might be going with this.

"He got a hit . . . on what?"

"Since you were a missing kid, your DNA is on record, Jess. The Wisconsin crime lab got a hit on your DNA. It puts you at that crime scene over twenty years ago."

"What?" Jessie grimaced. "I don't understand."

"I didn't either. That's why I put in a request for that DNA report. I could have our crime-lab boys take a look at it, decipher what it means. When I get it, I'll let you know."

"That's great . . . I think."

"I also called that local LEO in La Pointe. His name is Tobias Cook. I only asked questions and didn't tell him anything. I wanted to talk to you first," Sam told her. "According to him, that DNA hit on you was a dead-on match. Unless there's a serious mistake, it looks like you're connected to that murder somehow, but that's not all."

"Oh, great. The hits keep coming."

"Chief Cook was asking about your mother. He's looked into your story, Jess. He knows about Millstone and what happened to you as a kid. He asked why no one ever came forward and claimed you after the rescue."

"What did you say?"

"I told him I didn't know anything about that. And he'd have to talk to you about it."

"You did good, Sammie. Thanks." Jessie swallowed hard. "Did he say why he was asking about my mother?"

Hearing the word "mother" always flashed her back to a haunting memory that had been with her since she was a little girl. She remembered a sunny day with fall colors and a woman's smiling face. She held those images close to her heart, of a woman playing with her in a park. She must have been someone very special because the memories always made Jessie happy. Although she still couldn't be sure the woman in her dreams was really her mother, Jessie needed to believe she'd once had someone who loved her like that.

She'd always fantasized that if she saw the woman again, she'd know it. Something in her eyes would give it away. At least, she'd always hoped that would be true.

"The chief only told me that he was running down leads, something about kids being seen at the house where the murder took place."

"Was the murdered woman . . . my mother? I mean, did my DNA match . . . hers?"

She ached with the thought that her mother might have been dead all these years. And the very thing she'd longed for was never going to happen.

"Sorry. He didn't tell me anything more about his case. Believe me, I asked, but he got a call and had to jump. That's why I wanted to see that DNA analysis myself. I swear, Jess. The minute I get that report, I'll call you. Promise."

"Yeah, thanks."

"We don't know if your mother was there at all. Without a peek at the DNA report, there's no sense buying into more trouble. Even if she was there, she could have been a witness."

"Or a suspect."

Jessie had a hard time thinking about her mother after all these years, but she had an even tougher time considering what dark scenarios had put her at that crime scene.

"Don't go there, Jessie."

"Either way, I don't see a family reunion in my future. My luck doesn't work that way."

"You're still breathing, aren't you? I'd say your luck is better than most." Sam heaved a sigh. "Besides, if your mother had been connected in some way to a murder, that would explain why she never came forward after you were rescued."

What Sam said made sense. It had always pained her that no one had claimed her after her ordeal with Millstone, especially with all the national media coverage. Given the scant memories she had of a woman she believed to be her mother—a child's wishful thinking—Jessie didn't want to even think about the woman's being involved in a killing. The life she led before Millstone had been a black hole so far, but maybe this local cop could fill in the gaps. Jessie would have no way of knowing anything for sure unless she contacted him.

"So now what?" Sam asked. "People here at CPD know we have a connection. They're letting me handle this bulletin request for information, but I can't stall them."

"No, and I don't expect you to." Jessie chewed the inside corner of her lip. "Give me the 4-1-1 on this chief dude."

Sam gave her the man's name and phone number.

"Chief Cook asked you to call him. He thinks he can clear things up over the phone."

"Not good enough. Not for me."

"What are you saying?"

"I'm flying to Chicago as soon as I can arrange a flight, Sam. I'll call you when I get there."

"You want me to pick you up at O'Hare?"

"No . . . I'll get Harper to do that. But I'll call when I get a chance, okay?"

"So what are you going to do?"

"I'm driving to La Pointe. You can tell Chief Cook that I'll see him face-to-face late tomorrow. I gotta know what evidence he's got on that case. And if there's a connection to my mother, or a reason why I ended up with Millstone, I have to know."

"Look, Jess. I know this is hard for you, but if you need to talk, call me."

"Thanks, I will."

Her past never went away. For the first time in her life, Jessie had a future and prospects, working for the Sentinels. She wasn't just a bounty hunter drifting from case to case, living in a crappy apartment on the fringe of society in Chicago. And since Seth Harper had nudged his way into her life, she also felt good about herself. He had known about her past and accepted her. The scars she carried on her body and on her soul weren't an issue with a guy like Harper.

So why now? Why did this damned cold case in Wisconsin have to bite her in the ass now?

It scared her to think that her only memory of someone who could be her mother might have been wrong. Was she ready to kill the only good thing she remembered of her past?

"I can never catch a damned break," she muttered as she got out of bed.

Dressed in a tank top and boxers, Jessie trudged into her living room and logged onto her laptop to look for a flight to Chicago. She had breakfast plans with Alexa Marlowe that she could still make on her way to LaGuardia. Her new partner would need to know that she was leaving town, but Alexa didn't need to know everything.

Very few people knew the details about the nightmare of her childhood ordeal, and she preferred to keep it that way.

Two hours later

Norma's Restaurant in Midtown West was packed. Bright and bustling, the place had high ceilings, wood paneling, and faux-silver-edged tables that gave a modern yet comfortable feel. It was a popular café for breakfast and lunch, located in the Le Parker Meridien Hotel lobby. Norma's was too expensive and trendy for Jessie's taste, but Alexa knew her partner had suggested it for her sake. Being a former bounty hunter, Jessie had dealt with the dregs of humanity and would have been satisfied with any hole-in-the-wall greasy spoon.

When Alexa arrived, she noticed that Jessie had gotten there early and scored a table, a small carafe of coffee, and two shot glasses of the restaurant's complimentary smoothie du jour. After her partner waved her over, it didn't take Alexa long to notice the carry-on luggage under the table.

"Planning on staying the week? The blueberry pancakes are good, but come on," she joked to cover up her surprise . . . and disappointment.

"I'm on my way to the airport, heading for Chicago. Something personal has come up." Dressed in a T-shirt and jeans, Jessie leaned across the table. "I know this is short notice, but I don't have a choice."

Alexa narrowed her eyes and dropped her smile. "Anything I can do?"

"No, nothing." Jessie shook her head. "I've got it covered."

Jessie had hesitated, enough to tell Alexa her trip to Chicago wouldn't be for pleasure.

"And I'm guessing you probably don't want to talk about it."

"Bingo." Jessie grabbed her coffee cup and hid behind it.

Her partner was a woman with secrets, and Alexa respected her privacy. The scar over Jessie's eyebrow had a story behind it, one Alexa had never been privileged to hear. Even though not too long ago, Alexa had gotten a glimpse into something Jessie had barely survived as a child, her partner had never confided in her, and she hadn't pushed.

And Alexa also guessed that Jessie had feelings for the computer genius, Seth Harper. Maybe her trip had something to do with him. The guy was a new recruit for the Sentinels, but he'd opted to stay in Chicago rather than move to New York, so he could stick close to his mentally deteriorating father, who lived in a nursing home. Those had been her first thoughts about Jessie's trip; but with her partner, she might never know for sure.

"How long will you be gone?" she asked. "I mean, in case something comes up."

"Maybe a few days. Not long."

"Okay." She nodded. "Will you call me if you need anything?"

"Yeah . . . I'll do that. So what's good here?" When Jessie flipped open her menu, her eyes grew wide. "Oh, my God! They have a lobster-and-caviar omelet for a thousand smackers. Who the hell are they kidding? That's just . . . insane."

As fast as Jessie stuck her nose in the menu and changed the subject, Alexa knew her partner would never take her up on her offer. Jessie had a tough, independent streak. It was one of the things she liked most about her, but sometimes that made it hard for anyone to get inside. As a partner and a friend, Jessie was an acquired taste.

But with Jessie going out of town—completely distracted by her personal agenda—Alexa knew she'd be working with Tanya alone. Once her partner got back and could focus, Alexa might ask for her help, but for now, Jessie was out of it. And there was no sense telling her anything about Garrett. Jessie had enough going on in her life without adding the guilt trip of leaving her in the lurch—because that was exactly how Jessie's mind worked. She'd feel guilty over something she'd have no control over.

As if she'd read Alexa's mind, Jessie looked up from her menu, and said, "You look tired. You getting enough z's?"

Alexa ran a hand through her blond hair and heaved a sigh as she propped her elbows on the table.

"I'd be doing better if you'd dose me up." She forced a smile as she shoved over her empty cup. "Pour me some coffee, will ya?"

While her partner filled her cup, Alexa turned her thoughts to Garrett. Something was terribly wrong. As an experienced operative, she sensed it in her bones, especially after talking to Tanya and hearing that Garrett's top analyst hadn't heard from him either. That clinched it. She had to do something.

When they were together, Garrett had been an attentive and aggressive lover and quickly become her obsession after she'd come off the high of her near miss with fellow operative Jackson Kinkaid. Her one-sided feelings for Jackson had been tough to let go. They had chemistry, no doubt, but she needed more than he had to give. And, after working with him on a hostage-rescue mission in Cuba not too long ago, the emotional roller-coaster ride with him had not changed for her. She still had it bad, especially after Jackson told her why he'd kept her at a distance.

There had been another woman. A dead one.

Jackson was still deeply connected to his murdered wife and the child he had lost. He had nothing to give her, or anyone. He'd changed. He wasn't the same man she had known years before. It broke her heart to walk away from him after the Cuban op, but she had to. Forcing Jackson to deal with his grief before he was ready to let go wouldn't have been good. He would always resent her for it. And that was no way to live, for either of them.

After she'd first met Kinkaid years before, Garrett had been a rebound fling for her, but he'd been a distraction she needed at the time. He had unleashed her insatiable need and been a much-needed diversion after the pent-up feelings she had for Jackson. And even though the urgent passion she had with her boss, Garrett Wheeler, had run its course, she still cared for him deeply. She owed him more than her unflinching loyalty.

Where are you, Garrett?

Somewhere in Mexico

"Is it . . ."

"Is it . . ."

" . . . him?"

A woman's voice echoed in his head and filtered through the fog in his brain. Her words overlapped like undulating ripples across still water, mixed with the faint distant echo of a child's laughter. The sounds nudged his faltering consciousness or tapped into a sliver of memory. He didn't know which, nor did he care. He had to concentrate to hear anything at all. He didn't know where he was or how he got there. In this place, he had no past, no future, and barely remembered his own name. Yet in his shadowy existence, he felt certain that he was completely deserving of whatever fate had in store.

When he felt a cool velvet touch on his fevered

cheek, he heard a moan, unsure if the sound came from him. He forced his eyes open a crack and caught a glimpse of light. Shadows eclipsed a dim glow, but he was too weak to move. With the drug still so strong in his system, he wavered on the razor's edge of darkness and took the only comfort he could. He imagined the woman's voice he had heard morphing into a more familiar sultry one and pictured running his fingers through a soft tumble of blond strands as he gazed into pale blue eyes.

His lover's throaty voice stirred him, and her haunting eyes lingered, along with a trace of her perfume. He felt her kiss and her whisper in his ear as she trailed a finger down the bare skin of his chest and onto his stomach. Her touch made him flinch, and his body reacted.

He wanted her. He needed her. And when he willed the beautiful woman to stay—*she did*.

CHAPTER 2

New York City

After breakfast, Alexa arrived at the Sentinels' headquarters and went through the high-tech security measures to access the elevator that would take her to the belowground stronghold. Running on autopilot, she had her mind on Garrett as she headed for Tanya's office and walked through the massive computer area, where analysts manned global surveillance systems.

Black walls encircled the room, and the overhead lights were purposefully dim, so computer jockeys could better see the array of colors on their monitors. And with the tight acoustics in the room, the cavernous space had the feel of a planetarium.

With Jessie out of town, Alexa would be working alone with Tanya to dig into Garrett's whereabouts. Following the physical and electronic trail to find him would be tricky. Any search would cover sensitive information and involve tapping into restricted resources within the organization, something she'd be willing to chance if it meant finding him.

Plenty depended on her trust in Tanya's instincts and her own when it came to Garrett. And her experiences with the man and his covert organization told her their search should be low-key until they dug up something more substantial to go on.

When she got to Tanya's office, the door was open. She strode into the room but stopped when she saw that her friend wasn't alone.

"I'm sorry." Alexa stopped in the doorway and turned on her heels, heading out. "I'll come back later."

"No, please. Come in, Marlowe." A deep masculine voice called after her. "I was just leaving."

Alexa turned in surprise when she heard her name coming from the stranger. She narrowed her eyes and looked at the man. And from what she could see, Tanya appeared stressed. The analyst made eye contact and tried to communicate something Alexa couldn't read . . . yet. But knowing Tanya, that wouldn't take long.

"Have we met?" She stepped back into the office and closed the gap between her and a tall man dressed in an impeccable charcoal gray suit. "How do you know my name?"

"Your dossier." He flashed a slick smile and extended his hand. "Quite impressive. My name is Donovan Cross. I'm an old friend of Garrett's."

Alexa took his hand and fixed her eyes on him. Few people in the world knew her real credentials. Once she'd become a member of the Sentinels, her background had been sanitized or erased. If this man had seen her dossier, he had to be part of the organization—and a high-ranking agent at that. Yet this was the first time she'd heard his name or crossed his path. And she hated being at a disadvantage.

"Funny. He's never mentioned you. Why are you here, Mr. Cross?" She shifted her gaze toward Tanya, who only raised an eyebrow. When the analyst allowed it, her face could be an open book. And just then, she made for an easy read. Something about this man annoyed her.

"Please . . . call me Donovan. And as for why I'm here, Tanya can fill you in. I'm sure you'll have plenty to talk about once I leave. Good day, Marlowe."

Cross had an arrogant swagger, and he moved with the confidence of a man who had been in the business for a long time although he didn't look to be older than his mid-to-late thirties. In some ways, Donovan Cross reminded her of Garrett.

He had short dark hair and the same keen intense

eyes that took in everything, except that Cross's eyes were hazel, not the steel gray of Garrett's. He was tall and athletic-looking. And although he had the same taste for expensive clothing, he had a rougher edge than Garrett. His face told her that. He'd seen a fight or two and broken his nose more than once. He wasn't classically handsome, but any woman would notice him in a crowd.

"What was that all about?" she asked Tanya, after Cross left.

"I'm sorry I didn't have time to tell you. I only got the official word an hour ago, direct from Mount Olympus. And that's when he walked in, complete with access codes and security clearance."

Without Garrett at the helm, they had no one above his level to trust. Tanya was the only one who had communicated with the upper echelon, but she'd never met anyone face-to-face. Alexa didn't like what was happening. And maybe a small part of her knew what Tanya would say next.

"He's Garrett's replacement, Alexa. And I'm not sure it's temporary."

Chicago
Afternoon

Once Jessie exited the secured area at Chicago's O'Hare airport, she looked through the sea of expectant faces of those waiting for friends and family coming off flights. She searched the crowd for tall, lanky Seth Harper, a guy who wore his hair a little long in soft dark waves and had honey brown eyes that made her weak in the knees. His boyish good looks had always captivated her.

Jessie peered at dozens of faces, looking for him. When she didn't see him anywhere, she felt a twinge of disappointment. She couldn't believe how eager she was to see him. And, completely unlike her, she had primped on the plane and made sure her breath smelled minty fresh, behaving like such a . . . girl.

In her haste to leave New York, she'd only given Seth her flight number and arrival time, resorting to text messages after they'd played phone tag. And she'd told him if they missed each other—which would have been easy at the massive airport—that she'd see him on the curb outside baggage claim.

With airport security these days, it was easier to make arrangements to meet on the arrival ramp although a part of her had hoped he'd surprise her by showing up inside the terminal.

She hoisted her overnight bag over her shoulder and followed her fellow passengers toward baggage claim, but as she rounded a corner beyond security, she saw Harper leaning against a column outside a gift shop. He had a big grin on his sweet face and was holding flowers.

The boy looked damned good.

Without a word, she walked toward him. When she got close, she dropped her bag at his feet and collapsed into his arms. He smelled good—like soap on warm skin—and he felt even better. And all she thought about was how good it felt to be home.

Harper was home.

"Oh . . . you feel so good," she whispered into his shoulder. "You have no idea."

Her ear tickled with the sound of the soft laughter muffled in his chest.

"Yeah, I've missed you, too."

He pulled back long enough to raise her chin with a finger and kiss her. Sweet tenderness heated to a slow burn. People walked by, and the noise of the airport faded. None of it stopped her from showing how much she loved him.

"I've got a new place. And I can't wait for you to see it," he said, as his kiss turned into a big hug. "I got a deal on it."

"Yeah, I hear you're connected." She grinned.

When she reached down for her bag, he had already grabbed it and put his arm around her as they walked through the busy airport, with her holding the flowers he had given her. On the surface, they looked like a damned Hallmark card; but given their pasts, they were the polar opposite of ordinary.

"Tony carved out a piece of real estate for me downtown, one of his renovation projects, but the beauty of it is—I actually own it, Jess. Guess that makes me an official adult."

Harper said that like it was a good thing.

"You've done it now. You've crossed the line, Harper. I'm not sure I can hang with someone like you. Too rich for my blood."

Tony Salvatore was a local business developer in town, head of the Pinnacle Real Estate Corporation, a major player in the real-estate market. And he'd been a good friend to Seth and his family.

"Don't worry. It hasn't gone to my head. I have a roommate. He needed a place to stay for a while." Harper stopped and reached into his jeans pocket. "I better give him a call now, let him know we're on our way."

Jessie stood with her mouth open as Seth hit speed dial and walked away. *Harper has a roommate?* He was the original lone wolf. When she had first met him, the guy lived off the grid. With his computer expertise, he'd wiped his background clean and avoided any way to trace him. And he lived out of luggage as he moved from place to place with Salvatore's vacant high-dollar real-estate ventures.

Keeping a low profile had been Harper's way of dealing with the strained relationship between him and his father, a former cop who suffered from a form of dementia, the aftermath of a job that had consumed him. Seth's actually putting down roots shocked her, but the whole roommate thing was really over the top. Way too normal for Harper.

Living in downtown Chicago was expensive. Giving him the benefit of the doubt, Jessie knew it made sense that Harper had someone to share the cost, even if it was only "for a while," whatever that meant.

But it was hard to deny she had been disappointed when he told her about his roommate. She had high hopes of spending real alone time with him. And Harper was excited about her coming to Chicago, too. She'd seen it in his eyes. Before she arrived, he'd loaded up her phone with text messages, telling her about his special plans for their time together.

She chalked it up to bad Karma. A dark, surreal cloud had followed her from New York, after Sam's phone call. And after seeing Harper, she didn't have the heart to blurt out the real reason she'd come. Eventually, she'd have to; but before she ruined everything by leaving town again, all she wanted was to enjoy his company.

When Seth rejoined her after calling his roomie, she took a deep breath and shook her head, trying to hide her disappointment in sharing her quirky computer genius with anyone else. He had connections in Chicago, and not all of them were wealthy land barons.

Harper was a magnet for anyone strange. His innocent charm had a lot to do with it. Like her, he knew more than his fair share of fringe dwellers. And curiosity had her wondering whom he trusted enough to share his place.

Harper led a weird life. He was a guy she still thought had a borderline aptitude for crime. His sense of right and wrong was squishy and . . . adaptable.

In a word, he was "perfect" for his new employer, the Sentinels. Garrett Wheeler, the head of the clandestine organization, had recruited him personally. And as for her, Harper was like a pistachio. She couldn't get enough of him.

Jessie narrowed her eyes. "Does your new roomie know what you do for a living?"

"Yeah, he's got a vague notion, but he doesn't hold it against me. Someone's got to work." He shrugged. "Besides, I trust him."

Typical Harper. And she wouldn't have him any other way.

Jessie rolled her eyes. "If you say so, Harper."

New York City
Sentinels' Headquarters

When Alexa Marlowe crossed the threshold of Donovan Cross's new accommodations— Garrett's office—he was expecting her to make an appearance. The tall, athletic blonde made a point not to make an appointment or call ahead. He knew he'd have to earn her respect, and that would be a difficult task. And if the woman had something on her mind, she would say it. Marlowe had a reputation for being anything but subtle.

Cross didn't bother to stand. He slouched in his chair behind the desk, staring at the woman who he knew would not be intimidated.

"Good, you saved me the trouble of sending for you." He forced a smile. "Your work is exceptional. I've been looking forward to meeting you, Marlowe."

"I wish I could say the same. All I've got is your word that you have a pedigree. You've seen my dossier. The least you could do is return the favor and show me yours." The striking woman stood in front of his desk with arms crossed, not bothering to sit.

"And if I say no, what then?"

"Then you would seem like a man with something to hide."

"Well, here's a novel concept. You could give me a chance. I assure you, I'll grow on you."

"Look, I just want to know what happened to Garrett. Is it true you're replacing him?"

"Yes. I follow orders, same as you."

"Where is he?"

Cross raised his eyebrow and didn't answer at first. He made her wait, until he finally said, "I can't say."

"Can't or won't?" She leaned across his desk and fixed her icy blue eyes on him. "Big difference."

Cross smirked and rocked in his chair.

"We work for a covert agency. Everything is on a need-to-know basis. Surely you understand how that works."

"I do, but surely you understand a man like Garrett doesn't just disappear, not without people asking questions."

From what he'd read of her file, a woman like Alexa Marlowe wouldn't let her questions go unanswered. She was stubborn. Her inquisitive nature and undaunted spirit made her a good agent. Cross knew he'd have to go beyond protocol to satisfy her. And what he had to do wouldn't be easy—for him or her.

"Sit down, Alexa." He softened his voice and gestured toward a chair. The woman begrudgingly complied and sat on the edge of her seat. Her eyes were fixed on him with a stern expression on her face. Cross took a deep breath before he said, "I hate to be the one to tell you this, but . . ."

"But what?" She clenched her jaw.

"Garrett is dead. He was killed on a covert mission." He swallowed and found it hard to look into her eyes. "I'm sorry. I know he was your friend."

She fought to stay in control.

"No, this can't . . ." She shook her head, and her eyes watered. "How?"

"I don't have the details. And there are things we may never know."

"What are you . . . s-saying?"

"I'm saying . . . that his mission was highly classified. And we may not even recover his body. Witnesses say he was killed in an explosion, Alexa. A bad one, but we've confirmed his DNA at the scene. I'm sorry."

Cross had delivered his message and waited for her reaction. With a trained operative, he'd only get a glimmer if he got any response at all. Alexa Marlowe stared at him for a long moment with only small flinches to her facial muscles. He knew she was deciding what to believe, but when she gritted her teeth and stood without another question, her move surprised him.

Without a word, she left his office.

It took all Alexa's strength for her to walk away from Donovan Cross when she wanted to scream. Screaming might wake her up from the living nightmare her life had suddenly become.

This couldn't be happening.

Numb, she shook her head as she closed the door behind her and headed down a hallway toward the elevators in a fog, not knowing where she was going. She wanted a stiff drink to dull her senses and slow the rush of emotions that crowded in on her, but her training and her loyalty to Garrett wouldn't allow it.

In all the operations she'd worked with Garrett, she found it hard to picture him dead . . . until now. He was such a resourcefully strong man who had lived through some amazing missions, many of those with her by his side.

Donovan Cross was another story. She didn't know him or trust him. Her first impressions of him weren't good. He was cagey and had a hard time answering a direct question, the opposite of Garrett.

But the biggest ache she felt was about Garrett

and the connection they shared. If he was dead, surely she would know.

Wouldn't she?

When he was alone, Donovan Cross picked up the phone and made a call. On the second ring, his call was answered by a familiar voice. Forgoing any customary greeting, he simply said, "I gave her the news, and she just left."

"Do you think she believed you?"

Cross leaned back in his chair and stared at the ceiling before he answered.

"Actually . . . I have no idea."

"Assign someone to tail her. If she finds out what's going on, she'll interfere, and we can't afford that. Not now."

"Agreed. And already done."

He ended the call and stared at the door Alexa had closed after leaving the room. The woman intrigued him. He suspected that she and Garrett had shared a special bond.

And he had no doubt Alexa Marlowe would be trouble.

Downtown Chicago

After Harper had parked his vehicle in underground resident parking, he showed Jessie to an elevator, and they rode up to his floor. His developer friend hadn't missed a trick. He'd built another urban retreat in the trendy heart of downtown Chicago, with a view of Lake Michigan and close to shops, restaurants, and bars.

"I hope you don't mind, but I made us dinner. Nothing fancy."

"You've never really cooked for me." She smiled. "You know I'm a sure thing, right?"

When Harper grinned, his face turned red. Blotches colored his cheeks as he ran a hand through his dark hair.

"I hope you like my place," he said. "I mean, it's not finished, you know. It's a work in progress."

"I think you've forgotten where I used to live. I'm sure your closet is bigger than my old dump. The trick is, always have low expectations, Harper. You'll never be disappointed."

Jessie found his shyness completely disarming. Innocent charisma came naturally for Harper. His physical beauty never ceased to amaze her, but he never seemed aware of his looks. And he never had to work at it. Harper was an original, always.

Driving from the airport, he had rambled about lots of stuff. He told her the latest on his dad. And he had funny stories about Tony Salvatore helping him find his new place. She'd never seen him so chatty, except when he talked about RAMs and gigabytes. In Harperworld, she usually needed subtitles, but not tonight.

His nonstop stream of consciousness meant only one thing. Harper was nervous.

When they got to his floor, Seth unlocked his front door. Still looking a little on edge, he let her walk in first. And her jaw dropped when she saw what he'd done.

"Oh, Seth. This is . . . beautiful," she gasped.

Harper had his place lit with white candles, flickering romance wherever she looked. And she smelled fresh flowers. He'd placed bundles of colorful lilies and roses throughout his loft. Wine had been poured. Music was playing softly in the background. And a silver tray of appetizers was on a bar near the kitchen.

Seth had staged everything.

"That call you made at the airport. Your roommate lit all these candles, didn't he? Either that, or you didn't pay your light bill."

"Someone else did it. My roommate isn't much of a romantic." He grinned. "So, you like it?"

"Like it? Harper, I love it." Jessie walked into the loft with her mouth open. "You did all this . . . for me?"

Everywhere she looked, he'd done something special. He'd enlarged photos of them in New York and placed them on shelves. And he'd framed striking black-and-white images of her favorite spots in Chicago and hung them on the walls, places she'd told him about. Even the music he had playing was more to her taste than his.

"Why not?" He shrugged with a smile. "You came all this way to be with me. I wanted your visit to be special."

The old Jessie would have beaten herself up with guilt. She hadn't come back to Chicago for Seth alone, not exactly. Even though she had missed Harper terribly since his trip to New York, she had another personal reason for coming, and she dreaded having to tell him. But the new Jessie fought the sting of tears and the lump in her throat, accepting Seth's beautiful gift.

No one had ever done something so thoughtful for her. And before she met Harper, she never thought she deserved to be happy. Her abused past had been a lifetime prison sentence, without the possibility of parole. But seeing herself through Seth's eyes had allowed her to hope things could change. Maybe it was okay to let someone good like him into her life.

Maybe she had a chance at being normal if she let it happen. Harper was a heaping helping of normal compared to *her* crazy standards.

"I want you to be happy." He wrapped his arms

around her and kissed her neck, as if he'd read her mind. "Actually . . . I was hoping that if you liked it, you might want to . . . move back to Chicago and live here with me. I've missed you, Jess."

She turned and looked him in the eye. Now his nervousness made sense. Seth had more on his mind than spending a few days with her.

"I've missed you, too, Harper." She heard the catch in her voice. "But I need to tell you—"

She wanted to explain the main reason why she'd come, but Harper stopped her. He touched a finger to her lips and pulled her close.

"You don't need to tell me anything. Not tonight. I just want us to be together. Keep things simple, you know?" He kissed her forehead. "I'm not pressuring you. Just promise me you'll think about it."

"I will. I promise." She nestled into his arms and breathed him in.

The truth was that she had thought a lot about moving back. She'd never gotten used to living in New York City. She was a Midwest girl, and Chicago felt more like home.

Until Harper came along, she'd never thought about putting down any real roots. Her old South Chicago apartment had been more of a self-inflicted wound. She never thought she deserved better, but Harper made her want . . . *more*.

"But if I move in, what will your roommate say?"

"Absolutely nothing. Beggars can't be choosers."

"So where is he?" she asked.

"I banished him for tonight. I wanted you all to myself." When he grinned, his cheeks colored pink. "You can meet him tomorrow."

Jess didn't have the heart to tell him she wanted to be on the road early. The trip to La Pointe, Wisconsin, would take most of the day. The police chief would be expecting her, but after seeing everything Seth had done, she kept that information to herself for a while longer. He'd asked to keep things simple, and she knew what he meant.

For one sweet night, no drama.

When morning came, she'd find a way to tell him. Harper would want to go with her, but this was one trip she had to take alone.

Mexico

Last night, Ramon Guerrero had awakened fifteen-year-old Estella Calderone in the middle of the night, the way he usually did lately. He took what he wanted like an animal, without saying a word.

When he was done, he forced her to get dressed and come with him, ignoring her questions. When they got outside his hacienda near Juárez, two cars were waiting in front with headlights blazing. And his men were nothing more than dark silhouettes, without faces.

"You ride with them." He waved a hand, barely looking at her. "Watch over the American in the back. He's your responsibility."

Guerrero gave his order and told her to ride in the van. That was the first time she had seen the wounded man.

"What's happening? Who is he?" she asked, but no one answered, not even Guerrero.

Estella was shoved inside the van and did as she was told. She would not be traveling with Guerrero. His car would follow at a safe distance behind the van. And she would be alone with two men she didn't know.

Now that it was hours later and nearly dusk, Estella had had plenty of time to think. She realized she was as much a prisoner as the American who lay unconscious at her feet in the back of the moving van. She stared down at the man with his hands tied behind his back, experiencing a strange envy.

One way or another, his incarceration would one day end. She could not say the same.

Her thoughts turned to Ramon Guerrero, the man who had owned her for the last two years.

He'd traded drugs for her. And her mother had been too strung out to say no.

At first, she had been glad to have a roof over her head and food in her belly. Guerrero had her clean his house, do his laundry, and cook for him and his men at his hacienda near Juárez.

But all that changed two weeks ago.

One night, Guerrero had staggered into her room without putting on the lights. He'd been drinking. She'd smelled it on his breath. He forced her to take off her clothes, and he hurt her, covering her mouth as she cried. After that, he didn't ask her to clean or cook for him.

She'd become his whore.

What she had done with him had been a sin. And now she was no more than a common criminal, too. If she got caught with the American, she'd spend the rest of her life in prison, blamed for what Guerrero had done. It would not matter to the authorities that she'd been ordered to take care of the wounded man and keep him quiet if he got delirious.

She'd been given a canteen of water and an old rag. Not knowing what else to do, she kept his lips moist and dabbed the wet rag on his forehead and neck to keep him cool in the sweltering heat. If the man died while in her care, she'd be accused of far worse than kidnapping.

Hot air swept into the open windows of the van and sucked in suffocating billows of dust, forcing her to squint and hold her breath. Every now and then, she gazed through the windshield and caught a glimpse of road signs, the only way she knew they were heading south, deeper into Mexico.

Estella made the sign of the cross and shut her eyes tight as her lips moved in prayer. She had her doubts that God listened to a whore, but it gave her comfort even if it was only for a moment.

"We'll stop for gas." One of the men turned and spoke to her in Spanish. "You stay put. If you have to pee, squat in the corner. And don't let anyone see you. Understand?"

The man's eyes trailed down to her breasts. She hated how he looked at her.

"What is your name?" he asked.

She gritted her teeth and took a deep breath before she answered him.

"Estella."

By the way the man stared, she wondered if there was another reason she'd been told to go with them—and taking care of the American had only been an excuse to distract her. She had a bad feeling that Guerrero had grown tired of her, and that meant only one thing. She was no longer just *his* whore. Maybe he'd promised her to these men.

"This one, she has a pretty mouth," the man said to the driver. When they both laughed, Estella crossed her arms and looked away.

That was when she saw that the American was awake.

One of his eyes was swollen shut, but with the other, he stared straight through to her soul.

Estella gasped.

Although she wanted to talk to him, she didn't dare. She waited until Guerrero's men stopped the car and got out at the gas station.

When she was alone with the injured man, she whispered in English, "Who are you?"

The man blinked and opened his mouth to speak, but nothing came out. She reached for the damp rag and held it out to him.

"This may hurt."

With a trembling hand, she dabbed his forehead with the rag and water trickled down the man's swollen cheek. The American winced as he stared at her, accusing her with the unrelenting glare from his good eye.

"I did not do this. I swear. I am a prisoner, like you."

Estella didn't know if he believed her. He let her touch him and cool his brow before he slowly closed his eyes again. Before he drifted to sleep, she leaned closer and brushed his damp hair off his face.

"If I can, I will stay with you, *señor*," she whispered, only loud enough for him to hear.

Estella didn't know why she had felt such a strong urge to comfort the man with a lie. If Guerrero was involved, the American was as good as dead, especially if he was being taken to Guerrero's powerful boss.

The American didn't stand a chance. And she knew exactly how that felt.

CHAPTER 3

Downtown Chicago
The next morning

Before she opened her eyes, Jessie couldn't help but nudge the corner of her lips into a faint smile as she remembered making sweet love to Seth Harper into the wee hours of the morning. Images of Harper in the shower, running his soapy hands over her body, melded into flashes of memory when they'd made love by candlelight in his bed under white sheets.

Harper had always been beautiful to her, but by candlelight, he was unforgettable. And her skin flushed hot with the thought of him inside her, the urgency of his body filling her need for him. He made her feel wanted and loved and . . . beautiful. In the dim glow of candles and seeing herself in his eyes, she could forget the scars on her body and the deeper wounds she carried in her heart.

Even now, with eyes shut, she sensed the gray of morning and moaned with pleasure as she rolled toward Harper, wrapped in his comforter. But when something wet and cold nudged her chin, she flinched and opened her eyes with a start.

"What the hell . . . ?" she blurted out, running a hand over her face to clear the cob webs.

"You know, in some states, you could get arrested for that." Harper's voice came from across the room.

If he was over there, then who was in the bed with her?

With eyes wide, Jess sat up and pulled the sheets over her naked body. And she found herself staring into the face of the ugliest dog she'd ever seen—a brown-and-black-striped, brindle-colored pit bull with a large square head marred with scars. Its muzzle and paws were white, and the tip of one bent ear was gone. The dog sprawled on her lap and cocked its head, whimpering. Its tiny dark eyes were dwarfed by the size of its huge, panting grin.

"Meet my roommate, Floyd." Harper grinned. "I know you're gonna find this hard to believe, but he's not just another pretty face."

Dressed only in worn jeans, Seth joined her on

the bed. His hair was damp from the shower, and he flopped down on the mattress. Not even his enticing aroma of citrus soap cut the smell of warm dog breath.

"Floyd?" she asked.

"Yep, that's it. No last name. Just Floyd." Harper ran a hand over the dog's head. "He adopted me."

"Lucky you."

Jess scratched behind the dog's ear. The pit bull moaned and leaned into her hand until it flopped onto the bed, chest up and legs flailing.

"He's easy," she said.

"Yeah, he takes after me." Harper brushed back a strand of hair from her eyes. "Have I mentioned how much I love having you here? I love it even more than my towel warmer."

"Thanks, I think." She did a double take. "Wait a minute. You have a towel warmer?"

He grinned. "Come on. I've got breakfast started. Hope you're hungry. I couldn't decide what to make, so I kinda got carried away."

"Ah, Seth. You didn't have to . . ."

"I know, but I wanted to."

She opened her mouth to tell him what was on her mind, about the trip she had planned to Wisconsin, but Seth's face was an open book, and he looked like he had something more to say.

"Listen, Jess. Tanya Spencer assigned me a new

project. Sounds pretty important to her, something below the radar. I'm expecting her call. I wanted to spend the day with you, just the two of us, but I may have to work, so I'm officially apologizing now."

"Well, get in line, Harper, 'cause when it comes to official apologies, I owe you a big one."

Seth ran a hand through his wavy damp hair and shrugged.

"Not before coffee. House rules." He got off the bed and headed toward the door, with Floyd close on his heels. "Come on. Get dressed, Jess. Sounds like we've got talking to do."

Before he left the room, she called out, "Hey, Harper. Have I told you how much I love you?"

When he turned, he flashed a crooked grin, and his cheeks blushed pink. "Not today, but feel free to make that up to me."

Jessie knew Seth would be disappointed that she couldn't stay, especially after he surprised her with his new place—a home he wanted to make with her. She wished things could have been different, too, but she couldn't stop thinking about the mother she never knew and a dark past that still haunted her.

Harper would want to help, but she knew that he'd respect her wishes. This trip was something she needed to do alone.

New York City

Alexa had stayed up all night, working her own contacts. She'd made countless phone calls and even worked local sources by hitting the streets and visiting old haunts of Garrett's. No one knew what he'd been working on before he vanished.

"Damn it, Garrett," she muttered as she checked her cell for messages.

She resisted the urge to stay angry at him. The bastard had always been secretive. It was his nature, but that made it hard for her to feel the intimacy she had always craved with him—a closeness he probably had never shared with anyone—not even with lovers.

Sipping Starbucks coffee that she'd grabbed on the go, she navigated the Upper East Side on foot, heading back to her home. It would be the first time since yesterday afternoon that she would cross her own threshold, but not before she talked to Tanya to see if the analyst had had any better luck in tracking Garrett.

After she hit speed dial, Tanya picked up on the second ring.

"Hey, Tanya, it's me. I suppose you heard?"

"Yeah, I heard what that man is sayin'."

Alexa heard the contempt in Tanya's voice, contempt meant for Donovan Cross. The Sentinels had replaced Garrett without causing a ripple on still water. It was business as usual, but not for her or Tanya, maybe others. Replacing Garrett would be hard, but she didn't trust Cross. Something about him left her wary. Call it gut instinct. And she had to admit, trusting anyone after the tight connection she had with Garrett would be next to impossible.

"Do you believe his story . . . about Garrett being dead?" she asked Tanya, resenting the doubt she heard in her own voice.

"Do you?" the woman shot back.

Before Alexa answered, her friend softened her tone.

"Look, I don't know what to believe, except that I want all this to go away. All I know is that if he's dead, I need proof. That's all I'm sayin'. Guess I don't trust that wannabe, Cross. Garrett Wheeler he ain't, honey."

Tanya's Southern drawl always intensified whenever her attitude flared.

"Yeah, guess I'm not willing to give up hope either. Thanks for the pep talk."

"Anytime, sugar. Now what have you been up to? Talk to me."

Alexa tossed her empty Starbucks cup into a trash bin on the street, happy to get back to business.

"I've covered all my contacts, locals and otherwise. I've come up dry so far. If anyone knows anything, they're not talking. Something's up. I can feel it." As the traffic light changed ahead, she found a quieter spot away from the crowd. "How about you? You got anything?"

"Yeah, maybe. I've got a lead, but you're not gonna like it."

"Why?" Her voice edged with worry. "What did you find out?"

"A guy in Logistics told me Garrett had taken a small team on a mission, but he can't find any record of it. Whatever he had seen is gone now. And there's no trace of the cover-up either. He's working from memory."

"And how good is that? Can we trust this guy?"

"I trust him, but I'm also looking for confirmation. Give me a little time. If there's something out there, I'll find it," Tanya said. "My contact thinks Garrett was working off book, something I haven't seen him do before. And according to my guy, no one knows anything about it, not even those who should. It's really strange, Alexa. It's like he's dropped off the planet, and no one is talking."

"So did your contact have the names, the guys he took on his team?"

"Not yet, but he's working up a list of operatives who are AWOL without a specific assignment. A process of elimination. He'll call me later with that intel. It's the best we can do without more to go on. What are you thinking?"

"Garrett is too cagey to leave a trail, but maybe someone on his team wasn't so careful." Before Tanya could respond, Alexa heaved a sigh. "The thing is, why would he do anything without you knowing about it, Tanya? What could be so damned important to break protocol?"

"Good question, honey. I wish I knew." Tanya commiserated with her in silence before she said, "There's something else I have to tell you. I got a call five minutes ago. And you're not gonna like this either."

Tanya had mastered the art of the understatement. If she was concerned, that meant things were usually far worse.

"What's up, Tanya? Spill it."

Alexa shut her eyes, feeling a headache coming on. Her brownstone apartment was a few blocks away. She'd be home soon and could use the second wind that a long hot shower could deliver.

"Donovan Cross is looking for you. He wouldn't tell me what it was about, but I don't like it."

"Why didn't he call my cell?"

"He strikes me as someone who'd rather come at you sideways rather than head-on, like one of those sidewinder snakes." Tanya was spot-on with her analogy. "What do you want me to tell him?"

"If I was a suspicious person, I'd say he's working you to get to me. I don't trust him."

"You got that right. As far as I'm concerned, the jury is still out on Cross. I don't trust him either," Tanya said. "So what do you want me to do?"

"Stall him for now. Tell him you can't reach me. That'll give me time to get really lost, but I'll need you to be my eyes and ears. And when you find a lead on Garrett's last-known location, I'll need a way to get there. I'll call you when it's safe."

"You got it."

When Tanya ended the call, Alexa made up her mind to avoid her apartment and rely on her instincts to work off the grid. No one could know what she was doing. No one, not even Tanya. She didn't make such a decision lightly. There was risk in what she planned to do, but she'd already set up for such a contingency. Most covert operatives had a similar backup plan, out of necessity.

Heading west, she walked across the street, tossed her cell into a trash bin, and took the first step to sever ties to her life. An operative always had a fallback plan if all hell broke loose. Cash was stashed away with prepaid cell phones, fake IDs, and passports stowed in safe-deposit boxes. It was time to utilize what she'd set up long ago.

And it was time to find out what had happened to Garrett, even if the news wasn't what she wanted to hear.

Outside Guadalajara, Mexico

Estella crept down the murky corridor but ducked behind a stone wall when she noticed the guard outside one of the jail cells. If she got caught, Guerrero would punish her, whipping her for disobeying his order to stay in her room. She had no doubt that she wouldn't have been alone for long. Guerrero's men would finally come for what their boss might have promised, and Estella would rather die than sit and wait for that to happen.

But why she had come to find the American, she had no idea. The man had one foot in the grave. He wasn't strong enough to help her escape her fate, yet she followed her instincts to find him. She'd come to see where they had him. And even from where she stood, cowering in the shadows, she heard what they were doing to him. And it made her sick.

One voice stood out from the rest. And the sound of his cruelty raised the hair on her neck.

"Do it. Now!"

With the help of another man, Ramon Guerrero followed orders and grabbed the head of the naked prisoner. He shoved the man's face into a tub of filthy water. With his hands in shackles, Garrett Wheeler bucked to break free, sloshing water to the stone floor. When he stopped struggling, and the last bubbles erupted to break the surface of the water, Guerrero looked over his shoulder at the man who had given the order.

Miguel Rosas, number two man to the head of the Pérez cartel, had a reputation for brutality, with the body count to prove it. The Pérez cartel was a splinter group making a name and expanding its reach. And Rosas had played a big part in the Pérez family's growing reign of terror in the country. Guerrero had no appreciation for the politics within the organization. He was only a soldier within its ranks, only wanting to carve out his piece of the pie. A manageable piece.

Guerrero had transported the drugged American to a heavily guarded villa outside Guadalajara, Mexico. Being allowed to remain with Wheeler had been a good sign that powerful men had taken notice and trusted him to get the job done. Participating in the interrogation was another good sign. He didn't care if Wheeler died, but it made no sense to kill him before they got him to talk.

Finally, Rosas nodded, and the prisoner was yanked from the water. A loud, guttural gasp reverberated off the walls, but when Wheeler said nothing, his reprieve was short-lived.

"Again," Rosas demanded.

"No," the bound man gagged as his head was shoved back under the murky water. This time, when he was brought up, Rosas stepped closer and looked down at the gasping man.

"You make this harder than it needs to be. Who have you come to kill? And why are you here, in my country?" When Rosas spoke, his voice echoed. "Tell us what we need to know, and your misery will be over. Are you not hungry? Would it not feel good to sleep?"

Wheeler had not been allowed to rest after the drug had worn off. He'd been forced to stand naked in his cell and had been drenched with water every time he could no longer open his eyes. And he'd not been given food or drink. A local doctor had been on call to keep the American alive as the torture escalated.

And still, Wheeler had not told them anything.

Guerrero grabbed the American's hair and yanked his head back. The man's jaw fell slack as he panted for air, his chest heaving.

Mustering his contempt, he glared at Rosas. "Go to . . . hell."

"Very well. You leave me no choice."

In Spanish, Rosas gave an order, and the American was hung by his arms, suspended in chains from a massive wooden beam, and his body was doused with water. When an electrical generator was powered up, Guerrero knew what would come next.

Garrett Wheeler would be taken to the edge of death by electrocution. The American flinched when he saw one of Rosas's men touch two metal paddles together. A loud pop erupted, and a spark of electricity cast an eerie light into the murky cell.

The American narrowed his eyes and glared at his tormentor, Rosas. When Wheeler tensed his jaw, he didn't say a word, mustering what little defiance he had left. All that changed after the order was given. When the paddles sparked, volts of electricity shot through the American's body, making him jerk like a macabre puppet. Smoke drifted in the stale air, and the smell of burning skin and hair hit Guerrero's nostrils.

With a dismissive wave of his hand, Rosas eventually ordered his men to stop. Wheeler's body collapsed, still rippling with spasms. After he grunted in pain and fell unconscious, Rosas walked toward Guerrero and stood at his shoulder, speaking in a low voice.

"You do not approve of my methods. I can see it in your eyes."

Guerrero kept his dislike for Rosas in check. Looking into the man's eyes reminded him of the time he had confronted a rabid dog, an animal he would never turn his back on. With a man like Rosas, he had to tread carefully. One wrong word could ruin everything he had hoped to gain, or worse, put him in the crosshairs of a man he would rather not cross paths with again.

"It is not my place to approve or disapprove." Guerrero avoided looking at the man standing next to him.

"It is good that you know your place," Rosas said.

If the man had not looked so smug, Guerrero might have kept his mouth shut. But when Rosas ordered one of his men to awaken the American with a bucketful of water, Guerrero said what was on his mind. He could not help himself.

"It's just that this American, Garrett Wheeler, has many secrets worthy of your efforts. My sources tell me he is the leader of a very influential U.S. agency sent to spy on us. And who knows what someone would pay for a man like this."

"Yes, I know what you reported, but Pérez believes this American might be a diversion for a bigger assault on the cartels. The United States would do anything to stop the violence in our country."

"What are you saying?"

"What if the CIA or this agency Wheeler works for is planning to assassinate the leaders of the cartels, pick them off one by one, making it look like a drug war? Pérez doesn't care about what happens to the other cartels, but having advance information is very important."

"And I suppose if the competition is eliminated, that would not be a bad thing."

"Yes, of course." Rosas smiled. "So as you can see, our job here is very important."

Before Guerrero replied, the man looked over his shoulder at the waking prisoner hanging in chains. He ordered his men to hit him with the paddles again. Wheeler's body jerked with another jolt of electricity. He cried out, unable to hold back.

In reflex, Guerrero grimaced and noticed that Miguel Rosas was watching him. With the American dangling and jerking like a caught fish, Rosas only smiled at Guerrero, displaying a strange cruelty that caused the hair on the back of Guerrero's neck to stand.

At that moment, he knew that Miguel Rosas was a man who truly enjoyed his work.

Outside Guadalajara, Mexico

"We lost his signal, sir," his man reported as he knelt by him in the dark.

Following a burst transmitter signal, Hank Lewis and his team had crossed the border into Mexico and were positioned on a nearby ridge overlooking a large hacienda near Guadalajara. The estate was located on the northern shore of Laguna de Chapala, where his team was conducting a covert surveillance operation for the Sentinels, tracking an operative under deep cover who was being held prisoner inside.

As to who their operative was—or the purpose of their mission—Hank had no clue.

His team had been monitoring thermal imagery, tracking the movements of the men inside the compound, when he got the bad news about the transmitter. The device sent a burst of data at regular intervals via satellite, transmitting coordinates for his team to follow once an hour, but it also served a secondary purpose. It recorded the operative's vitals to make sure the unlucky bastard was still alive. From what Hank had been told, the transmitter had been implanted under the skin of their target.

The tracking device was damned small, an upgraded, high-tech version of the ones used to track the migratory patterns of wildlife. And unless someone knew what to look for, the transmission frequency was very hard to trace since it wasn't a constant signal. This version passed a bug sweep without a problem for the same reason. It only powered up once an hour, long enough to gather vitals, compress the data, and transmit it. That also meant the battery power would be minimal, which translated into a tracking device that could be injected under the skin with a hypodermic needle. A perfect piece of technology for this mission, until it failed.

"What do you think happened?" he asked his man.

"Don't know, sir. I'm trying to figure that out. Got cut off midtransmission."

"Keep trying, son."

"Yes, sir."

Hank didn't like being in the dark on a sensitive mission like this one. His team was on the front line of the op. If they couldn't find out what had happened, the mission could be scrapped. And Hank didn't want that to happen on his watch.

"What about our target's vitals, Doc?" Hank directed his question to the medic on his team. "Did we get a reading before we lost the signal?"

"I saw enough to know the target is an extremely agitated state. His breathing is irregular, and his heart rate is erratic. Up one minute and down the next. From my experience, the lower heart rate comes when the body is fighting off torture. It's a natural instinct."

"Is he in danger from a medical standpoint?" Hank asked. "Do we need to pull the plug?"

"I can't tell you. I didn't get enough of a data feed to form an opinion other than his body is under a great deal of stress, and one other thing." The medic fixed his gaze on Hank. "If we had to attempt a rescue, we'd probably have to carry him out."

Hank narrowed his eyes, considering what the man had told him.

"Thanks, Doc." And to his communications man, Hank said, "Let me know if Guerrero leaves the compound. We're still tracking his cell-phone GPS, right?"

"Yes, sir. If he moves, I'll know it."

Ramon Guerrero was their backup plan. Intel tracked a cell-phone signal from the moment the target had been taken hostage. One of the gang members had initiated a call to report what had happened. And Hank's team was already set to take advantage of that mistake. His team monitored any cell-phone signal detected in the general vicinity. Once they eliminated any legitimate cell-phone user through a background check, they narrowed their search to phones that could not be linked to a name. It was a surveillance tactic that had paid off in the fight against al-Qaeda.

Coupled with ground surveillance of the abduction, they eventually tracked the signal into Mexico, near Juárez, the stronghold of Ramon Guerrero, a known drug-cartel leader. After another sweep of cell-phone usage inside the compound, they used the process of elimination to isolate Guerrero's cell phone and had followed him and his men to Guadalajara, to the estate of another drug kingpin in the organization. Odds were that if the target was still alive, Guerrero would be close by. It was the best they could do without knowing more.

Hank's team had been fed coordinates through a handler, a man who monitored the transmission via satellite. Until now, they had stuck close to the target, moving as ordered. But with the target being in danger, and the burst transmitter potentially compromised, Hank knew the handler would have to kick the problem to the next level, the decision maker who was running the op.

Hank reached for the encrypted phone he'd use to communicate with his handler, a middleman in the operation. Although Hank was in command of the ground team, he didn't know who they were tracking inside the drug cartel or why the mission had required the secrecy. That bit of intel was on a need-to-know basis. Only one man knew all the details and would make the final call on every aspect of the mission. Communicating through the handler, he would direct Hank's team to carry out his orders.

But if the burst transmitter's signal was gone, they were flying blind. And the poor bastard on the inside would be on his own.

"Damn it," Hank cursed.

CHAPTER 4

New York City
Evening

Instinct had Alexa fixing her eyes on the reflection in a store window as she walked down Broadway. Display lights and neon signs cast enough light for her to see something she didn't like. She'd stopped suddenly, pretending to have an interest in a pair of Jimmy Choo stilettos.

That was when she caught the exchange.

A man had stopped short and looked across the street. Two men were following her, one in a dark business suit and the other in jeans, a Yankees ball cap, and a white T-shirt with a logo across his chest, too small for her to read. Their reaction had been subtle, but it was enough to trigger her survival instincts. From experience and training, she knew to trust her gut and take action. Indecision was not an option. And in the field, to hesitate might get her killed.

Without turning around, Alexa assessed her situation. If the men were connected to a surveillance team, they'd have a backup plan if she hailed a cab. And they could track the cab through the taxi company. Without thinking, she quickly ducked into the store and made her way to the back. When she saw a salesclerk heading for her, she smiled and waved her off.

"You got a way out back? I'm trying to avoid an old boyfriend. You know how it goes."

"Sure do, honey." The sharply dressed saleswoman pointed toward the dressing rooms. "We got a loading dock through those doors, and good luck ditching the jerk."

Within a minute, Alexa was on foot down an alley. She cut through another store and changed course again until she had lost the two men tailing her, but that didn't mean she was in the clear.

When she found a main thoroughfare, she took a risk and hailed a cab. She was already late. If she didn't rush, the bank would be closed when she got there.

And without the contents of her safe-deposit box, she'd be dead in the water.

Sentinels' Headquarters

"She tried to ditch us, but we picked her up again."

"Where is she?" Donovan Cross asked the agent who headed the second surveillance team tracking Marlowe.

"Bank of America. We've got eyes inside the bank. She's in the vault, accessing a safe-deposit box. What do you want us to do?"

Cross didn't like the sounds of this. If Marlowe was like any other good agent, she had a plan to ditch her identity and become someone else. And the contents of her safe-deposit box would help her do that. He knew from personal experience that she'd have fake passports and IDs, cash from several countries, and myriad ways for her to stay off the grid. A seasoned field agent like Alexa Marlowe would have stashed plenty of ways for her to get very lost.

"Don't let her out of your sight, do you understand?" Cross found it hard to keep the urgency from his voice.

"Copy that. When she leaves the vault, we'll be on her sweet ass."

"Just call me when she leaves." Cross ended the call and tossed his cell onto Garrett's desk.

Arrogant son of a bitch! Cross had more respect for Alexa than the pompous jerk following her, and he hoped he wouldn't regret giving the assignment to a young agent with something to prove.

"What are you up to, Marlowe?" He sprawled in his chair and stared across Garrett Wheeler's office. "And what have you got stashed at that bank?"

Cross had a bad feeling he wasn't going to like the answer to that question.

Sentinels' Headquarters
Twenty minutes later

"We lost her." Donovan Cross hated failure, especially when he had to be the one to admit he'd underestimated Alexa Marlowe. "I had a team on her when she left headquarters, but she gave them the slip."

"Do you think she knew she was being followed?"

The man on the other end of the line was his contact deep within the Sentinels' organization, one of the anonymous members of the elite council who secretly ran the covert group from a discreet distance.

"In a word . . . yes. Bank video footage showed

she entered the vault to access a safe-deposit box, but the surveillance team lost her coming out."

"How is that possible?" The man on the phone asked the same question he had only moments ago.

"Apparently, she had a change of clothes and a wig in that box. She ditched the stuff she had on in a vault trash bin. And the disguise she used was good enough to give our team the slip when she left the bank. She was dressed like an old woman."

Cross knew that field operatives could be real cagey and downright paranoid. If the hair on their necks got goosed, it wouldn't matter if they actually saw anyone tailing them. They'd follow their instincts and get lost in a crowd. And they had the training to carry out that slick maneuver easily enough.

"What about her apartment?"

"The surveillance team had someone there, too, but she never showed. We still have it staked out, but I don't think she'll go there now."

"This isn't good, Cross. What are you doing to rectify the situation?"

"We may have a line on her. When I get something definitive, I'll call you."

Cross told the man how his surveillance team had scoured digital camera feeds from all over the city after they'd hacked into the municipal traffic system. They'd picked up Alexa again—once they knew what disguise to look for—and although they hadn't pinpointed her exact location, they were getting close.

Very close.

"I don't have to tell you how sensitive our operation is at the moment. Find her, Cross. Do it, now."

After his call ended, Cross gritted his teeth. He hated losing. And Marlowe had bested him from day one, but with the success of the mission on his shoulders, that had to stop.

Outside New York City
10:40 P.M.

After Alexa felt safe enough, she grabbed a quick bite from a fast-food drive-through and hit a twenty-four-hour pharmacy before she found a place to spend the night. Without prying eyes, she changed her hair color to brown and took a quick shower. After a couple of hours' sack time, she'd hit the road again. But before that happened, she checked in with Tanya Spencer, her only lifeline.

"Hey, it's me." Alexa didn't say her name. "You got anything new?"

She'd used a prepaid cell, a number that Tanya

wouldn't know, but she figured the analyst would recognize her voice and take everything in stride like the pro she was.

"Yeah, I think I found something." Tanya dispensed with the usual formalities of asking questions and kept her focus. "But it doesn't make much sense."

"What do you mean?" With a towel wrapped around her wet hair, Alexa sat on the corner of her motel bed, a room she'd paid for in cash.

"Someone with access to our internal resources is using satellite time to track a cell-phone GPS signal in Mexico. And as far as I can tell, no one at the Sentinels has an operation in that country. Normally, I wouldn't make a big deal about this, but since we're looking for anything out of the ordinary, it piqued my interest."

"Do you have a name of the owner of the cell, or maybe the coordinates of that GPS signal?" she asked.

"No name, but I do have coordinates." Tanya gave her a location outside Guadalajara, Mexico. "And I've got Seth Harper working this on the QT. With him being located in Chicago, he's got no one looking over his shoulder to see what he's up to."

"Good call. Not many people connected to the Sentinels know Harper, and the guy can keep a secret." Alexa tightened the towel that she had wrapped around her body. "So what's near there? Can you tell if the signal is coming from a residence?"

"Did some digging on that. It's not just a residence, it's an estate, honey. And the property had a few layers of corporations heaped on top of the name of the real owner. I had to call in a few markers to dig that deep."

"And? Who's playing the shell game?"

"Manolo Quintanilla Pérez is the owner of record. He's the head of a drug cartel, an upstart group that's trying to make a name. What they lack in longevity, they more than make up for in brutality. A fun bunch."

"So if you can't find any record of this op, what makes you think Garrett is involved?" Alexa asked.

"My Logistics contact came up with those AWOL operatives who don't have a specific assignment. And one name got my interest. Hank Lewis. Besides you, Hank is one of Garrett's 'go to' guys. It's just a gut feeling, but I think this is the thread of information we've been looking for. We may not get anything better, Alexa."

For the first time since she had learned of Garrett's disappearance, Alexa felt the pang of regret. Whatever Garrett was involved with, he hadn't included her. He'd chosen Hank Lewis to confide in and lead the team that would back his play.

Why hadn't Garrett asked her?

"I know what you're thinking," Tanya said after her silence left an awkward wake in the conversation. "And when we find him, you can ask why he was so bullheaded about not making you a part of his team, but right now we've got work to do."

"Yeah, you're right." Alexa took a deep breath and rubbed her temple. The tension headache that had started earlier in the day had gotten worse. "I'm going to Mexico, Tanya. I don't think we've got another choice."

"Honey, I knew you'd say that."

Tanya had already worked out the logistics for her trip to Guadalajara. She'd leave at first light. If Garrett was in Mexico, she would find him.

She had to.

Northern Wisconsin

Jessie gulped down the last dregs of cold coffee from a lidded styrofoam cup and ate what was left of the Cheetos as she drove through Wisconsin. With orange fingertips, she gripped the wheel of her rented Taurus sedan and watched the center stripes roll by under its high beams.

The sun had gone down hours ago, taking with it the last of the scenery worth seeing. Rolling green hills dotted with picturesque dairy farms and placid lakes that mirrored the waning sunset had been replaced by darkness and miles of self-doubt. She had plenty of time to think. In her state of mind, that wasn't necessarily a good thing.

She had paid the price for getting a late start on her drive to La Pointe. Thinking of Seth had made the trip easier, but it was hard to ignore the nagging thoughts about her past. She had talked with Seth over breakfast and explained why she'd come to Chicago. And like she had expected, Harper had plenty of questions as they sat at his dining-room table.

"Do you really think this old case might give you a lead on your mother? That's huge, Jess." Harper leaned closer, elbows on the table, as he grabbed her hand. "I mean, how does that make you feel?"

Jess shook her head, and said, "I don't know, exactly. After all this time, a part of me wants to know what happened, but maybe this will make things worse."

If she had to let go of the only good memory she had—the only shining moment of the woman she believed was her mother—Jessie wasn't sure she could handle that. Her whole life had been about abuse—what one sick man had done to her and what she had done to herself when she didn't feel she deserved to be happy. Jessie wanted to believe she had gotten past it, but she knew that wasn't true.

She never would.

"I can come with you," Seth had offered. "I can have someone look after Floyd while we're gone."

"But what about that assignment you have with Tanya?"

Harper launched into geek speak, telling her about his new laptop, courtesy of the Sentinels. He had plenty of juice to keep in touch with Tanya Spencer on the road.

"My new laptop is ubersexy. I can stay connected with New York. No worries." He squeezed her hand and fixed his gaze on her. "I just don't think you should make this trip alone."

Looking into Harper's eyes made anything possible. Jess thought about his offer as they sat in silence. She'd have to keep her explanation simple and something Seth would understand. She would avoid telling him the real reason she needed to make the trek to Wisconsin alone, mostly because she didn't want to hear the words come out of her mouth.

If her mother had anything to do with how she ended up with a serial pedophile, Jessie wasn't sure how she would handle that. She'd rather face that reality alone and deal with it on her own terms. And if there had been a reason why she was never claimed by a family after her ordeal as a child, maybe Chief Tobias Cook might know what it was.

"I appreciate the offer, Seth, but I think this is something I'm gonna do on my own. I hope you understand."

Of all people, Harper would understand her need to uncover the truth about her mother by herself. For years, he'd been dealing with the fragile relationship he'd had with his father while growing up. In her eyes, Harper's father would always be a hero, but that hadn't been the way Seth saw it.

His old man was a retired cop who had been an AWOL dad when Harper needed him. It didn't matter that his father had sacrificed his personal life for the sake of his job. To a small boy, that didn't matter. And in a strange show of irony that life often dished out, now Harper was responsible for his father's care after dementia had sidelined him at a nursing home with no one else to take care of him. Seth had dealt with his burden on his own, too, even after he and Jessie had met and grown close. Sometimes, family problems hit too close to home to share with anyone.

"Yeah, guess I do. Family stuff can really mess with your head," he said. "But I want you to call me, anytime. You hear?"

"Yeah, I will."

"Don't say that unless you mean it, Jessie. Swear to me."

"Pinkie swear." She raised her hand and offered her pinkie. When Seth took it with his, she added, "I'll call you."

Under the table, Floyd sprawled at her feet and groaned. When he moved, the dog passed gas. Jessie tried hard not to take it personally.

"Oh man, Floyd. Give it a rest, big guy." Harper grimaced as he waved his hand. "Sorry about that. He must like you."

"I'll be sure and send him a thank-you note."

Although Seth had covered up his disappointment well with a soft chuckle, his eyes mirrored everything he felt. She knew he was worried about her and had been disappointed she hadn't asked him to come. In the end, he had to settle for feeding her, arranging for a reliable rental car, and stocking her sedan with Harper-worthy munchies. Field-tested eats, he'd called them. Jess didn't get on the road until early afternoon and had nearly nine long hours ahead of her.

She'd arrive well after dark at a remote location she'd never been to. And the only ferry making the trek to Madeline Island stopped at midnight. If anything went wrong, it would be close, but lingering with Seth in Chicago had been worth it.

She ached, having to leave Harper behind. Even Floyd had grown on her. She tried to imagine living with someone else, especially someone like Harper. She kept odd hours, took risks, and had never answered to anyone. The abuse she had suffered in the past was a strong driver for the woman she had become. Could she change the way she looked at the world for him? Despite the fact that she loved Seth, how would she feel about sharing her life?

Self-doubt had always been her number one enemy. It was easier to picture Harper getting tired of her than the other way around. When anything good happened, her first response was to beat herself up over it. And things hadn't changed much over the years. By the time she made it to Bayfield and the ferry, she had a wad of tension in her stomach the size of Floyd's head.

"Why do you keep doing this to yourself?" she muttered.

Jessie bought passage on the Madeline Island Ferry Line and pulled her vehicle onto the loading zone behind a guy in a red pickup. In no time, she was waved onto the ferry and told where to park. She could have stayed in her rental car for the half-hour ride to the island, but the moonlight dappled on the water was far too enticing. Jessie headed for the bow of the ferry and let the cool breeze tousle her hair.

In the distance, she saw the lights from La Pointe, a small town shining its beacon along the shoreline of Lake Superior. No big-city lights spoiled the incredible canopy of stars over her head. She took a deep breath and leaned against the railing, feeling incredibly small and inconsequential.

Whatever she learned the next day from Chief Cook would change everything she knew about her mother. She felt certain of that. She wanted to brace herself for what would come next, but she had no idea what that might be.

She had just begun to think her life had turned a corner, with Seth and Alexa and her best friend, Sam Cooper, in her life. And working for the Sentinels had been a step in the right direction, too. It meant she had a steady income and could leave behind her ratty Chicago apartment and the scumbags she had tracked for money as a bounty hunter, working one bail jumper at a time.

If she learned that her past was darker than she could have imagined, what new ways would she find to punish herself for coming from a crappy gene pool? Jessie shut her eyes when she felt the sting of tears. Wallowing in self-pity had its appeal, but the ferry had docked, and she'd arrived at La Pointe.

After she'd disembarked from the ferry, she got a better look at the small harbor town. The place wasn't much more than a few dimly lit streets that intersected. A visitor would have to work damned hard to get lost.

Except for a few bars, La Pointe was closed for the night. Most of the other businesses were geared for the tourist trade. Gift shops, quaint cafés, realty offices, and motels with self-serve Laundromats lined the narrow streets. When she located the police station, it was on the main drag across from a diner and a local watering hole, with a motel only a short walk away.

"Looks like I've struck the mother lode."

Jessie pulled into a parking spot near a motel that had a flashing red neon sign claiming it had a vacancy. Once she got out of her car, the sound of waves ebbing against the shoreline haunted her memory like a tune she was desperately trying to remember. La Pointe had triggered something in her that she couldn't quite put a finger on.

Only occasional laughter and jukebox music coming from a nearby bar interrupted her trip down memory lane. The remote location and the small size of the town made her wonder about her connection to it all. The place probably had a thriving tourist trade, and, during the day, it no doubt had its merits; but at night, it left her feeling lonely and on edge. Every shadow held demons from a past she needed to know more about.

How did you end up here, Beck?

Standing outside her car, Jessie looked around. There wasn't much to see this time of night, but she got a real hinky vibe when she thought about living in a town like this. There'd be no place to hide from who you were, and everyone would know your business, or think they knew it. Living in a place like La Pointe would be a disaster for someone like her. That was why living with hordes of strangers, like she had in Chicago and New York, had been a major relief. Except for Sam and Harper, no one knew her story. And she could reinvent herself whenever she felt the need.

Jessie looked into the window of the motel office and saw the light of a TV cutting the shadows in a room behind the counter. Someone was up. Her hiking boots crunched gravel until she hit the wooden boardwalk in front of the motel. When she stepped inside the front door, a doorbell tinkled overhead. The cramped space was filled to the rafters with knickknacks for sale, small-sized containers of toiletries, gum, and breath mints, and plenty of snacks even Harper would endorse.

"You come off the last ferry?" The motel clerk stepped out from the room where she'd seen the TV.

Jessie spied the clerk's name posted on a wall plaque behind the counter. Byron McGivens.

"Yeah, as a matter of fact, I did. You got a room, Byron?"

"Sure do." He worked the keyboard of his computer and kept talking. "If you came off that ferry, did you drive from somewhere or just walk on?"

"I drove up from Chicago." She was tired enough to let Byron's prying get to her. "What's with the twenty questions?"

"I didn't mean anything by it." He shrugged and had a hard time looking her in the eye. "Living in a small town, you get curious, that's all."

Jessie hadn't noticed before, but the guy got a little antsy when she pushed back on his questions. She'd probably overreacted.

"Sorry. Guess I'm a little tired."

After an awkward moment, the guy broke the ice.

"Okay, I've got another question, but this one's business. How long you stayin'?"

"Not sure." Jessie narrowed her eyes. "Can I tell you later?"

"Yeah, no problem."

The guy had on a royal blue T-shirt with the name Madeline Island printed in white across his chest. He looked to be in his thirties, with dark thinning hair and a day's worth of scruffy growth. After she handed him her credit card, the clerk had another request.

"I'm gonna need to see some ID."

"Sure." She fished for her driver's license and handed it to him.

"You can never be too careful these days," he said after he'd taken a good look at her ID and handed it back. "I've got you in number 12. Less road noise there. You can park around back."

"Thanks."

Jessie took her room key and headed to her car. She drove around back and carried in her one bag. The motel room was basic. Near the front door was a window with an air conditioner below it. One table was tightly squeezed next to the queen bed, with the bathroom toward the back and plenty of shag carpet in between. The room smelled moldy, like every other low-rent place she'd ever stayed in.

"Just like home."

Before she unpacked, Jessie reached for her cell phone and hit her speed dial, making a call to the one guy who could make her feel better.

Harper.

"Hey," she said quietly, finding solace in the sound of his sleepy voice. "It's me."

Shoreview Motel
After midnight

"You told me to call. A woman checked in just now."

Byron McGivens spoke low. Even though no one was within earshot at this hour, it seemed like the thing to do. He didn't expect the rapid-fire questions that came at him before he had a chance to think. This time of night, his brain wasn't working on all cylinders.

"Yeah, I checked. Her name's Jessica Beckett. And I verified that by her driver's license. She drove up from Chicago."

The motel clerk stepped out from behind the counter and walked toward the window, looking down Main Street.

"You need me to do anything else?"

Before he even got his question out, he was left listening to nothing but dial tone, with not so much as a good-bye. He would have been irritated with the rude way he'd been treated, but with the cash he'd been given, he overlooked it. Spying on a guest was easy money. And he hoped he hadn't seen the last of his newfound good fortune.

If his services were needed again, he'd be ready.

The Pérez Compound
Outside Guadalajara, Mexico

Estella had stayed as long as she dared, but after seeing bright light erupting from the make-shift jail cell and hearing the screams of a man in pain, she knew they were torturing the American, and she ran.

She tore down the stone corridor, back the way she'd come. There was nothing she could do for the man, not now. Tears clouded her eyes, and she had never felt so alone. When she hit the night air, she sucked it into her lungs, fighting back the sadness that threatened to choke her.

After Estella closed the door behind her, she leaned against it before she collapsed. Trembling, she made the sign of the cross and slid to the ground, clutching her arms around her. How did she end up here? And what would become of her? A small part of her had hoped the prisoner would be strong enough to escape and save her, but now she knew that would never be.

If her mother had known this, would she still have sold her to Guerrero?

Estella knew the answer to that question, and it made her sick. Her own mother had betrayed her. And she would've done it again if it meant more money for her next fix. When she had the strength to walk, Estella stood and headed for her room in a building next to the main house. She crept through an adjacent patio garden and stuck to the shadows, which would hide her from the guards patrolling the grounds. When she'd made it to the hallway—and knew her room was at the end of the hall—she breathed a sigh of relief. No one was waiting for her outside.

Her room was next to the maid's quarters, not much more than a closet, with only a bed and one lamp on a small wooden table. There was no lock on her door. Even if she wanted to hide, she couldn't do it.

She slowly turned the knob of her door and peeked inside. When she saw that the room was dark, she slipped in with hands outstretched as she fumbled for the lamp.

When she touched the chest of a man, standing in front of her, she screamed. An arm tightened around her neck, cutting off her air.

"No, please . . . d-don't hurt m-me," she begged in Spanish, not recognizing her own voice.

"You should have thought about that before."

When the man whispered in her ear, she recognized his voice. And his smell had haunted her nightmares. Ramon Guerrero had her by the throat. She couldn't breathe. In the dark, she never saw his face, but Estella knew Ramon took pleasure in her fear.

CHAPTER 5

The Pérez Compound
Before dawn

Ramon Guerrero had found a new way to get the attention of Manolo Quintanilla Pérez, head of his cartel. And the psychopathic tendencies of his number two man, Miguel Rosas, would aid him in doing so.

He had wanted to surprise Estella Calderone in her room, but when she wasn't there, Guerrero had waited. Every minute that ticked by made him angrier. With her disobedience, she'd forced him to punish her. He had no choice if he wanted to retain his reputation.

"Open the cell of the American," he ordered as he hauled the girl down the corridor, by her hair.

A guard did as he was told and stood back as Guerrero shoved the girl to the stone floor inside.

When she hit the ground, she cried out in pain.
And as he expected, Miguel Rosas was waiting in
the corridor.

"String her up," Guerrero demanded, but when
the jailer hesitated, he yelled, "Now!"

After the man reached for the chains, Guerrero
waved his hand.

"Use that rope, over there." He pointed. "Her
wrists are too small for the chains."

He didn't have to see Rosas's face to know that
the man was enjoying this.

"You surprise me, Guerrero, but in a good way."
Rosas smiled. "Since this is your idea, you take
the lead, and I shall watch. Please, carry on."

Although Rosas stepped into the shadows,
Guerrero felt his eyes on him. He would have preferred Rosas take charge and do what came naturally to a man like him.

Estella had disobeyed him. He owed her nothing,
but when Guerrero saw that Rosas wasn't going to
take over, he took a deep breath and thought about
what would come next. How far would he be willing to go to impress a man he didn't respect?

"Please . . . don't do this," the girl begged, with
tears glistening in her eyes. "I swear. I only left
my room for a little while. It was too hot inside. I
needed fresh air. Please."

"You're a lousy liar." He glared at her and pretended to be angrier than he truly was.

When the guard hoisted her off the ground, she cried out in agony. That was when Guerrero turned toward the American, who could barely lift his head. No matter what would come next, the blame would not be his.

"You see? You have done this," Guerrero yelled, and grabbed the man's hair, forcing him to look in his eyes. "Are you willing to let this innocent girl die in your place?"

Guerrero found himself pleading for Estella in earnest. He hoped the American would take pity on her, something he could not afford to do, not with Miguel Rosas watching. If the prisoner cooperated, he could release her without looking like he'd compromised. Sure, the girl needed to be taught a lesson; but if Rosas had his way, she would pay with her miserable life.

When the American opened his mouth to speak, Guerrero hoped he would let him off the hook, but that wasn't the case.

"Using that girl? You're a . . . c-coward, man." The prisoner could barely speak, but he'd said plenty.

Guerrero had no choice now. He had to save face in front of Rosas and his own men.

"Very well. This is on you."

He slid his knife from its sheath and slowly walked back toward Estella. Tears streamed down her face as she sobbed.

"Oh, no . . . Please. Don't do this, Ramon." Her plea echoed off the walls in the small cell. Guerrero gripped the hilt of his blade and clenched his teeth.

Whatever came next wouldn't be *his* fault. Estella had brought this on herself. And everything would depend on what the American would do next.

LaGuardia Airport—New York City
Dawn

The morning sun was making a valiant effort at its first appearance, but the night sky was conspiring with a menacing storm to keep dawn at bay. The dark clouds left Alexa feeling tense, as if nature foreshadowed the approach of something ominous.

Closing her eyes, she pushed the thought aside and sank into her seat on the US Airways jet as it pulled from the gate. She took solace in the fact that she was finally on her way to Mexico and breathed a sigh of relief. By late afternoon, after a change in carriers to Mexicana Airlines, she'd be in Guadalajara after layovers in Charlotte, North Carolina, and Mexico City.

Seeing herself in the reflection of the small window over the wing, she hardly recognized her face. She'd changed her hair color and used contact lenses to alter her distinctive blue eyes to hazel.

She had used fake ID to get past TSA security. And if someone came looking for her image on security cameras, she'd be impossible to recognize. On her neck and arms, she had fake tattoos applied with ballpoint pen, and she walked with a pronounced limp. And her secondhand clothes made her look like a homeless bag lady. Alexa had picked a disguise with layers of clothes in case she had to change on the run, literally.

In her line of work, being a chameleon came with the territory. And it was a skill that would come in handy where she was going. After a fitful sleep last night, she'd had plenty of time to think about her encounter with the two men on the streets of Manhattan. She knew they'd been sent to track her. And she also knew exactly who had sent them.

Donovan Cross.

She didn't have to know the man, only the type. He had pretended to be sincere when he'd told her how Garrett had died. That had been the mark of a real player with a streak of mean. She'd seen the act before. Hell, she'd played the part herself a time or three.

All she had to do was stay one step ahead of that bastard. And with the coordinates and location in Mexico that Tanya had given her, maybe she'd have an edge before Cross knew she was out of the country.

But one other thing was perfectly clear, and it was strangely comforting. If Garrett were dead, Cross wouldn't have sent a team to track her. More than ever, she felt certain her instincts were dead-on.

Garrett was in trouble. And Donovan Cross had no intention of letting her throw him a lifeline.

The Pérez Compound

With Miguel Rosas watching, Ramon Guerrero had to make it look good, even though he hated cutting into the tender flesh of Estella Calderone. She'd been a virgin when he first came to her bed. Her skin had been untouched and perfect.

But now, as he tightened his grip on the knife, he knew she would bear his marks forever. When the tip of the blade cut into her skin, the girl cried out.

"Please . . . don't do this. I beg of you, Ramon."

Under the flickering flame of a torch, he watched a stream of her dark red blood trail down her arm and leach into her blouse. And when she pleaded for him to stop, Guerrero saw the American flinch.

"Using that g-girl, you're a c-coward, Raymond."

"My name is Ramon. And you are the coward, not me. You are the one who is allowing this to happen to her."

"Turn your blade on me. I'm the one you want."

"And still, you do not talk. Why is that?" Guerrero turned toward his hostage and pointed the knife at his eye. "This girl does not have to suffer because of you. All you need to do is answer our questions. Is that so difficult? This could all be over if you would only cooperate."

"You mean we could all be friends? Well, why didn't you just say so?"

Guerrero clenched his jaw and glared at the man. He was tired of his insults.

"Always with the smart mouth. You think this is a game?" He shook his head, but when Guerrero turned his back on the American and stepped closer to Estella, the man spoke up again.

"You work for Pérez." He said it with certainty, as if he knew that for a fact.

"Who?"

"Now who's playing games?"

Guerrero took a risk and glanced at Miguel Rosas, Pérez's watchdog. The man's dark eyes glared back, yet he remained in the shadows, content to let him hang himself.

"Go on," Guerrero said. "What were you going to say?" He turned back toward the American and kept his face a blank slate.

"Before you go past the point of no return, you should contact your boss. Tell him about me."

"What makes you think you are worth his time . . . or mine?"

"You do, or you wouldn't have brought me here."

Without warning, Guerrero slashed his knife across the chest of the American. Caught off guard, the man cried out and gritted his teeth. Although his sudden show of violence seemed to redeem him in the cruel eyes of Miguel Rosas, Guerrero wasn't pleased with the fact that his hostage knew where he was. It made him all the more determined to push the man to talk. Everything he hoped for would depend on it.

"Pérez knows me. If you get him here, he'll tell you that." The American winced in pain as his chest bloomed with fresh blood. "I'll talk to Pérez, no one else."

Guerrero gripped the knife tighter in his hand, ready to cut the man again, but Rosas stopped him. He didn't say a word. He only tilted his head, ordering Guerrero to come with him. He resented being called like a dog, but he followed anyway.

When they got outside the cell, out of earshot of the prisoner, Guerrero spoke first.

"Do you believe him? You think he knows Pérez?"

"No. He's only stalling for time," Rosas said.

"But shouldn't we let Pérez decide?"

Rosas was an arrogant man who presumed too much. And Guerrero resented him for it.

"We don't need to waste his time." Rosas put his hand on Guerrero's shoulder and softened his tone. "You showed good instincts to bring the girl into this. The American reacted to her pain, I saw it."

"So what are you saying?"

"We let him think he has won, for now." Rosas smiled. "But I will return later, to pick up where you didn't have the stomach to continue."

Guerrero started to speak, but Rosas held up his hand.

"This is what I do, Ramon. Let me do my job, and we shall both get results."

Rosas didn't wait for his reply. He turned his back and headed down the corridor, back to the main residence. Rosas had dismissed him, like a servant who was beneath him.

Guerrero had no doubt that Rosas would kill Estella, just to make the point that he was in charge. And Guerrero would be no closer to getting recognized for his efforts than he was before. Letting Rosas take over wasn't an option.

Guerrero knew he had to do something, but did he have the balls to contact Pérez himself and go around the cartel boss's number two man?

"Hell, yes."

La Pointe, Wisconsin
Two hours later

Dressed in a Chicago Bulls T-shirt, jeans, and a hooded navy sweatshirt, Jessie hunched over her first cup of coffee, barely looking up at the waitress who poured it. She hadn't paid attention to the name of the hole-in-the-wall diner either, but she'd seen that kind of place many times on stakeouts. The clank of plates and the incessant chatter of the patrons were background noise to the thoughts roiling around in her head, thoughts that hadn't stopped all night long.

After spending the night staring at the ceiling of her motel room and catching the blur of red digital numbers on the nightstand alarm clock count down her boredom, Jessie was glad when dawn came. It gave her an excuse to be upright. And her motel was next door to the diner. All she wanted was coffee, but the waitress was hoping for a better tip.

"You know what you want, honey?" A woman with overpermed gray hair leaned across a Formica counter, popping gum. From the look in the woman's eyes, she'd seen it all and had lent a hand to invent the best parts.

"Not yet, but I'm sure it'll come to me."

"It'll come to you if I bring it. You see, that's how it works here. You tell me what you want. Joe back there cooks it like he knows how. Then you eat it, pay, and give me a big tip so I can retire to the Bahamas."

"What have you been smokin'?" Jessie mumbled as she took her first gulp of caffeine.

"What was that, darlin'?"

"Nothing." Jessie set down her mug and grabbed a menu, giving it a quick eyeball. "Gimme two eggs over easy with bacon and toast."

"You might as well take the hash browns that come with that. I hear they're sublime."

Jessie narrowed her eyes at the woman, who had polished her attitude to a fine sheen. And flinging it so early in the morning was a skill Jessie had come to respect.

"Fine." She held out her coffee mug. "Top me off, will ya? And keep it coming."

"You got it."

After the waitress called out her order, Jessie saw her own face in the mirror behind the counter. Under the fluorescent lights, she looked tired. Dark circles under her eyes made the scar across her eyebrow more pronounced and ugly.

The words "sullen" and "unfriendly" came to mind, which was fine by her. Not everyone was a frickin' ray of sunshine in the morning. When she gulped down more coffee, she noticed another pair of eyes staring back.

A uniformed cop with a newspaper under his arm was throwing bills on a booth table. She guessed that local law-enforcement officers kept an eye out for strangers sporting an attitude.

LEOs in small towns were like that. That was why she preferred the anonymity of getting lost in the masses of Chicago or New York City. She didn't appreciate getting rousted by the local law, especially before she had finished her coffee.

"You Jessica Beckett?" the cop asked as he walked toward her.

Before she said anything, Jessie looked down at the name badge on the man's uniform. Chief Cook, the man she'd come to see. She crooked her lips into a lazy grin, knowing from experience that the gesture would come off looking more like a sneer than hospitable. Even though she and the law seldom saw eye to eye, she reined back her usual cynicism to greet the man proper.

"Yes, that'd be me. How's it goin', Chief?"

The man ignored her attempt at small talk. With a stern face, he eyeballed her like the cops in Chicago usually did. And he got down to his agenda, the real reason he'd struck up a conversation in the first place.

"You have a permit to carry that concealed weapon under your sweatshirt?"

"Yeah, I do, but I guess you won't take my word for it." Jessie reached into the back pocket of her jeans and pulled out a wallet. "I'm a licensed fugitive recovery agent out of Chicago. Carrying a gun is part of the job."

"So you're a . . . bounty hunter."

"That's not what I said," she corrected.

For the police chief, her carrying a concealed weapon in his town had been like waving a red flag in front of a bull. And cops usually saw her former occupation the same way. The chief was no different. His disdain showed on his face and in the way he said, "bounty hunter." No, Chief Cook didn't bother to hide how he felt as he looked over her permit, but him seeing her as a bounty hunter was easier than concocting a lie to explain her current employer.

"Have a nice breakfast, Ms. Beckett. When you're ready, you know where to find me."

"Yes, sir. I do."

"And when we're done"—he leaned closer and lowered his voice—"I think it's best that you leave town. Am I making myself clear?"

"Abundantly. Guess you've got your welcome wagon in the shop, out of commission." Jessie raised her mug of coffee in mock salute.

Chief Cook gave her the stink eye and turned on his heels without saying another word. He left the diner, with Jessie watching him go. Even though her first encounter with the local police chief had been brief, she could tell already. Chief Cook had made a snap judgment about her. She saw it in his eyes because she'd seen it plenty before from other cops. He'd have no tolerance for any woman who would encroach on his territory and take up bounty hunting for a living. And a woman carrying a gun, legal or otherwise, got his testosterone all riled up.

"Great . . . just great."

"You know the chief, honey?" the waitress asked as she set down Jessie's breakfast and freshened up her coffee.

"Not yet, but that's about to change, unfortunately."

Before she'd finished her first cup of java, Jessie

had been kicked out of town. That had to be a new record.

Forty-five minutes later

Chief Cook made Jessie wait while he pretended to take an important phone call. Like most cops she'd known, the man liked being in charge and made sure she got that point. Jessie was on her second cup of the swill he called coffee when the chief finally gestured her into his office, shutting the door behind her.

"So how do you know Detective Samantha Cooper in Chicago?" he asked.

The chief sat behind his desk and invited her to sit in one of his visitor chairs while he made small talk and pried.

"In my line of work, I meet a lot of cops."

"It's just that she seemed to know you . . . beyond the job."

She could have offered him more, but the fact that she and Sam Cooper had been friends since childhood was none of his business, and her gal pal had nothing to do with why she'd come. Jessie had her secrets and had gotten really good at being evasive.

"Don't know what to tell ya." She shrugged. "Chicago PD told me you scored a hit on my DNA from an old murder case. I just came to check it out, see if I could help."

"What makes you think I need your help? From what I can see, your attitude could use an overhaul."

Something in his smug expression flipped a switch in her. And even though it would have been better for Jessie to keep her mouth shut and stifle her cynicism, she just wasn't good at that. Diplomacy was a skill set she didn't have.

"I'm a recovering smart-ass. Guess I've fallen off the wagon." After she realized how she sounded, Jessie heaved a sigh and tried to reel it back a notch. "Look, I think we've gotten off on the wrong foot. I'd appreciate seeing what you've got."

"That's not how it works around here." The chief leaned back in his chair and crossed his arms. Real defensive. "This is my case. I ask the questions."

Jessie held up both hands, and said, "I didn't mean to step on your toes, Chief. It's just that I'm an investigator. And I thought that having another set of eyeballs on the murder book might help."

Jessie had never called herself an investigator—until now—but if her argument swayed the stubborn man behind the desk, then she'd beef up her résumé to include anything that would get her a foot in the door of his case.

"No offense, but that murder book is off-limits to civilians. Now I know you were only a kid at the time, so I won't be needin' your help. All I need is your cooperation. Big difference." He narrowed his eyes. "Now what can you tell me about your blood evidence being found here in La Pointe?"

Jessie didn't know squat about how her blood had wound up in Wisconsin. She knew less about her past than most people since she'd blocked out the trauma of her childhood. And forget about old family albums. She didn't have relatives or the usual trappings that could help trigger a memory.

"When we got that hit on your DNA, I looked at your missing-persons file." The chief pursed his lips, letting what he'd said sink in. "Terrible thing happened to you."

Jessie saw the look of pity in his eyes, and she hated it. That look was the reason she never talked about what had happened to her.

"That Danny Ray Millstone case hit national news. I didn't need to read your file to remember that sorry excuse for a human being. He got what was coming to him."

Guess the chief thought that commiserating over the serial pedophile who had tortured her and so many other kids was a way of breaking the ice. Well, she didn't need that. *Ever.*

What she *did* need was a look at the chief's investigation. Seeing what the local law had accumulated would give her a glimpse into a past she knew nothing about. And maybe, for the first time, she'd get a lead on the woman who might be her mother.

The way she figured it, she had a fifty-fifty chance of discovering that her mother had been involved with Danny Ray Millstone and given her up or had loved her the way a mother should and hadn't been given the choice to keep her child.

But to get a look at the cold-case file—or gain the trust of the man behind the desk—would require her to do the one thing that didn't come naturally. She had to open up to a stranger, or her business in La Pointe would be done—over, out, *finito*.

"All that took place after your murder, Chief, but I don't know how your case would be connected to what happened to me."

"To find that out, you may have to talk about things you don't care to. You okay with that?" He furrowed his brow.

When the chief leaned forward in his chair, she knew she had his attention, making what she was about to ask him more difficult.

"Since you did DNA tests, was the woman who was killed . . . was she related to me?" Jessie cleared her throat, unable to look him in the eye. "Was she . . . my mother?"

"You don't remember anything about your mother?" His voice softened.

"Bottom line is that I don't know how my blood got here in La Pointe because I've blocked out a big chunk of my past. Either I was too young to remember stuff, or I didn't want to know what had happened. I don't know which, but I came here to see what you had, hoping I might learn something about my family . . . my mother, actually. That's why I want to see what you've got on this case. Do you think you can help me, Chief?"

At first, the man stared at her as if she had two heads. Like the boy who cried wolf, she was about to find out if the guy believed her when she finally told him the truth. When his expression softened, he leaned back in his chair and heaved a sigh. He kept up his silent stare as if the truth would appear on her forehead.

Eventually, he broke the stalemate. "You have time to take a ride with me?"

The Pérez Compound
Outside Guadalajara, Mexico

Ramon and his men had left them alone, for hours now. Estella Calderone listened to every sound coming from the corridor outside, waiting for the footsteps that would signal that her nightmare wasn't over.

And in the stillness of the cell, she also heard the labored breathing of the man next to her. They'd given him loose-fitting clothes to wear, pants that tied at his waist and a shirt that had not been buttoned. Since they'd taken his shoes, his feet were bare. Suspended by chains, he looked more like a ghost in the darkness of their cell. That was why Estella was shocked to hear the American speak to her for the first time.

"I'm s-sorry."

His voice had been so soft, she almost missed what he said.

"For what, *señor*?" Estella found it hard to breathe. Hanging by ropes made it hard for her to fill her lungs. And when she tried to relieve the pain by moving, her body ached with every exertion.

"What they've done to you, it wasn't s-supposed to go d-down like this."

Estella didn't know what he was talking about, but she heard the sincerity in his words. The man looked at her with his face half-swollen and saw the knife wounds Ramon had cut into her arms. The sight looked as if it truly pained him.

His reaction made her more aware of what Ramon had done to her. She would never be pretty to another man. Ramon had ruined her in more ways than one.

The smell of her own blood filled her nostrils in the small cell. And whenever she moved, she opened the wounds and more warm blood oozed down her skin. Estella felt the sting of new tears and fought them off by talking to the man she shared the cell with.

"I was born under an eclipsed moon. No good can come from that, my mother used to say." If her hands hadn't been tied, she would have made the sign of the cross. "Besides, Ramon owns me. He can do whatever he wants. My mother sold me to him."

It had embarrassed her to admit what she was to this stranger, but since they were both about to die, she did not see the point in hiding the truth.

"That bastard might've given m-money to your mother," he mumbled, trying hard to catch his breath. " . . . but he can't own you."

The American was weak. She strained to listen to him, barely hearing his words when the sound of his voice echoed off the stone walls.

"He's got n-no right to do w-what he did to you." He grimaced with the pain of speaking. "What's your name?"

"Estella Calderone. And you are Garrett Wheeler, is that right?" She'd heard his name when he was being tortured, before Guerrero had come looking for her.

The American barely nodded.

"If we are to die today, then it is good we know who we are." She felt a single tear roll down her cheek. "But in God's eyes, no names are necessary."

He knew the girl was scared even though she was trying to sound brave. It was one thing for him to withstand torture, but seeing what they had done to Estella had ripped him up. Any plans he had for revenge had been challenged the minute Ramon Guerrero touched that girl with his knife. It left him with a burning question that he had not yet found an answer for.

How badly did he want to kill the man who had taken everything from him?

La Pointe, Wisconsin

"So this is where it happened?"

Sitting outside in the passenger seat of Chief Cook's patrol car, Jessie stared through the windshield at a dilapidated old clapboard house that was set back into the woods, off an unpaved road. The yard was overgrown, with vines and weeds making an effort to reclaim the property.

Massive old trees dwarfed the abandoned house, casting the place in shadows. And old crime-scene tape fluttered in the wind, a sad reminder of what had happened. A strong feeling of déjà vu hit Jessie, even though a day ago, she would've sworn she'd never been to La Pointe.

"Yeah," the chief said. "It's been on the market a few times, but they haven't had much luck in selling it. In a small town, rumors get more exaggerated as time passes. And it's damned hard to whitewash a murder."

"Well, that's true enough." Jessie got out of the squad car, keeping her eyes on the old house. "What was her name? The woman who was murdered here."

"Angela DeSalvo. She was twenty-eight years old." When the chief got out of his car, he had a file with him. After Jessie got caught staring at the manila folder he had under his arm, Chief Cook added, "I was a rookie at the time. Didn't know her, but she was a pretty little thing by all accounts."

After an awkward silence, he said, "Let's go inside, and I'll show you where it happened. And you can ask your questions."

She nodded and walked in silence to the front steps. When she got closer, she stared up at the second-floor windows. One in particular caught her eye. Something about it was familiar, but it also stirred a tight knot in her belly.

"You look like you've seen a ghost," the chief said. "You okay?"

Without taking her eyes off the window, she replied, "Yeah, guess so."

When they got inside, the chief didn't say a word at first. He let her walk through the musty old rooms by herself, with her boots echoing in the emptiness. And every time a flash of memory hit her, she shut her eyes and clung to it as if she'd lose it forever if she let go.

Too much was familiar. As she walked through the rooms, too many recollections bombarded her for the unsettling feeling to be purely coincidental.

"I think I've been here . . . before," she whispered, hardly realizing that she had spoken at all. "Where did it happen?"

"Up here," the chief called to her from another room. When she joined him, he pointed up a set of stairs.

As Jessie followed him, her stomach tightened, especially when she got to the second floor and made the turn she knew would come. If Chief Cook hadn't been leading the way, she still would have known where to go. That window she had seen outside had been important to her for a reason.

She'd been there before.

"She was found in her bedroom. Right there."
He didn't need to point to where Angela DeSalvo
had died. Bloodstains marred the old floorboards.
The pooling wasn't red anymore. It had turned
dark brown with age.

When Jessie knelt by the stain and put her
hand to the floor, she felt an overwhelming sense
of loss. And flashes of violent images came from
nowhere, bombarding her with a past she didn't
realize she had buried. The darkness of it gripped
her hard. And she fought a lump in her throat. She
didn't want to break down in front of the chief,
but a part of her didn't care.

"You ready to see a photo?"

Jessie looked up in shock, unsure what to say.
After she took a deep breath, she stood and waited
for him to fish out a photo from his file. When he
handed it to her, she looked into the face of Angela
DeSalvo.

"Oh, my God." Jessie couldn't help it. She gasped
with a hand to her lips, her fingers trembling.

"You recognize her?"

"I don't know. I'm not . . . sure."

The woman in the crime-scene photo stared
back at her, forever immortalized in black and
white, a look of shock frozen on her face. The
photo was a close-up, and a dark pool of blood

was congealed under her head. Despite the image being graphic, Jessie had lied to the chief.

She'd recognized the woman from the many times she'd come to Jessie while she slept.

A flash of her smile and the sound of laughter jarred Jessie from her stupor, memories of the only happy moments she had when she was a child. The woman in her dreams had played with her in a park, on a swing.

When Jessie heard a steady squeaking sound coming from outside the bedroom window, she turned her head, trying to listen for the noise, and her breath caught in her throat.

"What's that?"

It took the chief a minute to realize what she was asking.

"That squeaking sound is from an old swing out back. You want to go see . . ."

Jessie didn't wait for him to finish. She ran down the stairs and headed for the backyard until she stood next to an old rusted swing, blowing in the breeze. The play set stood under a large tree, squeaking every time the wind blew. An eerie trigger for her memory.

Jessie knew right then that she had been there before. This had been where Angela DeSalvo had pushed her on the swing. That memory hadn't been from a park. It had come from right there, within steps of where Angela would later be murdered.

"Was she my mother? Can you tell me that?"

Avoiding the chief's eyes, Jessie looked down at the swing as she wiped away a tear with the back of her hand. He'd never answered her before when she questioned him on the DNA found at the scene, but now she had to know.

"Not sure how to answer that." The chief's voice was low. Feeling numb, she really had to listen to hear him when he said, "Biology doesn't always determine a real parent, but if you're asking if your DNA is a match to Angela's . . ."

Jessie found that she was holding her breath, waiting to hear what he'd say.

" . . . I'm sorry to say . . . No, her DNA didn't match yours."

Jessie was crushed. She couldn't help it. If Angela's DNA had matched, it would have meant her mother was dead, which would have felt just as bad. Yet without having a biological connection to Angela, everything she thought she knew about the sliver of memory she'd always associated with her mother was gone.

She had a strong feeling that Angela had loved her, but if she wasn't her mother, then who was she?

And why had she crossed paths with a killer?

CHAPTER 6

Guadalajara, Mexico

Situated twelve miles southeast of the city, Guadalajara International Airport had only one terminal, with domestic and international flights coming into the same facility. That meant more traffic for Alexa to blend into. A tall blonde would have stood out in a sea of brown skin and dark hair, but after the dye job from last night, she was a brunette. Having changed disguises at the last two layovers and scrubbed off her fake tattoos, she now looked like a conservative schoolteacher on vacation.

She didn't need to fight the crowd at baggage claim since she carried only one bag. Keeping things simple also got her through Customs without a hitch. Now she stood on the curb, waiting in line for a cab.

But she couldn't shake the feeling that someone was watching.

As a trained operative, she had learned to pay attention to her instincts. Using every tactic she had in her arsenal of tricks, she discreetly searched the crowd outside the airport. Tourist buses and yellow-and-green-striped taxicabs lined the arrivals ramp outside baggage claim, with the vehicles clouding the muggy air with diesel fumes. And men in uniform blew whistles and waved traffic through, yelling out orders in Spanish. Nothing looked out of the ordinary.

Yet she had the unmistakable sensation that someone was keeping tabs on her. If they had followed her to Mexico, after the many ways she'd covered her tracks, they were plenty good. Whoever got the hair on the back of her neck to stand at alert, they had her complete respect. She'd have to find a way to lose them, *pronto.*

"You need a taxi, lady?" A short, brown-skinned man in uniform smiled at her.

"Yes . . . please." Alexa adjusted her dark glasses and didn't look him in the eye.

She could have told the man she was also looking to rent a vehicle, but the fewer people who could trace her movements, the better.

"And can you recommend a good hotel in the city?" she asked.

"Oh, yes. The Hotel de Mendoza is very popular."

The man grinned and rattled off a location in the heart of Guadalajara—a place Alexa had no intention of staying. If anyone had eavesdropped or traced her movements, they'd be running down bogus leads. She needed a good smoke screen to ditch whoever was watching her now.

"Thank you," she told the man as she tipped him and got into the cab that he'd waved to the curb.

"*Gracias, señorita.*"

After the taxi pulled into traffic, Alexa told the driver to take her to the Hotel de Mendoza. From there she would find another place to stay. On pure reflex, she moved to where she saw the traffic behind her, using the driver's mirror. Although nothing looked out of the ordinary, Alexa had been in the field long enough to know looks could be very deceiving. And instincts carried much more weight than merely trusting her eyesight.

"How long to the hotel?" she asked the driver, to distract him from noticing her obsession with his mirror. As the man talked, she thought about her next steps.

She planned to get lost in the city of Guadalajara, traveling off the grid, using her fake passports and paying cash for everything. Once she got situated in town, she'd lease a rental car and make contact with the local Tanya had given her. For a price, he'd have what she'd need to conduct surveillance in a foreign country. She needed the right gear and enough firepower to make a good first impression.

Soon she'd be on the hunt for Garrett Wheeler, staked out near the compound of Manolo Quintanilla Pérez, the leader of a ruthless drug cartel. But if she couldn't shake whoever was following her, she had to come up with a better plan. No one was getting in her way, not when she was so close. If Garrett's life was at stake, she'd never forgive herself if she did nothing.

La Pointe, Wisconsin

"Were there any witnesses?" Jessie asked Chief Cook as she stood by the swing set in the back-yard behind the abandoned old house where Angela DeSalvo had been murdered.

"Only a yardman who found the body three days later. The smell, you know. His name was Luke Brenner."

"Was?"

"Yeah, he died three years ago. Hunting accident."

"What about neighbors? Did anyone see anything?"

The deserted house was on a spur off the main road. And given the rural setting, the nearest neighbor would have been too far to hear much, but asking the question was worth a shot.

"When we get back to the station, I can let you look at the case file, but I don't need an outsider second-guessing the work of my men. I've had my guys go over every detail, and I questioned most of the key people who were living here at the time. I came up empty. DNA evidence is my last shot at reviving this case, but without anything to compare it to, this investigation has run out of gas."

Jessie believed Chief Cook when he told her that he'd been over the case, reexamining every scrap of evidence. A murder like this would have been a black eye on his years of service. And it probably still haunted him, like it would have bothered her. But even if she wouldn't get a long look at the murder book back at the station house, she had another way to look into the case. If the local library carried old newspapers in its archives, she might find something intriguing to look into.

"When I talked to Detective Cooper about your case, Chief Cook, she mentioned something about children being reported at the DeSalvo house. What can you tell me about that?"

"Not much. We interviewed folks who lived close to the crime scene and one or two mentioned something about seeing kids at the residence the week prior to the murder, but none of that could be substantiated." He pursed his lips and avoided her eyes. "Now that I think about it, if your DNA was found at the scene, what those folks saw was probably you."

"But kids doesn't mean one child," she argued. "And with my DNA being at the scene, there's proof that at least one child was there. Doesn't that give a new perspective on all those people who claimed to see children there?"

Chief Cook heaved a sigh and shook his head.

"Like I said, none of that could be substantiated. We saw no evidence of a child or children at the DeSalvo house. For all we know, if there were kids there, they could have been visiting one day. That's it. We just don't know. And, quite frankly, I don't see how it factors in."

"It factors in because I ended up in the hands of a serial pedophile, Chief. If I was in La Pointe, how did I end up in Chicago? Someone had to take me there."

Cook narrowed his eyes as he leaned a shoulder against a tree.

"I don't mean to sound insensitive, and I certainly wish I had answers to your question, for your sake, but backtracking who brought you to Chicago won't solve my murder." He softened his expression. "That would bring closure to you. And I pray you find it, but I'm not sure what more I can do for you."

"Can I see a copy of the DNA analysis?"

Sam had already sent for the analysis, but Chief Cook didn't know that. Jessie wanted to see how forthcoming he'd be.

"I'll see what I can do. After I got a look at it, I sent it to be filed. It should be in the evidence box, but maybe that hasn't gotten done yet. Why do you need to see that?"

"DNA brought you the first lead you've had in the case in nearly twenty years. Bet that made you feel pretty good." After he nodded, she made her point.

"Well, think how I felt when I finally got a lead on a past I'd given up on knowing about. After I got rescued in Chicago, no one ever came forward to say they knew me. The Chicago PD posted my face in the news all over, and no one contacted them except the lunatic fringe. This is the closest I've come to knowing where I came from. I just can't walk away from this. I can't."

"I'm sorry, Ms. Beckett. I truly am, but I'm not sure what you expect me to do for you."

"You said you'd let me look at the murder book, that's a start. I don't want to interfere in your investigation, but maybe I could talk to those people who reported kids at the DeSalvo house."

"You can read the interviews. I don't want you talking to the people of this town unless I'm with you. But after nearly twenty years, the memory of some of these folks may not be so good. The best you'll get is probably in those interviews, when their minds were fresh."

"You're probably right. And thanks, Chief."

Jessie followed him back to his squad car in silence. For the first time in a long while, she was stumped for anything to say. The harsh reality was that the death of Angela DeSalvo might only be another piece to the puzzle of her life. The case had gone cold for a reason. Getting her hopes up now would only make it harder later if the answers she'd hoped for couldn't be found.

She knew she had been at that crime scene before. That had been real, but none of this explained why she'd ended up with Danny Ray Millstone.

At least, not yet.

Guadalajara, Mexico
Two hours later

After Alexa had been dropped downtown, it didn't take her long to find suitable accommodations. She'd checked into the Villa Ganz, a quaint boutique hotel on the west side of the city near

Avenida Chapultepec and the beautiful Zona Rosa district.

With the hotel catering to a discreet clientele, the average tourist couldn't afford the luxury accommodations, but she'd picked the hotel for other reasons. Her room had a good view of the street, and there were plenty of ways to bail in a hurry if she had to. And anyone who came looking for her, without an invitation, would get noticed if they weren't a guest.

While she waited for the sun to go down, Alexa had gotten familiar with the hotel layout, looking for viable egress plans in case she needed them. She had also made a few calls and arranged for a rental car to be brought to her. A dark SUV with tinted windows was waiting downstairs, but before she left the hotel, Alexa called Tanya to check in.

"I'm here. Anything new?"

"I had Seth do a little digging into the use of that satellite. Whoever is behind this off-book mission isn't only using it to trace one cell GPS signal at the Pérez compound. Harper backtracked their trace."

"Oh? What else are they working?"

"Something happened in El Paso that triggered all this. And from the satellite imagery, they were following a moving signal that ended up at the Pérez estate."

"Do we know what they were interested in?"

"Yeah, and Harper sent me the images. From what I can tell, a man was abducted on the U.S. side in El Paso and taken over the border to Pérez. We're trying to figure out who he is, but that's a long shot."

"You think it's Garrett?"

"Don't know. He's been missing longer than this man was abducted, but no telling what this off-book job is. I've forwarded the images to you on your cell. There's not enough detail to see faces, so no luck there."

Alexa couldn't help but let her disappointment get to her. They had plenty to be concerned about but nothing real to go on.

"Harper told me one other thing," Tanya added. "It seems phone chatter inside the compound was picked up once the hostage was delivered. Whoever this man is, it's a big deal to the men who took him."

"Do you think our team is there to rescue this guy?"

"From what we can tell, they haven't made their move," Tanya said. "It's like they're waiting for something."

"Or someone," she speculated.

"Maybe, but none of this makes sense from where I'm sittin'. I'm worried."

"Yeah, me too. Thanks. I'll call you when I can."

"Be careful."

After Alexa ended the call, she sat on the edge of her bed, thinking about what Tanya had told her as she stared at the satellite image she'd been sent. Tanya was right. There wasn't enough detail to see faces. All they had was proof of a kidnapping. Only her gut made her believe that Garrett was the abducted man.

But if this was a Sentinels' operation, why would anyone sit on the sidelines watching a kidnapping and do nothing about it? She had a feeling Donovan Cross knew about this mission. And since he'd tried to stop her, that had given her another reason to fear that Garrett was the guy in the hands of that drug cartel.

But something else bothered her.

If Hank Lewis was on the ground in Mexico, why would he sit still and let anything bad happen to Garrett? Like Tanya said, none of this made sense.

No matter how things played out, she was in the right place to do something about it.

Alexa grabbed her stuff and headed for the lobby and her rental car. Dressed in dark jeans, hiking boots, and windbreaker, she tipped the valet and dropped the nearly empty duffel bag she carried on the passenger seat next to her.

Before she headed for the coordinates Tanya had given her for the Pérez compound, she'd make contact with a local that the analyst had given her, an arms dealer who would have what she needed to fill the bag she'd brought.

She wanted to acquire a com unit to keep in touch with Tanya, a full surveillance package, body armor, grenades, two MP-5s, and a couple of handguns with ammo. If someone was tracking a cell-GPS signal inside the compound of a drug cartel, they'd soon have a shadow.

Alexa only hoped her efforts would lead her to Garrett—and that when she found him, he'd still be alive.

Police Station
La Pointe, Wisconsin

"You plannin' on stayin' the night?"

Jessie looked up to see Chief Cook standing in the doorway of the small conference room they'd allowed her to use. She'd been poring through the murder book and had photos, interview notes, and other evidence spread over the table.

She'd officially taken over part of his station house.

"Oh, wow."

When she looked past him toward a window, she saw that the sun had gone down, and it was dark outside.

"Sorry. I didn't realize what time it was."

"You've been so quiet in here, I didn't want to interrupt," he said. "You have any questions before I head out for dinner?"

The chief told her he would be working a little OT, catching up on paperwork, but eventually when he left for the day, she'd have to leave the case files behind.

"I noticed a folded map with notes on it. What did you use that for?" she asked, pointing to the aged paper map that she had pinned to a corkboard near the door. The town map had been laminated with red circles and notes in black marker on it.

"That map was used by me mostly. I kept track of who we'd interviewed, the neighbors who lived closest to the crime scene. With the properties so sprawled out, I wanted to make sure we got everyone."

"Looks like you did make contact with everyone who lived around the DeSalvo place."

"Yep, all those red circles. Once my men told me they'd made contact, I circled the location. What are you getting at?"

The chief narrowed his eyes, and she felt a distinct chill in the room after she questioned his investigation. The map had been loaded down with small, abbreviated notes from the chief. A lot of detail, but something was missing.

Before she answered the chief, one of his deputies poked his head into the conference room. Deputy Tyrell Hinman had introduced himself before when he got her a coffee refill.

"You need me, Chief. I'm fixing to head out."

"Ah, no. You go on, Tyrell. I'll see you tomorrow."

"Sure thing. Good night, Ms. Beckett. It was nice meetin' you."

"Yeah, you too." Jessie barely looked at the deputy. She had kept her eyes on the chief. While the deputy interrupted, she saw the wheels of Cook's brain working. The man was leaping ahead, trying to figure out where she was going with this.

"What's wrong with my map?" he asked.

"Nothing's wrong with the map exactly. It's just that when I went through the evidence box, I sorted everything by type. All interview notes are here." She put her hand on a stack of papers. "But when I matched up the interviews to the neighbor's residence and this map, that was when I noticed one interview was missing. Can you help me locate it?"

"What? No, that can't be." He stepped toward the table and looked down at the map where she pointed. "Which one is missing?"

"There's a note here. See it? The Tanner place. Sophia Tanner." Jessie stepped toward the table and pointed to the interview-report pile. "But I can't find an interview with her, just references that one of your guys missed her, a couple of times. Do you know if anyone actually conducted that interview? Maybe it was misfiled."

One missing interview wasn't exactly a home run, out of the park, but Jessie had scored a solid base hit. A murder investigation had a lot of moving parts, especially one as shocking as the DeSalvo killing would have been in a small town. The chief would have had a lot on his mind. And with the evidence spread out in the conference room, the magnitude of his job was very clear.

Jessie wanted to give him the benefit of the doubt that he might have missed something minor, but the neighbor living closest to the DeSalvo house was a key interview to miss. She hoped he'd tell her the paperwork had been misplaced and that he'd remembered it; but after seeing his reaction as he looked through the files on the table, Jessie had a bad feeling that a critical interview had never happened.

"Are you sure it's not here?" The police chief

helped her look through the paperwork, but they came up empty.

"I've searched through all this, too. Were there any other evidence boxes?"

After the chief shook his head, he slumped into a conference-room chair and stared at the papers stacked on the table in front of him.

"Well, I remember seeing it. It must have gotten misfiled . . . or something."

"If you saw it, what did she say?"

"Nothing. She didn't hear anything. And she hadn't seen any kids." Chief Cook shook his head. "I forgot about that map."

"What?"

"That was good detective work . . . you comparing that map to the interviews, I mean. I should have . . ."

He never finished. He only stared across the room, avoiding her eyes.

"Is Sophia Tanner still living in town?" she asked.

"Yeah, she is." Chief Cook looked dazed. "She used to work part-time at the police station a few years ago, after she retired from teaching. I can speak to her tomorrow . . . for all the good it'll do now."

Jessie knew what he was thinking. The chief claimed to have seen that interview, but he might have been covering up the truth. If that interview had never been completed, that was a pretty big hole in the investigation. And if Sophia Tanner was still in La Pointe, how much would she remember from so long ago?

Someone had screwed up, big-time.

Most people would have the urge to comfort him, but not Jessie. If he was anything like her, nothing would make him feel better. Chief Cook had owned responsibility for this case. Even if one of his men had dropped the ball, he knew it was all on him.

And she respected him for taking the responsibility.

"Who knows? Maybe something will come up," she said in commiseration. "You mind if I tag along when you talk to her?"

"No, I mean, yeah I mind. This is an official police investigation. I can't have civilians looking over my shoulder."

Jessie was dumbfounded by the chief's sudden about-face. She was getting the worst of his cold shoulder, and that was getting her hackles up.

"But I was the one who uncovered this missing interview. Some people might say you owe me one."

"Well, some people might be wrong. This is my case. And I'll handle it."

When Chief Cook stood, he grabbed the stacks

she had so carefully put in order and stuffed them back into the evidence box, piling them up helter-skelter. If she'd been lucky, he would've been done talking, but that didn't happen. Cook opened the door to the conference room and waited for her to leave, but not before he said what was on his mind. And the attitude he'd shown her when they first met was back in full force.

"I'm sure you'll be heading out of town now since there's nothing more you can offer. Leave a number where I can reach you. And I'll call."

"Be still my heart."

Jessie glared back, but the man wasn't intimidated. She walked out the door with her mind in overdrive. What the hell had just happened? She'd been kicked out of town twice in one day. A lesser person would have taken it real personal.

But unfortunately for Chief Tobias Cook, that wasn't Jessie.

CHAPTER 7

Alexa had parked down the street from a seedy-looking bar on the outskirts of Guadalajara, called La Cucaracha. A row of motorcycles was parked in front, with more parking in the rear of the stucco building that had been marred with black and red graffiti.

"Nice ambience." Alexa sighed. "Guess I can forget the umbrella drinks."

Tanya had told her about the bar. An arms dealer operated out of La Cucaracha, a man known by the street name, *El Puma*. In English, his name translated to Cougar. Clearly the man wasn't concerned with the negative image of his branding efforts, especially if he hung out at a bar named for the cockroach.

While she sat in her SUV, watching who came and went from the local watering hole, she pulled back her hair and tucked it into a ball cap that she'd brought in the canvas bag. Pulling the hat down over her eyes, she wanted to minimize the fact that she was a woman. In a dump like La Cucaracha, her precautions might not make a difference. Once she got inside, Tanya had given her specific instructions. If she did as she was told, *El Puma* would make contact with her.

"This better work."

After Alexa entered the murky bar, every head in the place turned toward her. At least, that was how it felt. She avoided eye contact and found an empty table to the left of the smoke-filled bar. The place smelled of cigarettes, sweat, and booze. Eventually, a waitress came over and dropped a napkin on the table and asked to take her order in Spanish.

"Sorry, I don't speak the language." Alexa kept her voice low, only loud enough for the young woman to hear. "Just give me a beer. Dos Equis with a lime, thanks."

After the waitress left, Alexa took out a pen and wrote on the napkin. When the girl came back with her order, Alexa handed her the note she'd written. The young woman looked at it, then locked eyes with her before she went back to the bar. Her exchange with the bartender left Alexa with little doubt that she'd gotten her message across. She wanted to meet with *El Puma* to talk a little business.

Alexa took a sip of her beer and kept her eyes alert for any sign of trouble. The place gave her the creeps. The only women in the bar waited on tables or looked like hookers working the room. La Cucaracha didn't exactly cater to the tourist trade. And with the abundance of ink in the bar, she was feeling left out, not having enough tattoos to fit in.

It took nearly twenty minutes before the bartender caught her eye and nudged his head toward the back. His gesture had been so subtle, she almost missed it in the dimly lit bar. Alexa noticed a doorway to the right.

"Showtime," she muttered.

When she got to the door, a man dressed in jeans and a black T-shirt stood in the hallway. He was armed and carried a Beretta in a shoulder harness. As big as he was, she couldn't see past him, making her edgy.

"Lead the way," she said with a wave of her hand.

"After you, *señorita*."

Although Alexa didn't like turning her back on *El Puma*'s man, she did as she was told and walked by him toward a door at the end of the hall. When she opened it, Alexa was surprised to see who was in the room.

A familiar face smiled back at her. And she couldn't hide her shock.

"Hello, Alexa. I usually prefer blondes, but seeing you as a brunette could change my mind."

Sentinels' operative Hank Lewis was leaning against the far wall of the office with his arms crossed. And a man she didn't know sat behind a desk like he belonged.

"What are you doing here, Hank?" She narrowed her eyes. "And who's your friend? *El Puma*, I presume." Alexa extended her hand to the guy behind the desk.

He had a wide barrel chest with broad shoulders and slicked-back dark hair. When the man stood to take her hand, Alexa noticed he was dressed in a navy sport coat, open-collar white shirt, and khaki pants. Except for his penchant for gold chains worn around his neck, *El Puma* looked like any businessman on the street.

"*Sí, Señorita* Marlowe. I have a street name for business purposes, but you can call me Victor, since we are all *compadres* here." The man remained standing. "Can I get you another *cervesa*?"

"Unless Hank gives me a good reason to stay, I'll pass on the beer, but thanks, Victor."

When she turned her attention on Hank, the short, muscular man with the burr haircut grinned, and said, "You mind giving us some time alone, Vic? We need to talk."

"No problem. My office is yours, *mi amigo*." Taking his bodyguard with him, Victor left them alone.

"Thought you were on assignment, Hank."

"Yeah, I was. Mission interruptus."

"Were you the one who's been following me since the airport?"

Hank furrowed his brow and shrugged.

"Sorry. Don't know what you're talking about."

Alexa watched every detail of Hank's reaction. His body language, and what she knew of her many missions with the man, made her believe he was telling the truth. And he had no reason to lie. Not now.

Had she gotten so paranoid that she'd imagined being followed?

"I've been . . . working, until now." Hank cocked his head. "I got pulled off an op to talk to you."

"Talk to me. About what?"

"I'm here to ask you to back off, Alexa. We're in the middle of a sensitive operation. We don't need the distraction."

"Just tell me about Garrett. Where is he, Hank? Is he involved in your assignment?" Alexa crossed her arms and stood her ground. "I just need to talk to him, make sure he's okay."

Hank thought about what she'd said before he answered, "As far as I know, Garrett isn't part of this."

"But you don't know for sure," she guessed. From his hesitation, she knew how things went when a mission was run on a need-to-know basis. Hank might not know who was calling the shots.

"Why are you here, Alexa? Straight up." He stepped closer and fixed his gaze on her.

Alexa had to give him enough so he'd believe her, but not so much that it would implicate Tanya's involvement. If anyone got pegged for interference, it would be her alone. She wouldn't let anyone else go down with her.

"Garrett's gone AWOL. He hasn't come up for air with me, and I checked with Tanya. She hadn't heard from him in a couple of weeks now. I'm worried, Hank. And I have reason to suspect there's an op going on down here off book. Is Garrett involved in any way?"

"I couldn't tell you that, Alexa, even if I knew myself."

"Did you know someone is using unauthorized satellite time to track a cell-phone GPS signal inside the estate of Manolo Quintanilla Pérez, a drug-cartel boss?" She pressured him to let her in on the mission by spouting what she knew. "Your op is south of the city at the Pérez compound, right?"

"I can't talk about the mission, Alexa. You know that."

"I just gotta know he's okay. That's all." Alexa took a risk and pretended to know more than she did. "Is he inside that estate? Is that who you're tracking? I've seen the satellite images of the kidnapping. What's going on, Hank?"

From the look on his face, she knew she'd hit on the truth.

"Damn it. How did you . . ." Hank shook his head but stopped before he said too much. "Look, the best I can do is run this up the food chain, see if they want to bring you into this."

"Who's running the show?" she asked.

"Don't know, but if they want you gone, you gotta follow orders." Hank headed for the door like everything had been settled. "In the meantime, give me a number where I can reach you. And stay put until you hear from me."

"Not good enough, Hank. I've got business with our mutual friend, Victor. Unless I hear from you, I've got my own agenda."

Hank turned and faced her, unable to hide his frustration. She'd seen that look before.

"Guess I knew that's what you'd say." He pulled a gun and aimed it at her, a move she didn't expect.

"Since I can't trust you to behave, you're coming with me."

"And just where are we going?" Alexa gritted her teeth, feeling more than a little pissed that she hadn't seen this coming.

"You'll see soon enough. Now move."

An hour later

Hank always did know how to entertain a woman. He had her stashed in a cheap motel room a few blocks from the sleazy bar he'd just abducted her from—at gunpoint. The place rented by the hour, which explained the low-rent décor . . . and the smell.

Slouching in a chair by the bed, Alexa had eavesdropped on a few of his cell-phone calls, but they were so cryptic, she hadn't learned much. The only thing she really knew was that after the last call to the handler for the mission, Hank was more nervous than she'd ever seen him.

When she saw a huge roach crawl across the floor, she watched it until Hank noticed it, too.

"Friend of yours?" she asked. When he didn't find her amusing, she said, "Hey? What's eating you?"

When Hank glanced at her sideways, Alexa cocked her head and batted her eyelashes, playing it real coy just to piss him off. Midpace, he stopped and did a double take.

"You're kidding, right?" he asked. "You come down here and mess with my op, forcing me to leave my men and make a call I never wanted to make to my handler. Now the head honcho in charge of this mission is coming here, breaking all protocol, to fix this screwed-up mess because you can't leave well enough alone. And you wanna know what's wrong with me?" He ran a hand across his short hair and shook his head. "That's just rich."

"Hey, you made the choice to bring me here. I had my own party goin' on." After Hank rolled his eyes, Alexa pressed him for more. "So why are you sitting this one out? You know they have a hostage. You've seen proof off the satellite. What are you waiting for? The guy could be dead, and you'd never know it. What kind of mission are you on?"

She hated grilling Hank, but she was bored and more than a little antsy.

"I'm following orders, Alexa. And if that hostage was in real trouble, we'd know it."

"What are you talking about?"

Before Hank could answer, a knock on the door stopped him cold.

"So who's at the door?" She leaned forward with her eyes darting between him and the closed door. "Come on, Hank. In a second, that won't be a secret anymore."

"That's just it, Alexa. I don't know." He rubbed his palms across his shirt to dry them off.

"Don't you know who's heading up the op?"

"No. I follow orders, Alexa, something you should consider doing from time to time." Hank reached for the door and pulled his weapon. After he nodded at her, making sure she was ready to back his play, Hank opened the door.

"What the hell . . ." He lowered his gun. "So *you're* in charge of this mission? Well, I'll be damned."

And Alexa stood with her mouth open. She couldn't help it. She was stunned.

"I thought you were . . ." She shook her head, staring at the man standing in the open doorway.

"You two better have a real good reason for risking this mission, especially you, Alexa."

Larger than life, Garrett Wheeler filled the threshold and lowered a weapon of his own.

CHAPTER 8

Alexa was completely shaken. After seeing Garrett Wheeler standing in front of her, she didn't know if she should be happy he was alive or be mad as hell. And he had the nerve to point the finger at her, accusing her of messing up his op.

"And you better have a damned good reason for breathing." She pulled him into the room by the arm and after she gave a quick look down the hall to make sure he was alone, she closed the door and turned on him.

"What's going on, Garrett? And why all the secrecy?"

"You ever look up the word 'secret,' Alexa? You should try it sometime."

"I was worried that something bad had happened to you. Sorry for caring." She glared at him. "If you're here, then who is Pérez holding as hostage?"

"What do you know about that?"

Typical Garrett. He had shifted gears by going on the offensive.

"Don't change the subject. Answer me."

She knew she was pushing it with the man who was her boss, but she was in no mood to be diplomatic.

"Give me one legitimate reason why I should? You're not part of this mission, Alexa. And from the way you've barged in here, I think that was a good call."

"Whoa, now. I don't wanna get hit in the cross fire." Hank raised both eyebrows and backed off. He found a corner in the room and crossed his arms, playing it as neutral as Switzerland. When Alexa saw Hank's reaction, she mumbled under her breath, "Coward," before she directed her anger back at Garrett.

"I was worried about you. If I had gone missing like that, what would you have done?"

"Touché, but jeopardizing a mission in progress? That's . . ." Garrett searched for the right word. " . . . irresponsible."

"So is disappearing without a word. And I refuse to apologize for caring about you." When Garrett softened the stern expression on his face, she knew he was finally listening. "Tell me about this mission. I'm down here. You might as well use me."

"I can't." He shook his head and turned his back on her. "The reason I didn't ask you to join us hasn't changed."

"What's that supposed to mean?"

"Damn it, Alexa. I need you to walk away from this. You came here looking for me. Well, you've found me. And I'm telling you to go home."

When Garrett looked her in the eye, he flinched for an instant. His reaction was enough for her to realize he was holding back. And it was personal.

"You're hiding something. What is it?"

When Garrett looked to Hank for support, the guy shrugged, and said, "Hey, don't look at me. This op is on a need-to-know basis. And, apparently, you didn't want me to know anything either."

"Not you, too." Garrett raked a hand through his dark hair as he thought about what to do next. His jaw tightened, and he avoided looking at either of them.

"I got a call a few weeks ago," Garrett began. " . . . a guy telling me that he had an operation already in play. He told me he would be infiltrating the Pérez cartel, the hard way. He had personal reasons for wanting to kill the son of a bitch."

"Who? Pérez?" Hank asked. When Garrett nodded, Hank narrowed his eyes. "Didn't know you needed a reason to kill that sorry bastard."

"Yeah, well, this guy had two good reasons. Pérez had ordered a hit on him several years ago, but his family got killed instead."

Alexa saw the pained look on Garrett's face and knew there was more to this story than what he'd told them.

"That's horrible, but why did he call you?" she pressed, moving close enough to look him directly in the eye.

"Because I owe him. I was the one who'd ordered the protection detail on his wife and little girl. His family was killed on my watch."

Alexa's next breath caught in her throat. She'd seen the same look of guilt on Garrett's face before. And a face from her past emerged from the shadows of her mind. Green eyes she'd seen not long ago, eyes filled with a never-ending sadness that had haunted her since she'd last seen him.

"I know this story," she whispered, not completely sure she had spoken aloud.

"Yeah, you do. And that's why you weren't asked to come along, Alexa. You're too close to this."

"Would someone please clue me in?" Hank asked.

"Jackson Kinkaid is the guy inside." Alexa felt numb. Saying Kinkaid's name made it all real. "He's on a suicide mission to kill the man who murdered his wife and child. And damn it, Garrett, you should've told me."

"Why? So you could watch him die? You're as crazy as he is, Alexa."

"I could've talked to him, made him listen to reason. Getting hijacked by Pérez, that's a one-way trip."

"You know how Kinkaid operates. He didn't give me any choice. By the time I got our team deployed, he was in the thick of it, with no way to back out. The guy doesn't know how to back down. I've known him longer than you have. He's been living for this. In his mind, it's all he has left."

Kinkaid wasn't with the Sentinels now, but he used to be. And after what had happened to his family while he had worked for their organization, she figured Garrett had authorized the mission based on the obligation he felt toward a man who had suffered as much as Kinkaid had.

"I can understand going after Pérez if the guy killed his wife and kid, but how do we know what's going on in there?"

"We have a burst transmitter on him, embedded under his skin," Hank told her.

"Don't tell me. Let me guess," she interrupted. "That was his idea, right?" When she looked at Garrett, all he did was nod and shrug.

"Unbelievable."

"That transmitter has been sending us his vitals, as well as his location, so we can track him via satellite," Hank continued. "I'm in charge of the ground team, and we're located right outside the compound, ready to go in once we get the green light. And as for his vitals? The medical doctor on our team thinks Kinkaid is being tortured."

"Tortured? What for? If they knew who he was, Pérez would just have him killed. I'm not arguing for that, mind you, but killing him would tie up a very big loose end. What am I missing?" she asked.

"That's just it. He got abducted when they thought he was someone else. And that's who they think they're interrogating, a bigger fish in their eyes."

"Oh, yeah. Who?"

"Me," Garrett said. "The Pérez drug cartel, they think they have me."

Shoreview Motel
La Pointe, Wisconsin

After the surreal trip she'd taken down a shadowy memory lane with Chief Cook at the crime scene earlier, Jessie was desperate for anything that closely resembled normal. And the chief's sudden change of heart, about wanting her help, had left her feeling more than a little lost.

She took a hot shower, got ready for bed, and made a call to Seth. He'd become her life preserver in the turbulent sea of her past. He steadied her and made her feel safe. With Harper, she had a shot at "normal," at least a taste of it.

When he answered her call on the second ring, she simply said, "Hey, it's me."

Jessie heard a soft rustle and knew he was in bed, too.

"Hey, you," he said. "What are you wearing?"

Jessie couldn't help it. She had to grin.

"Nothing but a smile. And you?"

"I'm wearing . . . Floyd, actually. He's such a bed hog."

"What did he do today? I could use a good Floyd story. And I know you've got one."

Harper told her that Floyd had learned how to open doors by standing up and flipping levers with his paws.

"I've got a reason for telling you this," he said.

"Oh?"

"Yeah, the next time you're alone in our bathroom and you feel a cold nose on your butt, you'll know who it is."

"A cold nose, huh? Why would I assume Floyd is the culprit?"

"Very funny."

She listened to the sound of his soft chuckle as she pulled the comforter over her shoulders.

"Should I be worried?" he asked.

"About what?"

"You seem to have this thing for Floyd. Do I detect a little canine envy?"

"That's it, Harper. You've nailed it." She sighed and ran a hand through her wet hair. "Have I told you how nice it is to hear your voice?"

"Yeah, but feel free to remind me whenever you feel like it."

After a comfortable silence, Seth had more to say.

"You've done a fine job avoiding what's on your mind. So what is it?"

"Can't fool you." She tried to smile, but couldn't. "This place, I know that I've been here before, but those memories are just beyond my reach, you know?"

"You met with that cop today. What did he have to say?"

"He kicked me out of town . . . twice. Is that what you mean?"

"Wow, that must be a record."

"Yeah, that's what I thought."

She told him about the police chief taking her to the crime scene and how he'd later allowed her to see the murder book until he erected a wall and suggested she leave town . . . again.

"I've seen you in action. Guess I'm not too surprised."

"Thanks a lot, pal. Whose side are you on?"

"Yours. You've got the gun. But what do you think happened? Sounds like you were BFFs until you mentioned that missing file."

"Yeah, that's what I thought, too."

Harper had the same take on the situation as she had. *Great minds . . .*

"You're gonna see that Tanner woman, aren't you?"

"You know me, Harper. Never leave a good turn unstoned."

"Wait, I gotta write that down," he said.

She heard him fumbling for a paper and pen, like he was seriously taking notes.

"Are you sure that Angela DeSalvo was the woman you remembered from your dreams?" he finally asked, taking a detour down Serious Lane. "Maybe seeing the dead woman's face forced you to make that leap."

What Harper had insinuated made sense, but

Jessie felt sure that she had remembered Angela's face on her own, without the help from an old crime-scene photo.

"No, I'm sure it was her." She sighed. "I've never felt so . . . down. Seeing her face and thinking she was my mother was the only bright spot to my childhood, and now all that is gone."

"I knew I should have gone with you. You shouldn't have to go through this alone."

"But I don't feel alone, not when I can look forward to your abuse. I mean, your support."

Even though she'd poked fun at him, hearing Seth's voice on the phone made her feel like he was right in the room with her. Of course, nothing would replace the feel of his arms around her—or the many other things he did to make her feel warm and happy—but having him to talk to at the end of her day was the next best thing.

"So, with the chief taking back his key to the city, what're you doing tomorrow?" he asked. "Is there something you need me to do?"

"I'm planning on making a royal pain of myself."

"Stickin' with your strengths. Always a good strategy."

"And thanks for the offer to help. I may take you up on that."

"For you? Anytime."

"I'll call you tomorrow," she said. "And give a big sloppy kiss to Floyd."

"That's an image I didn't need."

Even as lousy as she had felt that day, Harper could always make her laugh. And now he had an accomplice.

Guadalajara, Mexico

In the cramped motel room, Alexa listened to Garrett as he told what he knew about Jackson Kinkaid. And from the looks of Hank, he hadn't had a clue about any of it. She guessed that since she and Hank both knew Kinkaid, Garrett had kept the truth from them and added a higher level of secrecy to the mission.

"Kinkaid lied to them and set up a pretty big ruse, pretending to be me," Garrett told her. "He even made fake ID to back up his story."

"What made him think they'd believe that?" Alexa asked. "And how would they know who you are? You keep a pretty low profile."

"Actually, that was a thing of beauty." Garrett almost smiled. Almost. "He ran the whole thing like a con artist running a scam. He set up a fake online trail and made sure rumors got out on the street before he even got to El Paso. By the time he hit the ground, they were waiting for him, but that was what he wanted. All he needed was a way in, and a street gang on the American side of the border gave him that. He made himself a damned Trojan horse. Once he got inside, he had a plan to bring down the bastard who ordered the hit that got his family killed. Guess he wanted to look the guy in the eye before it all goes down . . . even if it put him at risk, too."

By the way Garrett shook his head, Alexa knew he hadn't had a say in how Kinkaid had orchestrated his own abduction.

"And in order for his plan to work, that meant you had to disappear," she said. "If anyone saw you living large in New York, word might get back to the border, and Kinkaid would be a sitting duck."

"Yeah. That's why I couldn't say anything. It had to look as if I'd gone undercover, on a mission of my own. If anyone knew what was really happening, Kinkaid's life would be more at risk than it already was. I backed his play because he left me no options."

"This is crazy. You gotta get him out of there," she insisted. "I mean, what are you waiting for?" Her frustration got the better of her, and she knew it. "There's gotta be another way to get at Pérez. We'll find it and bring him down."

"No, we're too close, Alexa," Garrett argued. "For now, we're doing it Kinkaid's way. All he has to do is hold out a little longer."

"Hold out, for what? He's not you. He can't tell them anything." She heard the anger in her voice and didn't care. Anything involving Kinkaid was personal. No wonder Garrett had left her in the dark.

"Yeah, but they don't know that. Kinkaid is holding out until Pérez gets there. From our intel, that son of a bitch is in Mexico City, conducting business as usual, but he's heading to his estate tomorrow. That's what Kinkaid has been waiting for."

"So what happens after Pérez is in the picture?"

"I know what I'd like to see happen, but I don't think Kinkaid has any intention of taking Pérez alive. He's got another plan that I don't know about."

"Then why did he ask you to back him up?"

"We're his insurance. If he can't finish what he started, he wants to make sure I do."

"That's insanity. We could have done this clean, with minimal collateral damage." Alexa shook her head. "But he doesn't care about that, does he? If he's got a shot at killing the bastard, he's gonna take it, no matter what happens to him. Damn it, Jackson."

She knew Kinkaid didn't care what happened as long as he got what he wanted. Garrett was right about his having nothing left but revenge. And how much of Kinkaid's mercenary days had been a part of his scheme to find the man who'd ordered the hit? Had he gotten involved with the drug cartels, hoping to find out who had been responsible for the murder of his wife and child?

His obsession had consumed him. That was what she sensed the last time she'd seen him on their mission into Cuba during a hostage-rescue operation, but after hearing what Garrett had to say, Alexa felt an overwhelming sadness for Kinkaid. *What a waste!*

"I want in." She turned her attention to Garrett. "I understand your concerns about my objectivity when it comes to Kinkaid, but I've got to be a part of this."

Garrett sighed and stole a glance toward Hank. The ground-team leader only shrugged his version of an endorsement.

"You're in on one condition. What I say goes. You're following orders, understood?" Garrett pointed a finger at her. After she nodded, he said, "And when this turns ugly, don't say I didn't warn you."

Alexa knew that if Kinkaid was on a suicide mission, odds were that she'd see him die. And that thought fueled an ache deep in her belly, but that was a far cry from letting him go it alone. The least she could do was back him up.

And that meant taking down Pérez on his turf—in the stronghold of his estate.

CHAPTER 9

La Pointe, Wisconsin
Next morning

Jessie had taken a chance and gotten up early to catch Chief Cook at the police station. She didn't intend to talk to him, knowing how far that would get her. This time, she parked down the street, playing a hunch. And when she saw his patrol car leave the station parking lot, she smiled.

"Gotcha."

The man could have been making a donut run, but Jessie had a gut feeling he was up to something else. When he headed toward the DeSalvo house and turned onto a back road, she knew her hunch had paid off. True to his word, he had gone to see Sophia Tanner, the trip he had wanted to make alone.

"Sorry, Tobias. You can't be the Lone Ranger, not today."

But before he turned into the Tanner driveway, the chief spotted her in his rearview mirror and stopped in the middle of the drive, blocking her way in. When he got out of his vehicle, she did, too.

"I'm not breaking any laws, Chief. This is a public road. And I'm a tourist."

"You're loitering."

"I'm bird-watching." She glared at him, going on the offensive before he did. "What changed, Chief? One minute you're talking to me, the next, you're ready to slather me in hot tar and roll me in feathers. What gives?"

"Look, I don't have to explain myself to you. What part of 'this is my case' don't you understand? Is English not your first language?"

"Oh, I'm getting your message loud and clear, Tobias. And for the record, if I were bilingual, I could ignore you in two languages." She stood toe-to-toe with him, her arms crossed. "Who's Sophia Tanner? And why are you protecting her?"

"What? That's ridiculous." Chief Cook glared at her and worked his jaw like it pained him. "Anyone ever tell you, you're a pain in the ass?"

"Yeah, but if it'll make you feel better, you're the first one today."

Before Cook could mount a second wave of

ornery, Jessie looked beyond him and waved her hand and smiled.

"She looks real friendly."

Chief Cook turned to see Sophia Tanner standing on the porch. She was returning Jessie's wave with one of her own.

"I might have to come back, to say hello."

"Now I told you . . ."

"I know what you said, Chief, but the way I see it, you have two choices. You could invite me to stay, and both of us talk to her, or I can come back later—alone. Your choice?"

"There is another way to go. I could arrest you."

"For what? Bird-watching?"

Cook dropped his chin to his chest and let his shoulders slump. None of this was going like he'd planned, but before he thought about things too hard, Jessie's mouth was making promises it couldn't keep.

"If I promise that I won't say a word, will you let me sit in?"

Chief Cook clenched his jaw, and finally said, "Fine."

The Tanner residence was the closest acreage to the house where Angela DeSalvo had been murdered. It was a mirror image of the DeSalvo place except that it was in better shape. The green clapboard house had a well-maintained yard with wooden steps that led to the front porch. Potted flowers hung from a cedar pergola near the front door. And Sophia Tanner was a collector of yard art, anything that spun in the wind.

By the time Jessie and Chief Cook parked their vehicles and got out, Sophia Tanner came out to meet them. She was wiping her hands with a washrag, wearing khaki slacks with a blue floral top.

"Hello, Sophia. Thanks for making time for me."

"I didn't expect you to bring a visitor, Tobias. Not with you wanting to talk about . . . that DeSalvo murder."

Mrs. Tanner did not look happy with the chief, but when she turned her attention on Jessie, the woman smiled.

"I'm Sophia Tanner." She extended her hand and waited for Jessie to reciprocate. The woman's hand was icy cold.

"My name's Jessie. Jessie Beckett."

"You're not from around here, are you?"

"No, ma'am. I'm not. I drove up from Chicago. I'm an investigator, helping Chief Cook with an old case."

The woman squeezed her hand and held it a little too long. And the way she looked at her, it made Jessie feel uncomfortable. Chief Cook must have felt it, too. He cleared his throat and put his hand on Mrs. Tanner's shoulder.

"Let's go inside. Would that be okay?"

Mrs. Tanner blinked, almost as if she hadn't heard him.

"Yes, of course. Please . . . come in." The woman led them into her living room. "How's that arthritis of yours, Tobias? You walking like I told you?"

"Sophia used to push me to walk at lunch when we worked together," the chief told Jessie. "And she wasn't a woman you could say no to, at least not often."

Mrs. Tanner listened to Cook and smiled, but when she thought Jessie wasn't looking, the woman stole glances at her. Jessie felt like a damned lab rat. The staring made her uncomfortable until she got distracted with the woman's house.

The Tanner house was real homey inside, especially with the smell of coffee and cinnamon lingering in the air. And she collected antique furniture, good-quality stuff, and had lace and pastel frills everywhere. But when Jessie saw all the family photos in the living room, the smiling happy faces reminded her of what she'd never had—a family.

She'd been a ward of the state of Illinois and had never been around a real family, except for those in the foster-care system that she'd stayed with when she wasn't in an institution or halfway house. All of her belongings had been kept in a trash bag, ready to move when the state ordered it. That was no kind of life for a kid.

"Can I get you some coffee?" the woman asked.

"None for me," he said.

Taking a cue from Chief Cook, Jessie shook her head and said, "No thanks."

"Please, sit." Mrs. Tanner took a seat and folded the washrag on her lap, something to do with her hands. "How can I help you?"

The chief sat in a wingback chair, and Jessie took a spot on the sofa.

"Like I said on the phone, I'm lookin' into the Angela DeSalvo murder case," he began.

"I don't know. That's been so long ago. I thought I read somewhere that you'd closed that case, Tobias."

"That case never went to court. And murder cases stay open until they do. You remember how that works, right?"

"Terrible thing." The woman shook her head. "I had nightmares over that for such a long time."

"I can understand that."

"So why are you here . . . talking to me, Tobias?"

"I hate to admit this, but we're missing some paperwork on the case. Everyone whose property was adjacent to the DeSalvo house got interviewed, except for you. And I've come to rectify that."

"But I did talk to someone. One of your men, I think." She wrung the cloth in her hand. "Maybe that old paperwork will show up. Maybe it was misfiled, is all."

"I understand what you're saying, Sophia, but while we're here, I'd like to ask you a few question. Will that be all right?" Without waiting for her reply, he continued as he opened a notepad, "What can you tell me about the night Angela DeSalvo was murdered? Did you see any strangers or hear anything out of the ordinary?"

Sophia Tanner told Chief Cook all she remembered. The more she talked about Angela De Salvo, the more her fingers worked the washrag she still held in her hands. And she avoided eye contact as she spoke. She was uptight about something more than recalling the murder of a neighbor.

While the police chief made a note, Jessie had a question of her own.

"How well did you know Angela?" she asked.

Chief Cook gave her a sideways glance, and, under his breath, he said, "So much for not saying a word."

When Jessie saw him raise an eyebrow, she ignored him and turned her full attention on Mrs. Tanner.

"I knew her as well as anyone would know a neighbor, I suppose. We didn't socialize, if that's what you mean. We talked on occasion, as neighbors. That's all."

"Do you remember seeing any children at the DeSalvo home?" From the corner of her eye, Jessie saw Chief Cook shift in his seat, and she heard his sigh, but that didn't stop her. "Maybe she had kids at her place that week prior to the murder."

"Tobias, what is she talking about? Kids? You never said anything about wanting to talk about children."

Sophia Tanner's eyes watered, and she looked confused. If Chief Cook had been doing his job, he might have attempted to calm her down, so he could continue his questioning, but that's not what he did.

"I think I've got everything I need." He stood and reached for Jessie's arm, heading her for the door. "Thanks for your cooperation, Sophia. If you think of anything else, give me a call."

"I will. I promise." The woman forced a smile. "Have a good day, both of you."

When they got outside, out of Mrs. Tanner's earshot, Jessie had plenty to say.

"You call that an interview? You clearly don't watch *Castle*, to see how it's done."

"And you clearly make promises you have no

intention of keeping. I think we're done here.
Have a good day, Ms. Beckett. And if I hear that
you've come back here to harass this poor woman,
I'll arrest you. Is that clear?"

The man was done talking. He got in his squad
car and waited for her to get in her rental. Any
hope she had for his cooperation had dried up,
and she had no idea why. She'd hit a wall that she
had never seen coming.

Now she'd have to scramble, and she had a
good idea where to start.

La Pointe, Wisconsin
Twenty minutes later

If Chief Cook wouldn't give her any more information on the murder of Angela DeSalvo, Jessie
knew how to dig up stuff on her own. And a good
source for a story nearly decades old was the town
library and the newspaper archives.

She took a corner of the archives and worked
over the digital images of old newspapers until
she was bleary-eyed. With only the occasional
bathroom break and a raid on the snack machine,
where she finished off the Cheetos and KitKat
bars, she searched the digital records, looking
for anything pertaining to the murder of Angela
DeSalvo. And seeing the newspaper evolve over

time gave her insight into the community and people of La Pointe.

TV detectives always had miraculous databases to help them solve cases in a make-believe world where DNA results could be done in minutes, and the killer always confessed in the last five minutes of the show. In real life, it didn't work that way. Most cases involved "beating feet" on pavement and tedious grunt work that could be butt numbing.

When she'd located a string of articles that encompassed months after the murder, Jessie made copies of the best ones with the most details. Since this was a small town, the newspaper took liberties with its reporting. It deviated from the typical sparse style of journalistic writing and sometimes focused on the more emotional aspects of the story.

She scanned the pages and didn't see anything that she hadn't expected, but she'd go over the articles later when she had more time to read.

When the last article had printed, Jessie sorted through her pile and placed the most important pages on top. Once she got back to her motel room, she wanted to read them first. And considering the stack of paper, it would be a long night.

She headed out of the library with her gold mine of old articles on the DeSalvo killing rolled up in her hand. When she got outside, it was the first time she realized that she'd spent almost the whole day ratholed in the archives. But after she filled her lungs with cool dusk air and caught glimpses of the sunset glittering on the churning waters of Lake Superior, she got a second wind. And her stomach reminded her that she hadn't eaten much all day.

She followed the main drag, walking toward the water. From what she remembered of her ferry trip, the harbor area had some inviting restaurants near the shore. That made her belly rumble, but as she turned down a side street, she caught a glimpse of movement in the waning sunlight. A shadow had moved behind her.

La Pointe was small, a tourist town. Why she flinched at the sight of someone behind her, she didn't know. Maybe her wariness had been a by-product of digging into the DeSalvo murder all afternoon. And being in the very town where it had all happened had caused her jumpiness.

The way Jessie figured it, it didn't hurt to be careful. When she picked up her pace, she paid closer attention to the sounds coming from behind her and kept a watchful eye on any suspicious movement. Under her windbreaker, she carried her Colt Python. And with the adrenaline coursing through her veins, she felt the weight of her weapon as she ducked around another corner. If someone was following her, she'd have precious seconds to expand the gap between them and look for a place to confront the bastard.

Jessie had no intention of losing him, not when she wanted to look the son of a bitch square in the eye.

CHAPTER 10

La Pointe, Wisconsin

Jessie spotted a darkened alleyway ahead. The sun was low enough on the horizon to leave shadows in its wake. The alley separated two storefronts. One place was still open, a small gift shop. And the other had lights out and was closed for business. Before the guy who was tailing her rounded the corner, she darted into the alley and shoved her back against a brick wall.

Come on, you sorry son of a . . .

She didn't have to wait long.

When the guy thought he'd lost her, he'd picked up his pace. The sound of his footsteps grew louder. Jessie waited for him to run by the alley where she was hiding. All she saw when he jogged by was a blue plaid shirt, jeans, running shoes, and a navy baseball cap pulled low over his face.

After she'd turned the tables on him, she fell in pace behind him, tailing him instead. But the guy must have seen her make the move, because with barely a look over his shoulder, he made a run for it.

"Damn it!" she cursed under her breath as she chased him. "If you make me break a sweat, I swear . . ."

There was only one good thing about the guy hauling his ass down the street. With him running, it confirmed that he'd been following her. She hadn't been overly paranoid after all.

But with the guy having a lead on her, Jessie had to make up ground. Her lungs were burning, and the muscles in her legs were on fire. With her arms pumping, she carried the rolled-up newspaper articles clutched in her hand. And when the bastard ducked around a corner without hesitating, she saw that he was taking her through a deserted part of La Pointe, a place she didn't know at all.

The guy knew where he was going. It was his town. He had an advantage. And with him out of sight, she had to be careful. Jessie slowed up, bracing her body in case he reached out and grabbed her. With her chest heaving, she tucked her newspaper articles in the waistband of her jeans before she pulled out her Colt. She gripped the weapon in her sweaty hand as she neared the street corner.

Jessie slowed her breathing and stepped lightly so he wouldn't know exactly where she was, but once she made her move, that was the end of her game of finesse. When she swung around the corner, with both hands on her Colt, she saw that the street was empty. An abandoned old gas station was positioned on her right and an auto repair place stood on her left, secured by a cyclone fence that was locked.

Jessie walked slowly down the street, keeping her gun aimed into every shadow. And after she'd checked both sides of the street, she lowered her weapon.

"Damn," she cursed under her breath.

The bastard had found a place to hide, like the cockroach he was.

Pérez Compound
Outside Guadalajara, Mexico
10:20 P.M.

On day two of surveillance, Alexa had changed her clothes to more practical attire—camo BDUs. Garrett always came prepared and had brought extra gear. She was hunkered down in the foot-hills outside the Pérez estate, with her elbows propped on a boulder, using high-tech night-vision binoculars to monitor the security patrols inside the compound. On instinct, she timed and tracked the intervals at which the armed guards patrolled the grounds and how many men made the rounds.

She felt dirt on her skin, but she kept perfectly still and didn't fidget. And when something crawled up her ankle, she didn't panic. She brushed the scorpion away by moving with slow deliberation to avoid any sudden moves, a practice honed from years of training and discipline. Hasty moves and unexpected noise in the stillness could make her a target.

She'd picked an isolated spot away from Hank's ground team and kept to herself. She melded into the terrain as the moon cast a bluish haze that looked like a dusting of fine blue powder over the rugged landscape outside the estate, covering trees, boulders, agave plants, and yuccas. And she listened to the sounds of the night, the forlorn hoot of an owl in the trees and the baleful cries of a pack of coyotes.

Most people might have been tense, hiding in the dark, but Alexa got off on the isolation, a complete departure from New York City. Yet despite the serene setting, she couldn't forget why they were there. Jackson Kinkaid had crossed her path once again. And she hoped, given the situation, that it wouldn't be for the last time.

Rapt in her thoughts of Kinkaid, she hardly noticed that Garrett had joined her. He hadn't said a word, and neither of them felt uncomfortable with the silence between them. He'd only slipped next to her and didn't feel the need to say anything at all. The reason for his secrecy had vanished, so he joined Hank and his men, and Alexa had become part of the team. Having Garrett with her felt comfortable, and it reminded her how close she'd come to losing him. But swapping her fears from Garrett Wheeler to Jackson Kinkaid wasn't exactly making progress.

It wasn't until she heard a steady thump in the distance that she'd realized the intruding noise was man-made and mechanical, and stood out from the sounds of nature.

"What's that?" she whispered, only loud enough for Garrett to hear.

"Helicopter."

As if on cue, lights in the distance cut through the darkness. She lowered her night-vision binoculars—not wanting to be blinded by the onset of the bright lights on the horizon—and watched as a helicopter rose over the mountains. The aircraft circled the estate below and hovered behind the hacienda, kicking up dust as it landed.

"Pérez," she said under her breath and edged closer to Garrett, feeling the warmth of his arm against hers.

Without responding to her, Garrett spoke into his com unit to Hank and his men.

"Anyone with confirmation, speak up. If the big man is there, I want to know it."

"Copy that."

Alexa watched as Hank's team shifted positions to utilize long-range surveillance gear. Even with her night-vision binoculars, she couldn't see well enough to ID a face. Not even the full moon helped. All she could do was sit back and let Hank's men do their jobs.

"What now?" she asked Garrett. "How do we know when to move in?"

"If we can't make an ID, then Jackson has to confirm that Pérez is on-site. He said he'd give us a signal."

"What kind of signal?" she asked.

"He said we'd know it when we saw it, but until then, we're to stay put on the ridge outside the estate." Garrett gave her a sideways glance and didn't say anything more.

Even in the murky shadows, she saw Garrett tighten his jaw as he watched the estate below. He didn't like this either.

An hour later

No one on Hank's team had confirmed that Manolo Quintanilla Pérez had been one of the people who'd flown via helicopter to the estate outside Guadalajara. Too many men had rushed to the helicopter to usher the new arrivals inside. And so far they hadn't seen any sign from Jackson Kinkaid, if he was even still alive, that is.

"I can't believe you went along with Kinkaid's self-destructive idea of a plan." The words were out of her mouth before she could rein them back in. The instant she'd said them, she knew she'd done the wrong thing. It wasn't Garrett's fault that Kinkaid had a vendetta against a drug kingpin in Mexico and that he was being held by Pérez and his vicious pack of dogs. Jackson had done that on his own.

"It's not like he gave me a choice, Alexa," Garrett said, unable to hide his annoyance. "If we don't see anything soon, I'll make the call to go in. Understood?"

"Yeah, understood." Alexa took a deep breath. She only had to understand, she didn't have to like it. "So what now? We wait?"

"Yeah," he whispered back. "We wait."

She knew that waiting was a big part of surveillance, but she didn't have to like that either. While the team watched the activity below—with some of Hank's men closer to the action, so they could confirm any sighting of Pérez—Alexa took advantage of having Garrett next to her.

And she wanted to get her mind off Kinkaid's suicide mission.

"Was it you who followed me from the Guadalajara airport? At first, I thought it was Hank, but later he told me it hadn't been him."

She hated admitting she didn't know who had tailed her, but if it had been Garrett, that would explain why she only felt him and never saw him. Garrett was an experienced agent who could make himself a ghost if he wanted to.

"No, wasn't me." He shook his head and furrowed his brow. "Someone followed you? Did you see 'em?"

"No, only felt them. If it wasn't you, I have a pretty good idea who ordered it."

"Who? What are you talking about?" he asked.

"Donovan Cross." She fixed her gaze on him, waiting to see if the name meant anything. "So what's up with that guy? What's his part in all this?"

"Donovan Cross? I know who he is, but what's he got to do with it?"

She stared at him for a long minute, trying to read if he was lying again. Since he'd clued her in and made her part of his team, now he had no motive for keeping her in the dark when it came to the mission with Kinkaid, but she had no idea if that extended to his past with Donovan Cross.

"He took over your job and told me you were dead, killed in a classified mission. He made up a story about how you got caught in an explosion, and your body would never be recovered. Ring any bells?" When he didn't say anything, she stared at him in disbelief. "You mean he wasn't part of your disappearing act?"

"No, he wasn't." Garrett narrowed his eyes and got strangely quiet.

When he finally glanced at her, he must have seen the worried look on her face, because he said, "I'll put out some feelers, figure out what's going on. It's probably nothing."

He tried for nonchalance, but she wasn't buying it.

"Yeah, right. It's probably just a coincidence. And you know how I feel about those." She sighed. "You better watch your back with Cross. He's got to have support within the Sentinels if he stepped into your job so quickly. Who would do that?"

"I'll take care of it."

The way Garrett said it—as if he had made a promise to himself—it left her cold inside. In a covert agency like the Sentinels, it paid to have solid support within the organization, from the top down. But if Donovan Cross had slipped easily into Garrett's job, she had to wonder. Who had undermined Garrett's authority? Doing something like that wasn't a one-man show. Who was backing Cross as the new head of the Sentinels?

And how far would they go to keep him there?

"Cross doesn't strike me as someone's puppet." She couldn't let it go. "And he's got to be working with people who have the balls to seize an opportunity when they see it, with you missing. I'm just . . . worried, Garrett."

"I know you are," he began as he stared into her eyes, "but I've got to handle this my way. I don't want you getting stuck in any cross fire. That would . . . kill me."

For the first time in a long while, Garrett looked into her eyes like he used to. She'd ended their relationship and moved on after she'd caught him with someone else, but the intimacy between them had never truly been severed. And that had never been more apparent. Alexa blinked and cleared her throat, breaking his connection with her.

"Just remember that you've got friends, too. Don't go it alone, tough guy."

Garrett smiled, a quick fleeting curve of his lips.

"Good to know. Thanks."

* * *

"What was that? That sound, did you hear it?" Estella's voice cracked.

She turned her head toward the only window in the cell and squinted into a piercing light that vanished as quickly as it had come. A powerful engine roared across the night sky as the sudden brightness stabbed the dark and left its phantom image in her mind.

Something was happening outside.

And after the engine noise faded, she heard the distant voices of Ramon's men and hoisted herself high enough to see out. But her sudden moves started the aching pain again. Her shoulders were on fire, caused by the weight of her body. And her wrists were raw from the ropes.

When her question about the noise went unanswered, she looked over to the dark part of the cell, where only a thin stream of moonlight doused the stone walls. Estella saw the silhouette of the American. He had not moved in over two hours. And she barely heard his breathing.

"Please . . . don't be dead," she whispered.

Saying the words aloud didn't make her feel so alone, even if the wounded man couldn't hear her.

"No such luck," he mumbled.

"Oh, I'm . . . sorry. I did not mean . . ."

"Helicopter."

"Excuse me?"

"You heard a h-helicopter. That was . . . the n-noise."

It took all her concentration to hear him. Yet even though the man sounded weak, there was something in his voice that calmed her. And since he had answered her first question, she ventured another.

"What are they doing? Ramon's men. I hear them outside."

Her whisper hissed across the cell and echoed off stone, sounding garbled. When he didn't answer right away, she almost repeated her question, thinking he had not understood her.

"This is almost over. I'm sorry for how it turned out." Even though he choked out words plainly enough, she didn't understand what he meant.

"This isn't your fault, *señor.*"

"I wish you were right about that." When he spoke, she saw the glint in his eyes, a reflection of the moonlight . . . and something else.

Estella didn't understand the strange man, but for the first time, she was afraid of what she saw in his eyes.

La Pointe, Wisconsin

After Jessie lost her footrace with the guy who had taken an interest in her, she had given up on her appetite. She'd stopped in at the motel office and scored enough snacks to satisfy her if she changed her mind. Byron McGivens wasn't behind the desk when she stopped in, even though his nameplate was still hanging on the wall as if he were on duty.

"Does Byron have the night off?" she asked. The minute she'd instigated the conversation, Jessie knew it had been a mistake. It only gave the guy behind the counter a reason to chat her up.

"Yeah, he had something to do. I fill in sometimes." The older man grinned back at her. "So . . . you new in town?"

Jessie fought the urge to roll her eyes. The clerk rang up the sale, between his attempts at making one-way small talk, and forced Jessie to smile as she headed out the door. When she got to her room, she set the brown bag with her snacks on the sidewalk near her door—and as a precaution—she reached for her Colt Python. After she unlocked her door, she flipped on the lights and aimed her gun from corner to corner.

Her room was empty. And her things were as she'd left them, except where the maid had touched. Jessie smelled the scent of pine cleaner, saw that the bed had been made, and noticed the maid had left her fresh towels. After she saw the room was clear, she went back for her bag of goodies and locked the door behind her, tossing her new stash of Fritos, Twinkies, and Red Bull onto the extra double bed.

She pulled out the newspaper articles from the waistband of her jeans and tried to straighten them, without much luck. Since the pages had gotten squashed and manhandled in her chase with the local yokel, she slipped them under her mattress to flatten them out while she got cleaned up.

Jessie took a quick shower and changed into the gym shorts and tank top she normally slept in if she wasn't spending the night with Seth. After she got in bed, she propped herself up on her pillows and spread out the articles she wanted to read as she ate a Twinkie.

Most of the articles about the killing were text-book journalism, but some were more dramatic, like an intriguing mystery. And some reporter even speculated on rumors. Anything was news in a small town.

Folks had wondered why Angela DeSalvo had kept to herself, not socializing much with the rest of the town. Someone had her pegged as a woman on the run from an abusive husband. And another local woman swore she saw her with kids and speculated that she was running an illegal adoption scam.

"Well, I'll be damned," she whispered.

Reading that, Jessie felt the hairs on the back of her neck rise. If Angela DeSalvo had been on the wrong side of the law, that could explain how she had ended up in the hands of a serial pedophile. The thought of Angela contributing to what had happened to her made Jessie sick.

"What were you up to? And did it get you killed?"

Jessie made up her mind to spend the next day talking to some of the locals mentioned in the articles, to see who was still living in La Pointe. And something about Sophia Tanner still bothered her. The woman had appeared edgy, and she had wrung the washrag so tight in her hands, it had made Jessie nervous just watching her. And when she'd mentioned kids, the woman freaked. She had immediately looked to Chief Cook for protection, and the local LEO obliged her, right on cue.

Jessie had no doubt that Cook would arrest her if he found out she had talked to Sophia Tanner one-on-one after he had specifically told her to leave the woman alone. When Jessie thought of how adamant he'd been, she smiled to herself.

Guess what he didn't know wouldn't hurt her.

Jessie turned out the lights and lay in the dark, her mind still working over all that she'd seen today, but when her cell phone rang, she had to get up to answer it. She had it recharging in the motel bathroom.

"Hey, Sam. What's up?" She'd recognized the incoming cell number and knew who it was. Her friend didn't call at this hour unless it was important.

"Hey, Jess. Sorry to wake you."

"Funny thing. I haven't been able to sleep lately. Imagine that."

"Well, don't kill the messenger." Detective Samantha Cooper forced a laugh, but since Jessie knew her well, she was familiar with Sam's strained attempt at humor. "Are you sitting down?"

Jessie looked behind her. The only place to sit in the tight bathroom was the toilet seat, and she had no intention of receiving bad news sitting on the commode. When she got to the bed, she took a corner and sat.

"Yeah, I'm sitting. Shoot."

"Remember that DNA report that I requested, the one Chief Cook claimed he got a hit with your DNA that tied you to his cold case?"

Jessie didn't like the sounds of this already.

"Yeah. What about it?"

"Chief Cook told me he got one hit on your DNA. Is that what he told you?"

"Yeah, he did. What's this about, Sammie? 'Cause you're shaking me up here."

Jessie's throat went suddenly dry. Her breathing had escalated, along with her heart rate. She had no idea where Sam was headed with her questions, but Jessie didn't like it.

"Sorry, Jess. I don't know why the chief wouldn't tell you everything. Guess you can ask him when you see him."

"Sam, spit it out. Please."

"I had my lab boys analyze that report, so I'd be sure of the findings. That's why I couldn't call you sooner, but Jessie, that report had two DNA samples on it. Your DNA wasn't the only one found at that crime scene."

"What?"

"The Wisconsin state crime lab found a second unidentified sample of DNA. And that sample showed a 95 percent probability match to yours."

"What does that mean?"

"It means that second sample doesn't have a match in the databases, so they can't ID who was there, but the DNA came from someone in your immediate family, Jessie. Your *real* family." Sam let that thought settle before she landed a second shocker. "And according to the crime lab and my CSI guys, that DNA has genetic markers that indicate it came from a male."

"You mean . . . my father?"

"I don't know, Jess. It could be your father or a

brother." Sam heaved a sigh. "I don't know if this is good or bad news, but maybe you can ask Chief Cook why he left out that second DNA sample. He didn't tell me about it. And apparently he never said anything to you either. I'd sure want to know why."

Terrible thoughts crossed Jessie's mind. And it left her reeling. She couldn't sit anymore. She had to stand, but when she caught a glimpse of her face in the mirror, she suddenly got nauseous.

With all the talk about kids being seen at Angela DeSalvo's place prior to her murder, Jessie had to wonder. She had to have been one of those kids since her DNA was found at the crime scene. And now it appeared her brother had been there, too. The joy of knowing she might have a brother mixed with a flood of dark thoughts.

Had her brother been taken the way she had been? Did Danny Ray Millstone torture her brother, too? Had he been in that house where she was held prisoner, and she hadn't even known it?

"No, that can't be." She swallowed, hard.

"What?"

"Oh, Sammie. Give me a minute here. I gotta process all this before I say anything." Her voice cracked as she paced the floor. "Just wait a minute."

Although Sam could check into the Millstone case, looking for names of the survivors or the names of the kids the bastard had killed, that would take time. Sam would have to pull the case files and do legwork to find out what Seth Harper would know in short order. Harper had his father's old murder book. And he'd been making contact with the Millstone survivors. That was how and why they'd met. Harper would know what she needed.

"I've got to talk to Seth," she muttered.

"What? Slow down, Jess," Sam urged her. "Take a deep breath."

"I know. And you're right, but I gotta think. What did Cook tell me? I gotta remember." As she ran through everything the chief had said, she paced the floor and searched through her mind.

Chief Cook had told her that he'd looked into the Danny Ray Millstone case and knew about what happened to her as one of his victims. Maybe he knew more than he'd let on. Or maybe he only wanted to spare her feelings. Either way, she hated that he'd kept the truth from her. And what she was thinking was far worse than if he had just told her what he knew.

Besides the possibility of having a brother who might already be dead—or a survivor of abuse like she had been—there was a darker scenario that lurked in the back of her mind, one that made her even more sick.

"Hold on, I gotta . . ." Jessie dropped her cell on the mattress and ran to the bathroom. She emptied her stomach until all she had left were dry heaves. Her face was hot, and beads of sweat clung to the skin of her arms. With trembling hands, she cleaned up. And when she could, she got back on the phone with Sam.

"Are you okay, Jessie? I'm so sorry."

It took her a moment to catch her breath and calm her racing heart.

"Can you do me . . . a favor?"

"Yeah, anything."

"Do you know if they have a sample of Millstone's DNA on file? I mean, maybe after he was caught red-handed and killed, no one bothered to collect it."

"That's hard to say. Back then, digital DNA records were hit-and-miss, and not every case got consistent treatment. Why are you asking about this, Jessie?"

"I need to know if Millstone was . . . my father."

It took everything she had to say those words.

She had no other explanation for how she ended up with the serial pedophile. Being related to that scumbag would be the worst she could imagine, and that was saying something. She knew it was a leap, one she didn't want to take, but if this trip had been about uncovering her past, she had to go the distance. She had to keep an open mind about the possibilities, or she'd never find the truth.

"Oh, my God, Jessie. I never thought . . . If Millstone's DNA wasn't on digital file that could explain why Cook didn't get a hit on that second sample. And if we can confirm that second sample is Millstone's, then odds are that Chief Cook can solve his old murder case." Sam rambled on for what felt like an eternity, trying to console her, but finally she said, "Yeah, I'll look to see what I can find. And I'll call you the minute I know something."

"Thanks, Sam."

Jessie ended the call, knowing she'd never get to sleep. She had too much to try to remember—and way too much she'd never forget.

She'd contact Seth in the morning, first thing, but confronting Chief Cook face-to-face weighed heavy on her mind. She had to know why he'd lied to her about the DNA analysis. Did he already know what Sam had promised to find out, about her possible connection to her childhood abuser?

According to Cook, his men had missed getting an interview with Sophia Tanner. The interview had been missing from the murder book, but what if that original document had been taken from the evidence on purpose, to cover up the truth?

And if Cook had been behind that cover-up, why would he have gone through the motions of interviewing the woman again? He could have blown Jessie off and made excuses. There was plenty for her to be suspicious about and not enough cold hard facts, but the chief of police in La Pointe would be the man to see.

Had he held back the truth to spare her feelings, or was he protecting someone? Either way, Jessie wanted to look Cook in the eye and dare him to lie to her again.

CHAPTER 11

Waiting had never been Alexa's thing. It gave her too much time to dwell on Kinkaid's predicament, but something else was eating at her. And she had to say something to Garrett. When she found him hunkered down next to Hank, she moved closer and spoke in a hushed tone.

"What happens when Pérez sees Kinkaid?" She didn't wait for Garrett to say anything. "If it's true that bastard killed Jackson's wife and kid, then he'd know Kinkaid on sight. Once he sets eyes on him, he'll know he's not you. The masquerade would be over. All Pérez has to do is pull the trigger, or order it done."

Garrett didn't act surprised to hear what she'd

said. He only heaved a sigh as he turned his back on Hank.

"I'm sure Kinkaid knew that going in," he told her. "I tried to warn you. He's not planning on walking away from this."

Until now, Alexa had thought of this as a rescue mission, but nothing could be farther from the truth. She turned away and didn't say anything more. She didn't want the moonlight to out her to Garrett as her eyes filled with tears. Whatever Kinkaid had planned, he was going out in a big way. And the odds were against him, even with Garrett's team being outside the stone walls of the Pérez estate.

Jackson Kinkaid was beyond saving.

1:10 A.M.

"What was so important that couldn't wait?" Manolo Quintanilla Pérez said in his native tongue.

Ramon Guerrero clenched his jaw as the drug-cartel boss stared at him and Miguel Rosas, his number two man. Pérez hadn't offered them a seat. He'd made them wait to see him while he relaxed. And now they stood in front of him as the big man sat behind a massive cherrywood desk in the study of his estate. He leaned back in his leather chair as he sipped a fine Cognac from a crystal snifter.

Rosas was about to open his mouth to speak first, but Guerrero couldn't let that happen. The American had been his to find, and he wasn't about to let Rosas take credit for his diligence or downplay his part, not after he'd made the call to Pérez that had brought him there.

"My men took a hostage in Juárez, a very influential American. His name is Garrett Wheeler and he claims that you know him."

"Oh? That name is not familiar to me." Pérez narrowed his eyes at Guerrero. "Tell me. How do I know him?"

When Pérez crooked his lip into a humorless sneer, Guerrero cleared his throat before he went on.

"He did not say, but I believe that if you see him for yourself, you can get him to admit what he's up to."

"So now, you want me to do your work for you?" The cartel boss cut a sideways glance at Rosas, who only shrugged with boredom.

"No, sir. That's not what I'm saying, but someone of your reputation has no doubt made an impression on this man. You have said that you fear this American is probably CIA, and my sources back this up, too. This man has probably been sent to assassinate the heads of the drug cartels for the U.S. government."

In an effort to make a big impression and beat out Rosas, Guerrero had blurted out a theory Rosas had told him about, something that had come from Pérez himself, but his boss's questions had rattled him. And now that his words hung in the air, without evidence to back him up, Guerrero had sounded like an idiot.

"Oh? How do you know all this?" Pérez asked, setting down his empty glass. "What proof do you have?"

Before Guerrero could answer, Rosas interrupted with a smirk.

"He doesn't have any. He is only trying to impress you. The American hasn't confirmed any of this."

"He carried a U.S. driver's license with him. I've seen it and so have you. It confirms his name and an address of his home in New York," Guerrero argued.

"Identification like that can be bought. It means nothing." Rosas looked at his boss with a dismissive shrug. "And do you think if he is some big spy, that he would have his real information so easily obtained? Like I said, his ID means nothing."

"Then you are also dismissing the messages I received from my contacts across the border? Wheeler was overheard, trying to buy information about the cartels . . . and you, in particular. He admitted who he was when he thought he was safe on the American side. And my sources in New York have confirmed that Wheeler is missing."

"That's the point. Only your sources say this, but I believe in other ways to arrive at the truth." Rosas narrowed his eyes. "When a man knows he is about to die, he will bargain any way he can to save his miserable life. That is the only source worth believing, forcing a man to tell you everything he knows when he faces death."

"Ramon, you told me that it was urgent I should be here. Is this all you have? That I should see this American for myself?" Pérez shifted his glare toward Guerrero once again.

"I assure you, sir. I believe the man has vital information that you can help us get from him. I swear on my sainted mother's head, it's only a matter of time before we get him to talk."

"So now you use the words 'us' and 'we.'" Rosas chuckled under his breath and leaned against a wall with his arms crossed. "A minute ago, you were running this show, single-handedly. Which is it?"

Guerrero suddenly saw himself between two very dangerous men. He'd gone around Rosas's back to have a face-to-face meeting with his boss, an encounter that had not gone as well as he had expected. If he didn't play his cards right, he would end up the big loser.

"You have been extremely resourceful in dealing with the American," Guerrero said to Rosas. "I'm sure he will tell us everything, in time. And my sources will be confirmed."

"Very diplomatic, Ramon." Pérez grinned and stood. "Cowardly, but diplomatic nonetheless."

Before Guerrero had a chance to redeem himself, Pérez focused all his attention on Miguel Rosas, his trusted death dealer.

"What has the American admitted so far?"

"Nothing of consequence, but he has told both of us that he has come to kill a man," Rosas admitted.

"Oh?" Pérez smiled. "Depending on who his target is, perhaps we should help him. Eliminating the competition, is that such a bad thing?"

"My thoughts exactly." Rosas glanced over his shoulder at Guerrero, rubbing in his advantage with the boss and taking credit where none was due.

"Take me to him then"—Pérez smiled—"this man I know."

Rosas escorted the cartel boss out of the study, toward the makeshift cells where the American was being held, with Guerrero following close behind. Without really trying, Rosas had made

him look like a fool, but maybe he still had a way
to redeem himself.

When Pérez came face-to-face with the American, perhaps the truth would come out, and his
boss would see who he had personally delivered
to his door.

1:35 A.M.

"I haven't told you the truth, but it doesn't
matter now. It's too late."

He looked at Estella and saw the questioning
look on her battered face. And before she opened
her mouth to ask what he meant, he kept talking.
He'd run out of time.

"My name is Jackson Kinkaid. I'm not Garrett
Wheeler. That was a name I thought would get
Pérez here."

"You mean . . . the man Ramon works for? He
is coming here?"

Kinkaid didn't have to see the fear in the girl's
eyes. He heard it in her voice.

"He's already here. He came in that helicopter.
And he's probably on his way to this cell right
now."

"He's a bad man, *señor*. A very bad man. If he's
here, it will not be good."

"If I had known you'd be dragged into my fight,

I wouldn't have done this. I would've found another way, but now everything is in motion. I can't stop it."

"What's in motion? What are you saying?"

From across the cell, Kinkaid saw Estella's eyes glistening with fresh tears. If this girl died because of him, he was no better than Pérez.

Grief and his urgency for revenge had blinded him. He had tunnel vision when it came to settling the score. There had to be a reckoning, where the dead got their due. That was all that had weighed on his mind and heart and soul since his family had been killed. The murder of his wife and his precious little girl had haunted him beyond reason.

Revenge was the air that he breathed.

Garrett Wheeler and his team were waiting for a signal—only it wouldn't be what they were expecting. Kinkaid's own men had confirmed that Pérez had been inside the aircraft at takeoff. And now that the helicopter had touched down at the compound outside Guadalajara, it had tipped the first domino, which toppled the rest to the point of no return.

And Estella would pay a price for his indulgence. But there was nothing he could do about it.

"Open the door," a man's voice bellowed from the corridor.

After a key slid into the lock, the door creaked open. And a torch nearly blinded him. Kinkaid squinted and turned his head with a grimace. He braced himself for more abuse, his body taut and seething with adrenaline.

He had lived for this moment. Despite his regret for what this meant for Estella, he couldn't do anything about that, not now. And his need to see this through to the end outweighed his good conscience.

Hidden behind the bright flame of the torch, the shadows of several men entered his cell, but the big man stood out. His face emerged from the dark, as in the many nightmares Kinkaid had had over the years. Manolo Quintanilla Pérez stood in front of him with a despicable smirk on his face. After all these years, it was really him.

The man who had murdered his wife and child. The man who had taken everything.

CHAPTER 12

Sweat trickled down Kinkaid's face and stung his eyes. And it took all his determination to lift his head and stare down the man who had killed his family.

It had taken him years to uncover the truth. And he had worked with other despicable men to find out who had given the order on the hit, an assault intended to kill him instead of his wife and baby girl. But after he'd learned the truth, that Pérez had put a price on his head, it was all he could think about and all he had lived for.

And it would be the reason he would die here.

"So you are Garrett Wheeler, a big man with the CIA." Pérez sneered and walked slowly, not taking his eyes off him. "I only want to know one thing."

The men standing behind Pérez shuffled and moved closer. They listened to every word the fat man said. They were waiting for the American spook to back down in front of their fearless leader.

"Why did you feel you had to lie to my men?" Pérez leaned in and whispered, "You are worth more to me than Garrett Wheeler."

"What?" The voices of his men echoed in the cell. "What do you mean? Who is this man?"

"His name is Jackson Kinkaid. He blames me for the death of his wife and child, but who is really at fault?" The man shrugged and shifted his focus back on Kinkaid. "You were the one who destroyed my first cartel. It took me years to rebuild. And what kind of man would I be if I didn't punish the one who nearly got me killed?"

Pérez grabbed Kinkaid by the throat and squeezed. "You are to blame for the death of your family. You brought that on yourself. I warned you what would happen."

After he let go, Kinkaid choked and gasped for air.

"Your beef was . . . with m-me, not them. You're a c-coward who murders innocent women and ch-children."

"So what did you hope to gain by getting

hauled here to me, like this? You are a stupid man, Kinkaid. A bullheaded one." Pérez grimaced. "And all this, for a mere woman? You are a young man. You could have had more children, no?"

"I missed killing you the first time. But now I'm here to finish the job."

"So the man you came to kill is Pérez?" Ramon Guerrero looked shocked, but it didn't take him long to make excuses to his boss. "I swear, I did not know."

"Unbelievable," Pérez said as he scowled at his man, but when it finally sank in what Kinkaid had intended to do, he laughed aloud. His men joined him, with each one looking at the other to make sure it was all right. In Pérez's eyes, he had the high ground—the advantage. Kinkaid was nothing, less than nothing.

"You turn me loose, and we'll see how unfuckin'-believable it is." Kinkaid mustered all his strength. He lurched at the man, rattling his chains. "You don't have the guts to face me like a real man. You're soft, Pérez. You've grown too fat and too old."

Pérez stopped laughing. And from the shadows, Kinkaid saw the man glaring at him in the darkness. He didn't know if the cartel boss would take him up on his offer, but he had nothing to lose.

Outside the Pérez Compound
2:05 A.M.

"What are you waiting for?" Alexa crowded
Garrett's space, grabbing the sleeve of his BDUs to
plead her case. "What if there's no signal? What if
he can't . . . ?"

She didn't have to finish. From the look on Garrett's face, he knew what she was about to say. Jackson Kinkaid could already be dead. And if Pérez
got into that helicopter again, he'd fly off and get
away with murder . . . again. Kinkaid might not
care what happened to him, but Alexa did.

"I'm telling you, Alexa, I have a gut feeling
Kinkaid has got more up his sleeve than us. If we
go in hot, it might get him killed or put my team at
greater risk." Garrett's commonsense advice contradicted the concern on his face.

Alexa knew he was right. Garrett had more to
consider than one man. Being in charge of the mission, he carried a great weight on his shoulders.
And heaped on top of that, his guilt over what had
happened to Jackson's wife and little girl had been
eating at him for years. Now this.

His training and his instincts were at war with
the regret he had over the brutal annihilation of
Kinkaid's family. And from the pained expression on his face, she knew none of this would be

easy. Before this day was over—no matter how it turned out—Garrett would pay a steep price for any mistake he might have made years ago, when he thought he had protected Kinkaid's family and hadn't.

"We got a read off the burst transmitter," Hank emerged from the shadows and huddled next to Garrett. "Our boy's in trouble again. His heart rate is up. Something is happening in there, but at least we know he's still alive."

Alexa breathed a sigh of relief. Even though the whole situation reeked, knowing Kinkaid was alive had taken the pressure off Garrett; but she still had no idea what he would do. Waiting was not Garrett's strong suit either.

"Kinkaid had asked us to stay in the foothills and keep watch." Garrett took another look through his night-vision binoculars. "But if anything happens to him, and Pérez leaves his estate in a hurry, we won't be able to stop him in time, not from here."

"What do you want us to do, boss?" Hank stared at Garrett, with half his face cast in shadows and the other half in moonlight. "My men are ready."

"We move closer. I want us within striking distance."

Garrett gave his order and pointed where he wanted his men positioned. They'd split up, with

Hank and Alexa taking one team and Garrett taking command of the other.

Alexa waited for Hank to leave. When she was alone with Garrett, she took off her camo boonie hat and looked him in the eye.

"You watch your sweet backside. I don't want to lose you twice."

Before he came up with his usual smart-ass macho comeback, she kissed him on the cheek for old time's sake. Feeling the warmth of his skin on her lips opened a floodgate of emotion that she hadn't expected. She'd moved on, and she knew that, but a part of her would always love him.

"I wish you hadn't followed me to Mexico, but now that you're here . . ." His lips curled into a lazy grin. " . . . I'm glad you did. Guess that makes me a selfish bastard."

"One of your better qualities," she said.

Giving her one of his devilish smiles made more seductive under the moon, Garrett left her and vanished into the darkness. This mission could cost her both of the men she loved. And no amount of training and experience would ever make her ready for that.

"Damn," she whispered to no one.

2:20 A.M.

Pérez glared at Kinkaid as he clenched his jaw in silence, leaving Ramon Guerrero dumbfounded at the stupidity of the man he worked for.

"Surely you are not considering this." Miguel Rosas stepped between his boss and Kinkaid, putting a hand on the man's chest. "He's simply goading you into letting him out of those chains. You have the advantage here. Give the order, and I will kill him for you. And I will take my time. He will regret his insults to you."

Still, Pérez didn't speak or take his eyes off the prisoner. Guerrero had a bad feeling this would not end well. The American—Wheeler or Kinkaid or whoever he was—had been tortured and was weak. But Guerrero had learned long ago not to count a man out who had just cause on his side. He slipped behind Rosas and moved closer to Estella, but not so close that it would draw attention. The girl hung from ropes and looked more frightened than ever. He could do nothing for her, not anymore, but he felt less like a bastard if he pretended he cared what happened to her.

"You should listen to him, coward," the American taunted. "You wouldn't want to ruin a good manicure, lard ass."

Guerrero was close enough to see the spark of anger in his boss's eyes. He knew the prisoner had hit the mark. He'd pushed as much as he needed to. Pérez would either order his men to kill the hostage—a long, slow death—or he would remove his restraints and free him to fight one last time. Neither of those options looked as if it scared the prisoner. The man was beyond caring.

Dead was dead.

"Don't do this, boss." Guerrero made his case, not wanting to be one-upped by Rosas. "Leave him to us. We will take care of this dog."

"Us? You brought this man to my door, Ramon. Don't think I will forget that." The cartel boss scowled at him. "But I will handle him myself. Uncuff him."

Guerrero was shocked by the man's order. And so were the other men. No one moved. Each of them looked at the other until Pérez broke the stalemate.

"What's wrong with you? Are you deaf?" he yelled. "I said free this man. And someone give me a knife."

His boss shrugged out of his suit jacket, unbuttoned his collar, and rolled up his sleeves. Miguel Rosas was the only man who moved. He handed his boss a knife and stepped back, glaring at the American, who would remain unarmed. Even in the shadows, Guerrero saw the faint smile on the face of Miguel Rosas. The man didn't care what happened or who died.

Like the sick psychopath he was, Rosas only wanted blood.

2:30 A.M.

Garrett's team was positioned outside the front gates of the Pérez estate. When his men got into place, he found a spot behind a boulder and lay flat on his belly atop a slight rise near the main entrance. He communicated to the rest of his team, and each one checked in. When their voices came over his com unit, it sounded like he was beside them. Hank and Alexa were last to move into position.

"We have two lone wolves, taking high ground. They're mine." Hank's cryptic message meant he had spotted a two-man sniper team in a tower overlooking the main residence. They had clear sight of the perimeter and the grounds.

"Two watchdogs every fifteen, front and back. Clockwork." Alexa had been monitoring the guards walking the grounds. Two-man teams walked their territory front and back of the property every fifteen minutes, without deviation.

"On my mark. In three." Garrett took one final look through his night-vision binoculars before he gave his order to launch their assault on the drug cartel's stronghold. RPG rounds would take out the front gate and cause a diversion for Hank and Alexa to launch their simultaneous assault from the rear.

But something made Garrett stop. He lowered his night-vision gear and listened with eyes closed so he could focus. A distant sound droned in the background. Something familiar made him hesitate. And when he recognized the noise, he had no choice but to call off their assault.

"Stand down. I repeat, stand down."

"What's happening?" Alexa was the first to speak over the com, but Garrett didn't have time to answer. Within minutes, they all heard it, and Garrett was the first to break silence.

"Fall back. I repeat, fall back," he ordered. "And take cover. Now!"

If what he suspected was right, they'd have to find cover fast. From the sound of the turboprop engine and the brief glimpse he got of its sleek distinctive design, an MQ-9 Reaper UAV had targeted the drug cartel stronghold. The unmanned aerial drone had hunter-killer capabilities. With its sophisticated surveillance, it could hunt a specific target. And with its payload, it could definitely kill. It was loaded with up to fourteen Hellfire missiles and GPS-laser-guided bombs. In seconds, the UAV drone would be over the estate and dropping its payload.

"Damn, Kinkaid. That's what you call a signal?" Garrett fell back with the rest of his team, praying that Alexa and Hank had gotten away clean. "You sure know how to send up one helluva flare."

Kinkaid had always been a gutsy operative. Garrett should have trusted him when he said to wait for his signal. If anyone died because he gave the order to attack too soon, that would be on his head, not Kinkaid's.

2:47 A.M.

Estella struggled to see over the men who stood in front of her, despite the pain it took for her to move at all. Flickering torches were the only light in the stone cell. And men's voice echoed loudly as they yelled their encouragement to Pérez. They wanted him to kill the American. She screamed, "No!" and thought no one heard her, but she'd been wrong. In the noise and confusion, it took her a moment to realize that Ramon had come to her. He leaned close enough to speak in her ear.

"If you know what is good for you, you will keep your mouth shut and stay put."

He raised a knife, and she flinched. It had been

the knife he used to cut her, but this time he used it to cut her down. She collapsed in his arms, too weak to stand on her own. Her arms were numb, and every muscle in her body ached. She didn't want to touch him or feel his hands on her again, but she had no choice.

"Can you stand?" he asked. Ramon smelled of sweat and dirt and blood.

She only shook her head. She didn't think he would hear her. Ramon held her for only a moment before he shoved her aside to lean against a wall in the shadows. He raised a finger of warning for her to stay put before he joined the rest of the men.

Where would she go? She had no one to help her and no place safe to run.

Estella dropped to the floor and crawled away from the men, so she could see. She watched Ramon's boss come at the American, Jackson Kinkaid. The man was weak. He could barely stand or even lift his arms, but when Pérez came at him with his knife, the American lunged for the big man. She knew the agony he felt to fight. And her pain was only a fraction of what he had endured.

Both men fell to the floor of the cell, kicking up dirt as they wrestled for the knife. The circle of men moved tighter around Pérez and the American until they blocked her view. Estella couldn't see any more.

She was trapped, and there was nothing for her to do but watch the American die. Tears streamed down her face. She could not blame the brave man for wanting revenge. Pérez had killed his wife and child.

It took Estella a moment to realize that she was already doing the only thing she could. She prayed for both of them.

3:05 A.M.

Kinkaid grappled for the knife Pérez had in his sweaty hand. All Pérez had to do was give in. If he ordered his men to kill him, his fight would be over, but the big man never opened his mouth. He was too stubborn, something Kinkaid had counted on.

But he was no match for the fat man, not in his condition.

Every time Pérez rolled on top of him, he cut off his air. Kinkaid shoved the man aside and used his weight against him. And he kept both hands on the knife. The blade cut into his skin. And with the adrenaline racing through his system, he used his rage to keep fighting. His lungs burned, and every muscle in his body was betraying him. He had nothing left.

"To d-die . . . f-fighting. It is g-good." The drug kingpin felt Kinkaid's hands give way. And when he saw the blood draining down his arm, he knew Kinkaid was losing his fight. One last time, he rolled over him. And the sharp tip of the blade hung over his eye, with Pérez putting his full weight behind the knife.

"G-glad you . . . think so." Kinkaid felt the sting of the blade cut into his cheek. In seconds, his warm blood rolled down his skin and filled his ear.

He was staring up at the last thing he would ever see—the red-faced, sweaty, drug-dealing bastard who had murdered his wife and child. Pérez looked like a madman. His eyes were bulging from his skull, and his jowls were trembling with his exertion. Kinkaid shoved at the man, using his legs to topple him, but that wasn't working. He had no more strength left.

"It w-would be . . . easy." Pérez whispered as he struggled to make one last thrust. "Just let . . . g-go. You will . . . die quick."

The drug-cartel leader's face blurred above him. The tip of his blade hovered over his one good eye. If he let go, Pérez would drive the knife into his brain. The drug trafficker was right. He'd be dead in seconds.

"No, don't. Please!"

Kinkaid heard a faint voice, mixed with the shouts of Pérez's men. The angry shouts echoed in the cell and nearly drowned out the girl's voice, but eventually Kinkaid heard Estella.

"No, please don't kill him." She was the only one who was on his side. And she had the guts to cry out, even in the face of an angry drug-cartel boss and his men.

Her voice gave him the strength he needed to hold on. All he had to do was last a little longer, but when a deafening blast erupted and shook the ground and walls around him, he knew the cavalry had arrived. When the first missile hit, he saw the brilliant flames light up the night sky through the barred window in the cell. And he heard stone walls topple. Dust filled the room, and Pérez's men yelled and ran for cover.

"What's happening? What was that?"

One blast had them scrambling, but the second and third blasts had them running to save their miserable lives, scurrying like vermin into the dark.

Pérez eased up on his grip long enough for Kinkaid to breathe. Air rushed into his burning lungs as Ramon Guerrero and Miguel Rosas emerged from the shadows.

"We are being attacked. If we don't leave now, we will be trapped. We'll die here." Guerrero's voice cracked.

"Give the order, and I will kill this man," Rosas yelled as he pulled his gun.

Kinkaid couldn't let that happen, not now. He heaved against the drug boss one last time, shoving him into his men. In the confusion, he grabbed for the hilt of the blade and twisted it, bending the man's fingers back. The weapon slipped from Pérez's hands before he had a chance to fight for it.

"Kill him. Do it now!"

The drug dealer screamed his order as he crawled away like the coward he was, but he didn't get away fast enough. Kinkaid gripped the knife and thrust it hard into the fat man's leg. Blood spurted from the wound before the cartel boss clutched his leg to staunch the bleeding. When he cried out, Guerrero rushed to him and grappled with the man, lifting his weight off the ground.

"We have to go. Now!"

The night sky lit up with more explosions. And when the sound of automatic gunfire erupted, Rosas aimed his weapon. Kinkaid had nothing to defend himself with except the knife in his hand. On his knees, he grabbed the tip and threw it at Rosas. The blade spun end over end until it struck the armed gunmen's flesh with a meaty sound. It embedded in his chest, hilt deep.

Wide-eyed, Rosas staggered back, his jaw slack, staring down at the knife protruding from the center of his body. The hilt of the blade pulsed, moving in time with his still-beating heart. And as blood blossomed from the fatal wound, it saturated his shirt with a deep crimson. The man dropped to his knees, still aiming the weapon at the prisoner.

Kinkaid held his breath. If Rosas had the strength to pull the trigger, he'd be dead before the bastard took his last breath.

CHAPTER 13

Outside the Pérez Compound
3:20 A.M.

Garrett watched the air assault from a distance as his team fell back to the designated rendezvous point and checked in. One by one, he heard from each of his men but still hadn't seen or heard from Alexa.

Where the hell are you?

Garrett and his team were firing back when the armed men behind the compound walls got off a few rounds, but the attacks were sporadic. The air assault had split the drug cartel's forces, and some of Pérez's foot soldiers were running for cover and scattering into the hills, the ones who had had enough fighting an unmanned drone that could target their positions with precision. In this attack, they weren't after the small fish.

"Whisky Two, reporting in, sir." Hank's voice came over his com unit. "Not that I'm complaining, but who's operating the Reaper?"

"Don't know. One of Kinkaid's men, I'd guess." Garrett couldn't tell Hank who was operating the UAV, but he couldn't help smiling. He had a grin on his face as he watched more missiles hit the Pérez estate.

"If you take fire, return it, but stay put until the UAV is done. Wait for my order."

Even with the Reaper UAV's sophisticated technology, Garrett knew his teams would have a hard time joining the battle. They would have no way to communicate they were "friendlies." And a thermal-scanner surveillance didn't have the capability of distinguishing his team from Pérez's men.

But from the looks of things, apparently Kinkaid had thought about that. So far, the UAV was only blowing the shit out of Pérez's estate and punching holes in his stone walls. The Reaper was paving the way for Garrett's ground teams to clean up. Within minutes, the unmanned drone would let them get to work.

"Martini One, come in." Garrett kept his voice steady. "Do you need assistance, Martini One?"

When Alexa didn't answer, Garrett took a deep breath and focused on the rest of his team.

"Whisky Two, are you getting a transmission

from inside?" Garrett knew it was a long shot, but he had to know. "Is our boy still alive?"

He was breaking protocol by saying too much, but he had to know. If he got confirmation that Kinkaid was still alive, he'd push his men to move in as soon as the last rocket was launched. While he waited for Hank's response, Garrett got out his binoculars and searched the flaming rubble below for any sign of Alexa. Her men had checked in, but she was still missing. And the longer she stayed that way, the more he worried.

"Where are you?"

He had a bad feeling that she hadn't waited for the air assault to be over. If she thought there was a chance she could save Kinkaid from the fate he had planned for himself, she would go in with guns blazing. And she wouldn't risk her team to back her play. She'd go it alone.

"Damn it, Alexa," he cursed.

Garrett had the rest of his team to think about. He couldn't give a command that he knew would put his men at risk. He had no idea why Alexa wasn't answering him, but either option wasn't good. She was either dead or badly injured, or she'd gone in after Kinkaid on her own.

Alexa Marlowe and Jackson Kinkaid were two of a kind.

* * *

With her binoculars, Alexa had seen movement and a flash of light coming from a barred window right before the air assault. From the belowground prison cell, she had heard men shouting until the UAV launched its deadly payload—and she and her men had run for cover.

But in that split second, she had made a decision.

When the missile had blown a hole through a main wall, the initial blast had blinded her. She saw her team retreat, and she should have followed. They motioned to her, and she saw their mouths move, but her hearing was nearly gone. Instinct told her she should have gone with them, but her heart sent a different message. She couldn't leave, not without knowing what had happened to Jackson.

In the noise and confusion, she made a run for it, only she didn't do the smart thing like her men had done. She ran toward the breach in the stone wall that surrounded the Pérez estate. And when a second rocket hit the main house and sent stone and debris flying, she felt rocks pummel her body, and she had no way to protect herself. She went down, and everything went black.

It had taken her precious minutes to recover. She'd lost consciousness. How long she'd been out, Alexa didn't know. By the time she got to her feet, she stumbled deeper into the hacienda, with everything a blur. She'd gotten caught in the fall-out, and shards of rock had cut her face. Smoke from the intense flames billowed black into the night air, making it hard to see and breathe. And it took all her concentration to hold on to her H&K MP-5 assault rifle. Men escaping the burning estate ran into her, but they never looked back.

"What the hell . . . ?"

When she realized where she was and remembered what was happening, she had no choice. The air attack had escalated. She had to look for cover and go farther into the compound. That was when she remembered the prison cell where she had heard the angry men shouting before. Since Kinkaid had a way of riling people, that seemed like a likely place to begin her search.

"Damn it." Disoriented, she raised a hand to her ear and looked down the front of her shirt. "Where is it?"

It took her time to realize she'd lost her com unit back in the rubble where she'd fallen. Alexa knew her decision to search for Kinkaid alone hadn't been her finest hour. She wasn't think-ing straight, but it was only her ass on the line now. Whatever consequences there would be, she would face them alone, and she could accept that. The last thing she wanted was to be responsible for anyone else getting dragged into the risk she was about to take.

"Kinkaid, I swear, you better be alive, so I can kill you myself."

3:32 A.M.

Kinkaid stared into the vacant eyes of Miguel Rosas. The crazed, bloodthirsty lunatic still had a gun pointed at his head.

Outside, the war raged on. Secondary explosions mixed with the staccato sounds of automatic gunfire. And dust and smoke clouded the stone cell. Wide-eyed, Estella stood frozen in place, staring at the man with the gun. Even Guerrero had stopped at the cell door. He had Pérez's arm over his shoulder as he helped the man escape, leaving a trail of the drug dealer's blood on the ground. He was bleeding like the stuck pig he was.

But all eyes were on Miguel Rosas.

And Kinkaid could do nothing except wait for the man to pull the trigger. He was too far away to lunge for the weapon. And he had nothing else to fight with.

"Kill him, Miguel. Do it!" Pérez demanded. "Pull the trigger!"

Rosas blinked. He gripped his weapon tighter

and steadied his aim. That left Kinkaid with nothing left to do but open his mouth.

"You're done, Pérez. This isn't the only place we hit tonight." Kinkaid forced a weak grin. If he was going down, he wanted the drug-cartel boss to know what he'd done. "We wiped you out."

MQ-9 Reaper UAVs had arrived in time to annihilate Pérez and his entire operation. Kinkaid's men had staged more than one attack, at multiple locations. By now, the second drug cartel that Pérez had worked years to rebuild was nothing more than massive holes in the ground.

Kinkaid and his men had been researching the drug dealer's strongholds and supply connections for years. Every key target that could be destroyed without jeopardizing innocent lives had been hit in simultaneous assaults across Mexico.

His taunt had been enough to force Pérez to make his move. The man grabbed for the gun Guerrero had stuffed into the waistband of his pants. He cursed and took aim. When Miguel Rosas saw his boss move, he turned and lowered his weapon as another missile tore through the stone wall near the makeshift cell.

That was the break Kinkaid needed.

As flames billowed through the barred window, and rocks rained down on them, Kinkaid lunged for Rosas and shoved him to the ground. He grabbed for the gun as he rolled behind the man. When Pérez fired his weapon, Kinkaid returned fire. And the only protection he had was Miguel Rosas. He heard the bullets as they riddled the man's body. And when he could, he shot back. He saw the drug boss stagger when he put a hole in his chest, but in the chaos, Kinkaid didn't know what happened.

He felt a punch in his shoulder, but kept shooting. Estella screamed and cringed in a corner, covering her head. When Kinkaid heard her, he got to his knees and shielded her from fire. And Guerrero had used the fat body of his boss to cower behind. Everything happened in slow motion.

Bullets ricocheted off stone, splintering wood and spraying shards of rock into the room. And when another blast shook the foundation, and the roof started to crack and break free, Guerrero had had enough.

"Let's go . . . let's go. Now!" The man urged his boss to move. And when the big man stumbled, Guerrero grabbed him by the collar and pulled him into the corridor, making a run for it. His motivation wasn't difficult to figure. Guerrero had no weapon. Pérez had taken it.

Guerrero had no choice but to get his boss moving, the man who was big enough to use as a human shield. And with the hacienda coming down, if they didn't get out now, the odds were they'd be buried alive where they stood.

"Move it! Now!" Guerrero yelled.

Kinkaid stood and looked for Estella in the haze of black smoke and suffocating dust. When he found her, he knelt beside her.

"Are you okay? Can you move?" When the girl nodded, he said, "We have to get out of here."

But it was too late. The minute Kinkaid had the girl on her feet, heading for the only way out, the roof caved in. He pulled her back and put his body between her and the falling rock. It was all he had time to do.

"Get down. Cover your head." He shielded the girl as best he could. Every stone that hammered his body sent a shock wave of pain through him. And after a brilliant burst of light blinded him, his body went limp. He fought to stay conscious, but lost his battle.

Darkness swallowed him whole.

CHAPTER 14

"The whole place is a house of cards, ready to come down. Heads up, people." Over his com unit, Garrett warned his men as they walked through the fallen stone wall at the entrance to the hacienda. They'd split into three-man teams and spread out, making tougher targets.

"Anyone who finds Martini One, sing out."

When the UAV had stopped firing, Garrett and his men breached the perimeter and went hunting for survivors. Most of Pérez's men had split, running for the foothills. And there had been only the occasional skirmish between his men and those still hiding within the walls of the estate.

The UAV flew wide circles around the vast property. Soon, the drone would have to leave.

Once Mexican authorities detected the battle, they'd have to evade capture. The longer they were there, the greater the chance of them getting caught, but Garrett hadn't found Kinkaid or Alexa yet. No matter how one-sided the attack might have been, any victory would be tainted if Jackson and Alexa had been killed in the assault.

And if he didn't have enough to worry about, what Alexa had told him about Donovan Cross had disturbed him. What was Cross up to? And who was backing him for the number one slot? One man couldn't do it alone. He had no doubt that Cross had help, but how far would Garrett have to go to protect his back? Returning to his old life, as head of the Sentinels, might be dangerous, especially when he had no idea who had supported Cross in his apparent attempt at a takeover. Someone within the Sentinels had made it easy.

"Found something. Over here." The voice of Hank Lewis came over his earbud, a much needed distraction from the conspiracies filling his head. When Garrett looked for Hank, he saw him waving in the glow of the burning hacienda. By the time he got to him, Hank was kneeling near a large pile of rubble, holding something in his hand.

"Found Martini One's com unit." Hank held the gear up toward the light and showed it to Garrett. "She didn't respond because she couldn't."

Finding her com link didn't mean she was alive. Her body could be under the pile of stones at their feet, but since they hadn't secured the compound, Garrett couldn't divert his men into a rescue mission for one agent. As he saw it, he had only one option.

"Put a team on this spot," he told Hank. "Have them trade off. Two men dig through this pile and one stands guard. Call out if they . . . find her."

"Will do, sir."

Garrett didn't want to think that Alexa was dead. She was a force of nature, a strong, intelligent woman who was a borderline adrenaline junkie. She thrived in his world, living on the razor's edge of danger. Imagining her dying before he had taken his last breath was something he couldn't handle. Even though he gave his order to Hank, it pained him to pretend he could conduct business as usual.

Loving her had been the reason he'd let her go. Neither of them had functioned in their jobs the way they should have. When the success of the mission should have been top priority, they each layered on the added complication of caring what happened to the other. They took unnecessary risks to protect one another, real over-the-top stuff like her risking her career and her life to come looking for him in Mexico.

So when Garrett had seen an opportunity to end it, he had let her find him with another woman, someone who didn't matter and could remain discreet. Although it had killed him to hurt Alexa that way, he had seen the writing on the wall and knew it was in her best interest to dump him so she could find a better man.

Quitting Alexa was the hardest thing he had ever done. And he'd failed at it. Now it would take all his concentration to focus on the rest of his mission, when all he wanted to do was find her.

But from the look on Hank's face, the man had more bad news.

"My communications guy just got a call from our handler," Hank interrupted his misery. "He's picking up chatter with the local police. They know we're here, and they're coming out to investigate. We've run out of time, sir."

Garrett stared across the compound. The Sentinels had survived for as long as they had because of their secrecy. He wouldn't break that code.

He knew what he had to do, but he didn't have to like it.

Before the last missile blew apart the main residence, Alexa had zeroed in on the prison cell she had seen from the outside. One corridor, partially belowground, had fit her memory of its location. But after the blast, the destruction had been devastating. Whole sections of the roof had collapsed, and flames lit the night sky. Clouds of dust made it hard to breathe, but she pressed on, aiming her MP-5 into every dark corner. With slow, deliberate steps, she made her way through the debris.

When she heard a moan ahead, and the sound of footsteps echoing down what remained of the stone hallway, she moved faster.

She peered through the dust and smoke and saw movement. The faint silhouette of a man caught her eye. She wanted to yell out, but she had no idea if the man was Kinkaid or the enemy.

The man she had seen hadn't been alone. Another wounded man was with him. With his back to her, the big man hobbled and needed help to walk. When Alexa got close enough to take aim, she shouted.

"Stop, or I'll shoot."

One man looked over his shoulder, the one helping the wounded guy, but neither of them slowed down. And when they disappeared around a corner, she'd lost sight of them.

"Damn it," she cursed under her breath.

But before she could chase them down, something caught her eye. When she crossed the threshold of the only chamber down that corridor—a room that had a massive door splintered by the blast and fallen rock at the entrance that blocked the way in—she saw a light.

A flickering flame burned through the debris. And eclipsing the fire was a barred window that had been cracked from its casing. The metal bars cut the light and were exactly what she had seen from outside. Gut instinct told her this cell was the one she had come to find.

"Kinkaid . . . you in there?" She took a risk and called out his name, but no one answered. While she kept her eye on the corridor where the men had vanished, she leaned closer to peer through the pile of rock.

Nothing moved inside.

"Jackson. Talk to me. Please." She yelled louder this time, but still, she heard nothing.

Alexa stood back from the cell and stared at the cave-in. Something made her stay. She couldn't explain it, but to move the boulders that blocked the door didn't make sense if there were no signs of life inside. She grimaced and shook her head as she held her assault rifle. She had the two men to follow. They were real. They should have been her target, but something kept her rooted where she was.

"Kinkaid. Give me a reason. Please!"

When her plea echoed in the room without a response and nothing else to show for it, Alexa reluctantly made up her mind to leave. She turned, but stopped when she heard it. The sound barely registered with her, and yet she knew she'd heard something.

A choking cough.

"Jackson, is that you? Come on. Answer me."

"Please . . . h-help him. I don't know what to do."

A girl's voice gripped Alexa by the throat. When she heard it, she didn't hesitate. She slung her weapon on her shoulder and dug into the rocks and debris blocking the splintered door.

"Hold on. I'm coming," Alexa cried out as she worked.

Sweat that had beaded on her skin now ran down her arms and back. It stung her eyes, but she kept working. And without gloves, the shards of rock cut her hands, and dust clotted the wounds.

"Is he alive? Please tell me," she begged the girl. And while she shoved at the door that hung off a hinge, she listened for any signs of life inside. When no answer came, Alexa worked harder. A minute later, she heard the weak voice again. The girl answered her, but Alexa didn't like what she heard.

"I don't know. I don't think h-he's breathing. Pl-please hurry. There's blood."

A slow rage burned under Alexa's skin. She hadn't come this close to Kinkaid to let him die. With her hands bleeding and raw, she strained to move the wall of stone that stood between them.

"Hang on, Jackson. Please . . . for once in your life, do as I tell you."

CHAPTER 15

Alexa heaved rocks one by one, trying to open a gap for her to squeeze through the toppled wall. Outside, she still heard the sounds of the skirmish, but things had died down. To avoid the Mexican authorities, Garrett's team on the ground and Kinkaid's UAV would have to clear out soon. She was running out of time, but she had no choice, not now.

The more she worked, the more her hands and shoulders ached.

She heard muffled sounds coming from outside. She tried calling for help, but no one heard her. Being in a collapsed part of the hacienda, Alexa knew it would take time for Garrett and his men to find her. And it would soon be dawn. In the harsh light of day, she didn't want to get stranded and have to explain to the Mexican government why she was there. Getting caught would land her in a Mexican prison, with the Sentinels throwing away the key. They wouldn't officially claim her, and that meant she'd be on her own, but all she could think about was . . .

"Jackson? Are you with me?" she called out.

"He's opening his eyes," the girl told her. "Can you hear me, *señor*?"

Alexa heard the excitement in the girl's voice when she began talking to Kinkaid. And with more of the rock shoved aside, Alexa heard the crunch of shoes on the stone floor. The girl was moving inside the cell. At least she was free and didn't have to be dug out. Alexa prayed that would be the same for Jackson.

"Is he okay?" she asked.

"I think so, but I see blood. I think he's been shot."

Alexa craned her neck to look into the cell. Torches had been tossed to the floor but were still lit. The flames gave off enough light for her to see a small girl kneeling by Kinkaid. Dust covered both of them.

"I'm coming. Hang on."

Alexa shoved at the last boulder that blocked her way. She squeezed through and worked her way back to where they were. The roof looked dangerously fragile. It wasn't safe, but she had to see how bad Kinkaid was before she moved them to a better location.

Jackson was sprawled flat on his back in a corner of the cell, covered in dirt and debris. Alexa had to lift rocks off his legs before she could get close enough. When she stared down at him, she saw his blood-covered shirt and went looking for the damage. He'd been shot in the shoulder, but that was the least of his worries. She'd seen men tortured before, but nothing like this.

She couldn't help but stare at him. He'd been beaten so badly that half his face was swollen, and one eye was nearly shut. His body was bruised with deep contusions, with knife wounds across his chest and stomach. He had to be in incredible pain even though he didn't let it show.

But Jackson was breathing. And that made him beautiful to her.

Alexa stared into his dazed eyes until she knew he recognized her. With trembling fingers, she touched his cheek, careful not to cause him more pain. She never thought she'd see him alive again.

She had walked away from him in Cuba when she saw in his eyes that he had nothing to give her . . . or anyone. He was too much in love with his dead wife and too empty inside from grieving over his only child. And from what she saw in him now, that hadn't changed, but she couldn't help how she felt about him. Loving Kinkaid had been her joy and her curse. And she wasn't sure she would change that, even if she could.

"You're a hard man to kill, Jackson." *Thank, God,* she wanted to add.

"You say that . . . like it's a b-bad thing." When he tried to smile, he winced from his cut lip.

"They tortured him. I heard it . . . and I saw what they did. It was terrible," the young girl said with fresh tears in her eyes. "When the rocks came down, he protected me."

"Don't make me out to be a hero, *chica*. No one who really knows me will believe you."

"He's got a point," Alexa said as she shrugged out of her shirt. "What's your name, little one?"

"Estella Calderone."

"Thanks for helping him, Estella. Now we need to get both of you out of here. Can you walk?"

"Yes." The girl nodded.

This time, she turned to Jackson. "And how about you? You look a little rough, big guy."

"Took one in the shoulder. Is the bullet still in there?"

She helped him rise enough to see his back. Without an exit wound, the bullet was still lodged in him. Someone would have to cut it out. But something else caught her eye.

"What's that old burn scar? When did you get that?" Before he answered, she remembered where she'd seen that burn before. "Actually, that looks like Garrett's scar. You didn't . . ."

By the look on Kinkaid's face, she knew what he'd done. He'd burned his own skin to make it look like a scar Garrett had, in case the drug cartel had heard about it.

"Seemed like a good idea . . . at the time." He shrugged.

"You're insane. Plain *loco*," she said, noticing that Estella was nodding behind his back. "And that bullet is still in there. Garrett brought a medic. He'll have you patched up in no time."

"No way. Pérez just left. He's wounded. I can catch him, but I gotta go now." When Kinkaid struggled to sit up, rocks and debris fell off him. Alexa helped him brush off as she thought about what to say.

"When I saw him, he wasn't alone. By now he could have plenty of help. And you're in no shape to chase after them, not anymore."

"Ramon Guerrero is with him," Estella told her. "He's a dangerous man."

"There, you see? Listen to her." When Jackson tried to stand, Alexa helped him to his feet, but the guy was real shaky. "Look at you. You have a bullet in you. Your face looks like raw hamburger meat. And you're barefoot. How far do you think you'll get like that?"

It took Kinkaid a moment to straighten up. And when he did, he looked her in the eye and ran a finger through her hair and tugged at a strand with a nod, his only acknowledgment of her changed hair color.

"I'll get as far as I need to." He softened his tone. "Now please . . . tell me where he went?"

When she didn't answer right away, he glared at her with his one good eye. No matter what shape Kinkaid was in, he still looked intimidating. His handsome face was battered and bruised, and his broad shoulders and tight abs were covered with bloody cuts and contusions. He'd been tortured for days, and it showed on every inch of his body.

He was barefoot and dressed in a thin pair of pants and an oversized shirt that made him look like a refugee from a prison camp, but the fire in his eyes was still there. Seeing him like that made Alexa a believer.

Jackson Kinkaid wanted revenge. He had come to take down Manolo Quintanilla Pérez and annihilate everything he stood for. Alexa understood that. The drug-cartel leader had brutally taken everything that Kinkaid held dear and loved—his wife and precious child.

From their last hostage-rescue mission in Cuba, Alexa had seen firsthand the pain of Kinkaid's self-imposed exile from the rest of humanity. He hadn't always been that way, but he'd changed after his family had been killed.

He'd alienated everyone who had mattered in his life. Her included. And he'd banished himself to live among drug dealers and the dregs of society as a mercenary for hire, so he could focus on the only thing he had left. She knew he hadn't thought about tomorrow because, for him, there wasn't one. Kinkaid hadn't counted on living beyond this mission, but with so much at stake, Alexa knew.

She wouldn't be the one who stood in his way.

"Come on. I'll show you. But not before I bandage that shoulder."

After Alexa had cut up her shirt to use as a bandage to stop Kinkaid's bleeding and give protection to his bare feet, she led him and Estella down the collapsed corridor that she'd seen Guerrero and his boss escaping. It was dark, and the going was slow. They had to be careful they weren't headed into an ambush. She'd followed a heavy blood trail. The big man Guerrero had helped get away was hurt bad.

But with Kinkaid barely able to walk with-

out her and Estella's help, they weren't in much
better shape. Jackson's bare feet were holding up,
but she knew he was in pain. And as they neared
a busted door that looked like it led to the outside, Alexa took the lead and aimed her assault
rifle.

"Stay behind me," she said, mainly for Estella's
benefit. "And don't move until I say so."

Gripping her MP-5, she found a bloody hand-
print on the doorjamb and knew Guerrero and
Pérez had come that way. She listened through the
door before she opened it, but what she heard had
disturbed her.

Nothing. She heard absolutely nothing, and the
stillness bothered her.

She had expected to hear the UAV making a run
overhead or the sounds of Garret's men outside.
When that didn't happen, she kicked the door
open and squinted into the first rays of sunlight.
Brilliant orange painted the top of the ridge where
they'd pulled surveillance. Alexa slowly stepped
out into the sun and looked around, clearing the
way for Kinkaid and Estella.

Inside the perimeter, fires were still burning,
and black smoke spiraled into the early-morning
sky. The smoke would make them an easy target
for the local cops, who would see the attack site

from a distance. And wherever Alexa looked, she saw no one to help them.

Pérez and his men were gone, but so were Garrett and his people. They were alone.

"Damn."

"Garrett couldn't take the risk. You know that. He had his men to consider." Kinkaid's low, gritty voice gave her comfort. "I'm sorry, Alexa. If you want to beat it, I'll understand. I can stall 'em until you and Estella get out of here."

"Stall who?" she asked.

Kinkaid answered by pointing, and saying, "The Federales. And unless you want to see a remake of Butch and Sundance, you better take me up on my offer."

On the horizon, Alexa saw a cloud of dust on the dirt road heading toward the hacienda. Several vehicles with flashing lights were barreling toward them. She didn't need binoculars to know that the Mexican Federal Police were only minutes away. Their time had run out.

"No way, Kinkaid. No man left behind, remember? Come on. We gotta go. Now."

When Alexa turned, she came face-to-face with Estella. The girl looked scared. And she didn't have to open her mouth. Alexa knew what was on her mind.

"You can't come with us," she told her. "It'll be too dangerous."

"But please, don't leave me here. They will put me in prison."

"You didn't do anything. Just tell them that. I'm sure after they question you, they'll let you go."

The girl grabbed her hand and begged.

"No . . . please. You don't understand. I was Ramon's whore, not by choice, but the police won't care about that. I don't trust them. They will lock me away to punish me."

Kinkaid could barely stand, but he gave her the eye again.

"Don't look at me like that. You know how this is going to play out. She's better off without us."

Alexa had hoped the girl would be questioned and released, like they would have done in the States.

"With the drug wars they've got down here, she could be right," Kinkaid said. "There's too much corruption and not enough good cops to cover the territory. They're overworked and underpaid. She could fall through the cracks, easy."

Kinkaid made good sense. It was possible Estella could pay a price no one would intend her to pay. They couldn't leave her behind and only hope she'd be okay. Without knowing for sure, they couldn't take that chance. The girl needed a break, and they owed her.

"Okay, you can come with us"—Alexa nearly got bowled over by a squealing Estella, who hit her with open arms—"but only until we find a safe place to drop you off. Understood? Did you hear me, Estella?"

The girl grinned and nodded. And without saying another word, she hugged Alexa again. With Estella wrapped around her, Alexa noticed the faint smile on Kinkaid's face, busted lip and all. He knew she wouldn't leave the girl behind.

He'd counted on it.

"I saw that, Kinkaid." She shook her head. "Now make yourself useful. We need a way out of here, *pronto*."

She followed Kinkaid's gaze across the compound as they looked for a way out. Pérez's helicopter was nothing more than a fireball, completely blown apart. If Guerrero had escaped with the drug-cartel leader, they hadn't flown out. The UAV drone had taken care of that. And Pérez wouldn't get far bleeding the way he was. They had to have wheels to get to Guadalajara and the nearest doctor.

"How else would Guerrero make his escape?" she asked Estella. "Do you know where they kept their vehicles?"

"Ramon had a van and another car. Over there." The girl pointed to an outbuilding that looked intact.

By the time Alexa got there, she found more blood and knew they were on the right track in trailing Pérez. She saw the building had been used as a garage, but the vehicles were missing. Without a car, they'd be on foot, with the Mexican police having every advantage.

Their odds of getting away clean sucked.

"Damn it. I can't catch a break. We could sure use some good luck about now."

"Will I do?" A man's voice came from behind them.

Alexa spun and aimed her weapon at the silhouette of a guy bracing an assault rifle on his hip. He wasn't threatening them with his weapon. His body eclipsed the sunrise behind him, making it hard to see his face until he leaned against the open garage door. Alexa hadn't heard him walk up on them, and Kinkaid hadn't either.

She only knew one man who could do that.

"Garrett? I thought you left."

Garrett Wheeler's face lit up with a grin that put the sunrise to shame. Alexa hadn't seen him smile like that for a very long time, but she knew exactly how he felt.

"And miss a good ass kicking? Never," he said

as he walked up to them with his usual swagger. "But I did send the team home."

"In case you haven't taken a head count lately, if there's an ass kicking, it's gonna be ours," she said. "And Kinkaid has a jump on us in that department."

"Everyone's a critic." Jackson gave her a sideways glare that softened into a smile.

Alexa knew they were in plenty of trouble, with more on the way, but she couldn't help it. Having Garrett and Jackson with her, alive and well, made her feel damned lucky. And being on the right side of the dirt was always a good thing.

"Then we better get a head start. I've got a car and a GPS signal to follow." Garrett's expression became more somber as he turned to leave. "Come on. We've got ground to cover."

CHAPTER 16

La Pointe, Wisconsin
Morning

"You want me to do what?" Seth asked. His sleepy voice told her that he was still in bed. "Sorry, I'm not awake yet. Worked late last night."

"Your assignment with Tanya?"

"Yeah."

Jessie was already working on her third cup of motel-room coffee. Dressed in jeans and a T-shirt, she'd been up for hours looking through the local phone directory, trying to locate the witness names she'd remembered from Chief Cook's murder book.

She heard Seth yawn, but he didn't say anything more about what he was working on for his direct-report boss at the Sentinels. And she knew better than to press him for details. They both would have secrets when it came to their mutual employer.

"What's this about my dad's old case file?" he asked.

Jessie knew Seth had kept a copy of his father's biggest case with the Chicago Police Department. Harper's dad, Max, had rescued her and the other kids that Danny Ray Millstone had kidnapped and tortured at his sprawling old Chicago home.

"You still have it, right?"

"Well, yeah. Sure. What's this about, Jessie?"

Seth's father had killed Millstone. He shot the man dead in front of her when the bastard had come to kill her. She was only a kid at the time, but she never forgot what it felt like to be carried out of that hellhole—from the darkness into the light—by a man she always had remembered as a hero. But the price Max had paid, when he became obsessed with the serial pedophile, had been the estrangement of his son, Seth. And that case had cost Max his marriage, too.

"I need to know if there were any boys held at Millstone's house?" She cleared her throat, having a hard time talking about her ordeal again. "And I guess that would include the bodies the police found buried on his property."

Harper had dealt with his rift from his dad by taking Max's casebook and had attempted to make contact with every survivor of Millstone's. Seth had needed to see with his own eyes that his father's obsession had been worth the sacrifice his family had made. At least, that was what Harper had thought when he first started his own fixation. Jessie had a suspicion that he saw things differently now, and that difference had brought him closer to his father, but if anyone knew about the victims of Danny Ray Millstone—then and now—it was Seth Harper.

"Wait a minute, Jess. Take pity on me. I haven't had my coffee yet. You better start from the beginning."

Jessie told him about Chief Cook's misleading her with his lie of omission, that there had been two DNA samples found at the old DeSalvo crime scene. Cook had gotten a hit on her DNA and made contact through the Chicago PD, a call fielded by her friend, Sam Cooper. Once she'd gotten Harper up to speed, she got around to telling him what she'd been thinking and asking her favor.

"So you think Millstone was your . . . father? Oh, Jessie. I'm so sorry you're going through this alone. I can drive and be there in nine hours. Just let me find a place for Floyd."

"No, Seth. Thanks for the offer, but I need you to help me another way. And no one can do this but you."

"I'd do anything for you, Jess. What do you need?"

She heard sympathy and commiseration in his voice. The old Jessie would have heard only pity and resented him for it. She would have sabotaged any relationship they had and dealt with her pain by pushing him away, but it felt good to have someone to talk to about the worst days of her life. Harper was her sounding board, a guy she could trust with her worst suspicions.

"Look into Millstone's list of victims. I need every boy's name—alive or dead—and their ages when they were found. And it would be great to have photos of the boys. Can you do that for me?"

"Yeah, will do. I only remember girls' names, but I could be wrong. And I haven't looked at the names of the dead kids in a while. I was more after the ones still breathing, but there could've been boys on that list. I'll let you know what I find out."

"Thanks. That'll help."

Once she narrowed down the kids' ages, she could show the photo of any boy who matched the description the witnesses in La Pointe had reported. From what she remembered of Cook's interview records, the witnesses were consistent in reporting a boy and a girl. And the descriptions had been similar enough to sound like the same kids had been seen by more than one witness.

"And what have you got Sam looking into?" he asked.

"Sam's checking out the evidence archives, trying to find any record of Millstone's DNA that might have been missed when they digitized the old cases. If we can connect that second DNA sample to Millstone as a direct match, then we can link him to the murder and ID who killed Angela DeSalvo."

"Wait a minute," Harper interrupted. "Didn't Chief Cook tell you he'd looked into the Millstone case? Millstone would've been a likely candidate for the La Pointe murder. Cook would've connected the dots to him if he could. And as a cop, he would've had access to the same information that Sam is looking for. Don't you think he would have noticed if Millstone's DNA matched anything he'd found at the DeSalvo crime scene? I mean, he'd say something to you, right?"

"Yeah, like I'd believe anything coming out of his mouth? He's already lied to me about finding more than one DNA sample at the scene."

"Yeah, but why? That makes no sense."

"I know. The more I look into this, the more questions I have."

"Maybe this'll turn out to be a good thing."

"Oh? Enlighten me."

"Cook found you when that DNA sample scored a hit on you as a missing person. Well, barring any fat-finger data entry, if that second DNA sample didn't come up on the hit parade, I'd prefer to focus on the positive."

"Yeah, what's that?" she said.

"That the DNA is from your brother. And that he's alive and had never been a missing kid. You've got a 95 percent probability match to family, Jessie. And if we can rule out Millstone as daddy dearest, then that could mean you have a brother who might've had a normal life, whatever that is."

Harper was right. Thinking positively gave her a warm feeling when she thought about having a brother, especially one who had a better life. But her cynicism didn't let her enjoy that moment long.

"Even if we don't match that second sample to Millstone's DNA, that doesn't necessarily mean that bastard didn't kill Angela DeSalvo. It just means we'd be back to square one without any evidence for our theory," she said. "And like you say, that DNA could belong to a brother I may never find. This could all turn out to be one big dead end. And I may never know how or why I ended up with Millstone in Chicago after being in Wisconsin."

Pessimism was an acquaintance she'd grown up with. After barely surviving her encounter with Danny Ray Millstone, she'd learned to deal with her peculiar emotional balancing game. On the one hand, she'd been fortunate to have survived him, but she had a hard time reconciling her bad luck in crossing his path in the first place.

"I'll do some digging into the case," Seth said. "You've given me plenty of food for thought. I'll let you know what I come up with . . . after I feed my java addiction, and Floyd gets his breakfast, and not in that order."

"Thanks, Seth." She smiled. "I love you."

"I love you, too, Jessica Beckett. Don't ever forget that."

Outside Guadalajara, Mexico

With Garrett driving a rented SUV, they had taken advantage of the vehicle and gone off road for the first hour. Once they got to a road, they took the long way around Leguna de Chapala and stayed off the main highways until they had ditched the local cops. Garrett kept driving northwest until he saw more traffic, a sign they were nearing Guadalajara.

"They've got to be heading for medical attention if Pérez is still alive," Alexa speculated, when they were twenty miles out. "From what I saw of the blood trail we followed, Kinkaid got his licks in."

"I'll check on that," Garrett said as he locked his gaze on hers in the rearview mirror.

Alexa had sat in the backseat with Kinkaid, taking care of his shoulder. She'd managed to stop the bleeding, and the wound looked shallow. Despite the pain he was in, Kinkaid was nodding off from sheer exhaustion and blood loss. The steady rock of the vehicle and the drone of the engine had lulled him to sleep.

The days of torture had finally caught up to him. When he didn't have to play the tough guy, he'd let his guard down and dared to shut his eyes as long as he was with friends who had his back. Alexa felt tired, too, but she couldn't take her eyes off the road. She was too wired and hyped on adrenaline.

"I think we're clear of the local LEOs," Garrett said into his cell phone after he'd called the handler for the mission. "If you still have that GPS signal, give me the coordinates when they stop. They're probably looking for a doctor."

Kinkaid opened an eye to listen, but that didn't last long. Sleeping was as good as any weapon, and Jackson took advantage of the downtime. Estella was sitting in the front seat next to Garrett.

The girl looked carsick. She probably hadn't eaten either. None of them had.

"Here." Alexa nudged Estella's shoulder with one of the bottles of water she had found stashed in the seat pocket behind Garrett. The girl savored each sip before she tried to give the bottle back.

"No, you keep it. That's yours." She waved her off, whispering in a low voice while Garrett talked on his cell, "And here's an energy bar. Even if you don't feel like it now, eat it."

The girl did as she was told. Garrett's backseat gear was a treasure trove. Alexa forced herself to eat and sipped on another bottle of water that she'd found. And she'd saved some for Kinkaid when he woke up and for Garrett once he got off the phone. They all needed to refuel.

Once they got to Guadalajara, they'd drop off Estella wherever she wanted to go before they would start their hunt for Pérez. They'd have to play it smart. The Mexican police would be on the alert, looking for them. And when they found Guerrero and his boss, they'd have to hit them fast and hard.

With her mind on the fight to come, she was surprised when Kinkaid laid his head on her shoulder to sleep. She held her breath, not wanting to wake him and spoil the moment, but eventually she cupped her hand to his cheek and nuzzled her chin against him. She was about to close her eyes, when something stopped her.

She saw Garrett staring at her from the rear-view mirror. He didn't say anything, and neither of them looked away. It was as if he was telling her it was okay or that he'd moved on, and so should she. And maybe his basic respect for Kinkaid had something to do with it.

Alexa had had a hard time reading Garrett lately, but she didn't look away. That wasn't her style. Of all people, Garrett understood what it meant to live on the edge, not knowing if there would ever be a tomorrow. So Alexa held Kinkaid as he slept, and she shut her eyes, sending Garrett a clear message of her own.

She wasn't ashamed for having feelings for Kinkaid even if Jackson didn't feel the same.

Downtown Chicago
Two hours later

Seth spent time digging through his father's old murder book and case notes, with Floyd's chin on his thigh. His new roommate didn't say much, but his company was appreciated, especially today.

When Seth's father had retired, he'd made copies of the case he would never forget. The pages had yellowed and smelled stale, but there was a familiarity to them that comforted Seth as he looked at his dad's notes and recognized Max's handwriting. It was as if he got a glimpse into how his dad's mind worked. And on more than one occasion, he had imagined Max writing in the margins of the investigative journal.

He thought he'd practically memorized the contents of the files, but each time he looked at them, he saw something new or read his father's notes differently. Jessie wasn't the only one who had mixed feelings about rehashing a past they both would have preferred to forget.

His part of that equation wasn't nearly as bad as what Jessie had been through—and was still going through. But he'd learned long ago that if a wound didn't heal, ignoring it wasn't an answer. Jessie's instincts were solid to deal with the darkness that haunted her, head-on. He admired her strength and courage, respected her tenacity, but he loved her for the vulnerability she had trusted him enough to show.

When he got to the list of Millstone's victims, the missing and the dead, he scanned every name three times. He didn't want to make a mistake. Boys' names didn't stand out. Only a few had first names that could go either way. After he made a note of them, he compared the gender-neutral names to the photos taken of the children who had survived and the ones who hadn't.

"Sick bastard."

Millstone had ruined so many lives. Even beyond the immediate names, Seth knew that being a victim of violence radiated out to affect the families, friends, and the community, which had suffered, too.

By the end of his search, he had trouble confirming the gender of two names—Jamie Littlefield and Cameron Harte. Both kids were dead, and their decomposed bodies had been discovered in shallow graves behind the old Millstone family home. He'd have to dig for photos or autopsy reports to confirm the gender or find any photos of those kids before they had died. But since the rest of Millstone's victims had been little girls, the odds were that the bastard wasn't into boys, too.

"This is good news, isn't it, Jess?" he muttered as he looked over the list one more time.

Seth wanted to give Jessie a lead to follow, but he had mixed feelings about that lead coming from the Millstone case. Would Jessie be better off not finding her brother at all if it meant the kid hadn't been taken by that sick pervert? He had a strong feeling Jessie would agree. Ruling out Millstone had its own merits, even if it didn't give Jessie something more to go on.

But before he pushed too hard on coming up with more from the Millstone files, he decided to talk to Sam Cooper. They both loved Jessie. And he knew Jess had asked them to work different angles of the case.

"Maybe face time wouldn't hurt," he muttered as he pulled out his cell phone.

Seth hit his speed dial for Sam. Flying solo had gotten him nowhere. It was time to join resources and make a better run at helping Jessie. Maybe kicking around ideas—with the only other person who knew Jessie's story better than he did—would make a difference.

Guadalajara, Mexico

Jackson had asked Garrett to drop Estella off at a local church. On the drive over, the girl had argued that the Church would not want her once they knew what she'd done. The girl was obviously embarrassed and had censored what she told Jackson in English, until he spoke to her in Spanish. Whatever Kinkaid said, he must have convinced her to keep an open mind about the Church. Alexa got the sense that he was telling her something private between them, and it must have worked.

When they got to the church, Alexa spoke to a priest and made a donation to care for the girl, at least until she got on her feet. When she headed for the car, Alexa saw Jackson with Estella near the front entrance. She didn't mean to eavesdrop, but their voices carried like an echo through the chapel.

Estella hugged him, crying. "I can't believe I am free of Ramon . . . because of you. God answered my prayers when he sent you to help me."

"Believe me, I'm not anyone's answer to a prayer. And God and me parted ways for good reason, but if it makes you feel better, put in a good word for me." He turned to go, but stopped and looked over his shoulder. "You have a chance to reinvent yourself and start over. Not everyone is capable of that, but you're a survivor, Estella. I think if anyone can do it, you can."

Alexa wasn't sure he was talking about the girl's future anymore, but he'd made starting over sound easy, for her sake.

"Put what Ramon did behind you, if you can," he told her. "He committed an act of violence against you. His sin is not yours."

Fresh tears ran down Estella's face. And when it took her a long, awkward moment to find the courage to speak again, she avoided looking at him.

"But what man will . . . have me now?"

Jackson didn't hesitate. He stepped closer, reached for her chin, and made her look him in the eye when he said, "A damned lucky one."

Kinkaid never said much. He was a man of few words, but Alexa knew he'd said enough to make the girl a believer in second chances. And he darned near convinced her, too.

An hour later

They had followed the GPS signal of Guerrero's cell phone until the signal had stopped in one location. Garrett had parked down the street from the home of a local doctor and was setting up his thermal imager. According to his handler, the home was the personal address of Dr. Carlos Hernandez, a physician who got paid on the side by the drug cartels.

Alexa liked the setup. The doctor's modest ranch-style home was at the end of a long block, with most of the surrounding land belonging to him. The grounds were gated, but no guards stood watch. With the house relatively isolated from any neighboring residence, the situation was perfect for minimal collateral damage. If they executed their plan with precision, they had a good chance of not firing a shot.

"Don't see a car or that van Estella told us about," she said.

"With Pérez wounded, they wouldn't have parked on another street and walked over," Jackson said. "They probably have their vehicle in that garage."

"Yeah, I agree." Garrett looked up from his surveillance gear. Even if he didn't have his high-tech thermal imager, Alexa would still know someone was inside. Drapes near the front door moved with regularity—a dead giveaway that someone was home . . . and downright nervous.

"Curtain moved again." Sitting in the front seat, Alexa had binoculars and got a closer look. "I can't be sure. That could be the guy I saw in the hall, the one who helped Pérez escape."

"Let me see." Kinkaid poked her shoulder from the backseat, where he had changed into BDUs Garrett had given him. She handed him her binoculars, and it didn't take long for Jackson to catch a glimpse of a face at the window. "Yeah, that's Guerrero. Looks like he's waiting for someone. How many are inside?"

Garrett had the thermal imager working in the front seat.

"Two in that front room. And someone is in back," Garrett said, not taking his eyes off the imager's display. "One in the front is stationary and hasn't moved much. He's alive, and that could be Pérez."

The thermal imager picked up on the heat signatures of people in the house, but it didn't give a layout of the rooms except for ghost images of walls that gave off heat. Although the imager gave them good information, without a schematic of the house, they'd be at a disadvantage.

"And I'd bet money the person in the back is a housekeeper or the doc's wife or kid. I can't tell, but that looks like an odd-shaped room, too. No telling where they're at until we get in there." Kinkaid had handed back her binoculars and was looking over Garrett's shoulder at the thermal screen. "Someone had to let them in. Guerrero probably has them locked up until the doc arrives. Where's Hernandez?"

"My guy tells me he works at a local clinic, but he's not there now. The receptionist didn't know where he went. He got a call and headed out. If that's true, he should be here soon."

"Got a car at six o'clock, moving fast." Garrett had his eyes on the rearview mirror. "Get down."

They all ducked and waited for the car to pass before Garrett slowly raised his head.

"If that's the doc, we give him twenty minutes inside before we move in. You gonna hold up your end?" Garrett looked over his shoulder at Kinkaid. When Alexa saw that, she turned and waited for Jackson to answer.

"I've waited years for this, Garrett. And I let those bastards beat the crap out of me to get

Pérez to think he had the upper hand." Kinkaid rummaged through weapons and gear that Garrett had stowed in the back, but he stopped long enough to say, "You're damned straight I'm gonna hold up my end."

Kinkaid looked like a different man than he had a few hours ago. Despite his shoulder wound, he had a new spark in his eyes that almost scared her until he caught her still looking at him. Kinkaid ran a hand through her hair and trailed a finger down her cheek. And he stopped long enough to smile.

"And thanks to both of you, I get the chance to keep a promise I made a long time ago."

Alexa had never known Kinkaid had a wife and child until their recent hostage-rescue mission in Cuba. Hearing about them had shocked her, mostly because he'd been so willing to entrust her with his life on any mission, but he hadn't trusted her enough to share his family. With something so important, Kinkaid didn't have faith in *anyone*, except Garrett, when he had no choice. And considering how *that* had turned out, she could understand how withdrawn he'd become.

The whole point to keeping his personal life secret was to keep his family safe. And when that didn't happen, he had lashed out at Garrett and anyone he thought had been responsible—but no one had taken the heat more than what he'd heaped on himself.

Finally, his vendetta would be over, one way or another. His act of revenge wouldn't bring back his wife and child, and she had no doubt that he knew that. He could kill Pérez a thousand times over and even the score, but that wouldn't fill the void in his life where his beloved wife and child used to be. And living with that cruel reality had to leave him feeling damned empty inside, no matter what happened in the next few minutes.

Her gut instinct told her Kinkaid might think that dying there would be easier than living with the aftermath of what had happened, when he had no one else left to blame.

She prayed she was wrong.

CHAPTER 17

Guadalajara, Mexico
Afternoon

Garrett had tried to assign Kinkaid the back of the house since he was wounded and not in the best of shape, but Jackson refused. He wanted to be first one through the door and nearest Pérez.

With Dr. Hernandez inside, Garrett had monitored his thermal imager to check his movements within the walls of his residence. The person in the back of the house had moved but was still there. Whoever was there was either hiding or had been confined to a room. Either way, no one could be ignored. And after the doctor entered the house, he went straight for the front room. The movements on the imager gave them more intel to plan their strategy.

"You cover the back. When you're in place, we'll make our move," Garrett told her. "With the doctor working on Pérez, Guerrero will be distracted. Since we don't know the layout, picking the lock might buy us time to get in tight and take them by surprise."

"When you get inside, let me know," Alexa said as she put on her com unit. "I'll secure the rear of the house after I hear from you."

"Kinkaid and I will focus on the three in the front. Guerrero is the one to watch. He'll be armed and nervous. If we hit them hard, this could be over fast."

"Guerrero doesn't strike me as someone who'd risk his life for Pérez," Kinkaid said. "If it comes down to him or his boss, I'd bet money he'd give Pérez up once he knows they're not getting out of this. We just have to convince him that he's not important to us. We're not cops. We won't arrest him or turn him over."

"Yeah, good point. Talking him down will be your job," Garrett said. "Anything else?"

Kinkaid and Garrett looked ready to go, but Alexa had something on her mind and she had to bring it up now, for Kinkaid's sake.

"Once we get Pérez, what then?" she asked. She shifted her gaze between the two men, but when neither of them said anything, she pressed. "I

mean, if he doesn't put up a fight, is this an execu-
tion . . . or do we have another plan?"

Given what she did for a living, Alexa found it
more than a little ironic that she'd suddenly become
the voice of reason when it came to morality. The
Sentinels were a covert vigilante organization. Their
operations were about doling out justice without
the red tape of the court system and jurisdictions.
When they went after a target, they had proof of the
crime to justify their actions, and they usually confronted criminal organizations who were clearly in
the wrong, but working for the Sentinels required
her to have an adaptable moral code.

She believed in what they did, or she never
would have joined the group and sacrificed
having a normal life for one mired in secrecy. But
this operation had been Kinkaid's vendetta. And
even though she completely understood Jackson's
motivation, if he murdered Pérez in cold blood,
would that trigger an even deeper slide into deso-
lation for Kinkaid?

She didn't care about a man like Pérez. The
man was a total waste of skin. He was a known
drug dealer and head of a brutal cartel. Assault-
ing his hacienda outside Guadalajara had been
easier because they knew the man had Kinkaid as
a hostage, and they had proof of that. And Pérez's
men had fought back, but here, that might not be

the case. If the cartel boss gave himself up, would they still execute him?

When Kinkaid was the first to speak, she thought she knew what he would say, but she would've been wrong. Jackson surprised her.

"I have to see this through, but I can take it from here if you can't stomach what'll happen in there." Kinkaid gave them a way out if they wanted it.

"And as far as I'm concerned, Garrett, the slate is clean," Jackson said. "You don't owe me anything anymore . . . if you ever did. What happened wasn't your fault. It's taken me years to see that. And killing Pérez won't bring my wife and little girl back, but I have to see this through. I destroyed Pérez's cartel before, and he only rebuilt it. He'll do it again, and I can't let that happen. I can't stomach the thought of that man thriving from all this, but I won't blame either of you if you decide this isn't for you."

"If Pérez gives himself up, what do you see happening?" This time Garrett asked the question. And only Kinkaid could answer it.

It took Jackson a long moment to think about what he would say, but eventually he did. And he did it as he looked Garrett square in the eye.

"I trust you. Both of you. I just want Pérez brought to justice. Whatever happens, you make the call, Garrett. I can live with that."

Kinkaid sounded as if he wanted to play nice. And Alexa hoped he meant it. If he did, there was hope for him yet. He might have a future if he lived through this. But a part of her remembered the ruthlessness in his beautiful fierce eyes that she'd seen in Cuba and how haunted he'd been when he finally told her about his wife and baby girl. Pain like that didn't just fade away. It lasted a lifetime.

People change. And she wanted to believe Jackson had, too, but the paranoid part of her wasn't so sure.

She could also see why Kinkaid would trust Garrett to finish this. Leaving the decision up to him didn't mean Pérez would walk. Garrett was the head of the Sentinels for a reason. He knew how to make the tough calls, and he'd killed plenty in the name of justice, but maybe Kinkaid would say anything to stay on the team and face Pérez one last time to play judge, jury, and executioner.

Without knowing what was in Kinkaid's head, Alexa had to make one last-ditch effort to reach him.

"I hear what you're saying," she told Jackson, looking him in the eye. "And I want to believe you can put this behind you when this is all over, Jackson. But revenge never lives up to its hype. Obsessing over it like you've been doing can make you an addict who never knows when to quit."

When he had a hard time meeting her gaze, she reached for his arm. "Will you know when it's time to let go?"

Jackson never answered her. He stared back with his battered face, a reminder how much he'd already been through, but he never said another word. She tried reading something into his silence but came up empty. It was time to go. And whatever would happen between Kinkaid and Pérez lay ahead of them.

Alexa wasn't sure why Jackson had handed Pérez's fate over to Garrett and had used the word "trust" to do it, but given the expression on her boss's face, he hadn't missed that point either.

Garrett only nodded, and said, "Let's move out."

In the study near the front door, Ramon Guerrero looked out the front curtain one last time as he aimed his weapon at Dr. Hernandez. The neighborhood was quiet this time of day, but Ramon knew the importance of being careful. He'd picked the doctor's library to hide his boss because it had two entrances. One door was off the foyer, and the other led to a vacant guest bedroom in another wing of the house. The study was a pass-through. After the doctor had come into the house, he'd accosted him in the foyer and escorted him to where Pérez was. He'd locked both doors and secured the room.

Now Ramon had his weapon pointed at the doctor's head as he told him what would happen.

"We have your wife locked in a room. If this man lives, you'll see her again. You understand?"

"Yes. Just don't hurt her. I'm here. I'll do what I can." The doctor reached for the leather bag he'd brought with him before Ramon stopped him.

"Hold it."

Guerrero grabbed the bag while he kept his gun on the man. He searched the contents to make sure the doctor didn't have a weapon hidden in his medical supplies. When he didn't find anything suspicious, he threw the leather case onto a coffee table.

"Get to work. He's lost a lot of blood."

"He needs a hospital. I brought a couple of bags of O-negative, but he'll need more."

"Just shut up and do what you can. We'll talk about that later."

His boss had collapsed on a sofa in the doctor's library and was bleeding all over the man's expensive furniture. His chest was heaving, and he had panic in his eyes.

"Ramon, don't let me die. When this is over, I promise you. Anything you want."

Pérez was making promises out of his delirium and fear. Earlier today, the man had accused him of betrayal when he brought the American to his hacienda. Now that his life was in Ramon's hands, the man promised him anything he wanted.

He'd helped Pérez escape his fate once today. A second time might ensure him a higher rank within the cartel. As he saw it, Ramon had nothing to lose by letting the doctor do his job, no matter which way things turned out.

"Get to work. And he'd better live, Doctor, for your wife's sake."

Pérez heaved a sigh and shut his eyes as the doctor hovered over him, checking his condition and preparing to remove the bullet from his chest. Ramon knew the doctor had been right about his boss needing a hospital, but they couldn't afford to take the chance. If the police got word he was wounded, they would arrest him while he was vulnerable.

But while the doctor was filling a syringe with medicine, Ramon thought he heard something.

"Shush." He aimed his weapon at the doctor and whispered, "Don't make a sound."

"What's happening?" Pérez lifted his head and shifted his gaze around the room.

Guerrero handed his boss a weapon and forced the doctor to his feet, putting a gun to his head. He moved toward the door near the foyer, clenching his hostage by his collar.

Was he being paranoid, or had he heard something? Guerrero held his breath and tensed his body as the hair on his neck stood on end. Instinct had sent him a message.

Someone was in the house, and he was no longer in control.

Garrett had used shrubs and hedges in the front of the private residence to get closer to the front door, with Kinkaid close on his heels. Without a nearby neighbor, they had a good shot at not being seen.

Once they got to the front entry, he'd picked the lock in seconds. Before he went inside, he whispered into his com unit to Alexa.

"We're going inside . . . now. When you hear us, make your move."

"Copy that," she said.

Garrett used a hand signal to give the order to Kinkaid to enter the premises of Dr. Hernandez and follow his lead. The front door was the closest point to where the thermal imager had shown activity. And when Garrett found double doors to the right of the foyer, he knew Guerrero and Pérez were only steps away.

He put his back to the nearest wall—with Kinkaid taking the other side—and listened at the door. When he heard nothing, he gave a nod. No words were necessary. Jackson reached a hand across and tested the lock.

When Kinkaid shook his head, Garrett knew the door was locked. This time stealth wouldn't do it. They'd have to break through clean in order to get the drop on Guerrero and his boss. Garrett gripped his assault rifle, the muscles in his body growing taut as he stared at Kinkaid.

In seconds, this would all be over, one way or another.

CHAPTER 18

Guerrero didn't wait for what he knew would come.

"Keep your mouth shut," he whispered into Dr. Hernandez's ear. "And do as I say."

"What's happening?" Pérez kept his voice low. But when he tried to sit up, he couldn't. The man even had trouble holding the gun he'd been given.

If they were about to be attacked, his boss would be of no use to him. Ramon was on his own. He put his arm around the doctor's neck and squeezed, pulling him back. He kept the man's body in front of him as he moved deeper into the room and away from the foyer door.

"Unlock this door," he hissed into the doctor's ear, only loud enough for him to hear, and pointed at the door behind him. When the man did as he was told, Pérez spoke louder.

"Something's going on. What is it? Talk to me."

The bastard was talking too loud now. If someone was outside the study door, Pérez was making it easy for them to locate where they were. Ramon moved back to the center of the room, closer to his boss. His mind reeled with the scenarios racing through his head. And when he saw a dim shadow move under the threshold of the library door, he knew he'd been right.

Someone had come in through the front and was outside the study. In seconds, he would know who they were, but that would be far too late.

Garrett gestured to Kinkaid. On the count of three, he'd kick the door in. Jackson would cover him with his assault rifle and be first through the door, with Garrett close on his heels. They'd done the maneuver countless times, but everything hinged on how clean he hit the door and busted it open. And with the doctor inside, they had to be careful. Opening fire without a clear target might get the man killed.

When Garrett moved into position to kick the door in, he heard gunfire.

One shot. Two.

He lunged for the wall and ducked for cover, talking fast into his earbud to Alexa. "Shots fired. Not us."

"Copy. You okay?"

"Yeah," Garrett whispered. "Secure your target before you assist, is that clear?"

"I copy."

When Garrett was done talking to Alexa, Kinkaid nudged his head toward the door. He'd heard a noise coming from inside, and so had Garrett. He gave him the signal. They'd go on three . . . again.

This time when Garrett kicked the door, it crashed open, and both he and Kinkaid rushed into a library with assault rifles tight at their shoulders. They aimed at the man on the sofa, and another man screamed and held up his hands. He was cowering on the floor near Pérez.

Dr. Hernandez had been gagged. And blood ran down his cheek from his temple. Another door across the room gaped open. It led into a bedroom. Garrett kept his rifle on the doctor and the big man on the sofa while Kinkaid got a look into the bedroom. When he didn't see anything, Jackson shrugged, and said, "Clear."

Garrett stepped closer to Pérez and stared down at the man. The cartel boss had his mouth open, with his dead eyes glazed over. Two bloody holes had dented his skull, and bigger exit wounds spilled brains onto the couch cushions.

Pérez was dead.

When Kinkaid stepped back into the room, he helped Dr. Hernandez with the gag as he stared down at Pérez.

"Please . . . don't shoot me. They have my wife. I only did as I was told . . . so they wouldn't kill her. You have to believe me."

The doctor had stayed on his knees to beg for his life. He had no idea who they were. All he saw were their guns.

"Where's Ramon Guerrero . . . the other man who was here?" Garrett asked.

Before the doctor answered, Alexa came into the room, escorting a frantic woman in a house-dress and apron, who was crying.

"Carlos, thank God you are safe." The woman rushed to her husband's side and fell to her knees, hugging the man who had nearly gotten her killed, all because he wanted to earn extra money working for the cartels.

But Garrett got his answer on where Guerrero had gone when an engine started. And after they heard a loud crash of grinding metal, Kinkaid rushed to the window.

An SUV burst through the garage door and ripped it apart, with Ramon Guerrero at the wheel. It didn't take a genius to figure out that Ramon had given himself an edge—at the expense of his boss, Pérez. And if he was going to run, he didn't want Pérez coming after him for his betrayal. That was why he'd killed the man.

"That's my wife's car. He's stealing my car." The doctor stared at them, like they should care. He actually looked as if he expected them to give pursuit.

"You've got a dead cartel boss on your sofa. A stolen car is the least of your worries, man."

Garrett shook his head and fought a smile as he gave Kinkaid a sideways glance.

"But I had nothing to do with that," the doctor argued. "That man killed him, not me. He shot him in the head twice, in cold blood. You have to believe me."

"Oh, I do. But I don't think you've fully grasped the situation."

"What do you mean?"

"That"—he pointed to the dead man on the couch—"that could've been you and your wife."

The doctor looked stunned as he clung to his sobbing wife, but not half as stunned as when Garrett, Kinkaid, and Alexa turned to go.

"Wait a minute. Are you leaving? The police . . . what do I tell the police?"

"I'm sure you'll think of something. Doing what you do for the cartels, I'm sure you're good at lying to cops," Garrett said as he walked through the foyer on his way out, with Kinkaid and Alexa beside him.

"We've done as much as we can do here," Garrett said.

And as they left out the back of the house, he stopped before they made their exit. He grabbed Kinkaid by his good shoulder.

"It's over, Jackson. Pérez is dead. I know it's not the way you wanted it to end, but there's nothing more for us to do here."

It took Kinkaid a while to respond, but eventually he nodded, and Alexa did the same without saying another word. They had no choice. After Guerrero's gunshots, any neighbors within earshot would have heard the noise and reported it. The police would be coming soon.

Ramon Guerrero hadn't been their target. Like the other men who had dropped their guns and run from the hacienda—not wanting to die for Pérez—Guerrero was no different. They hadn't come for him.

Kinkaid's vendetta was over, and he'd done what he came to Mexico to do. He'd brought down the Pérez cartel, and their actions had cut off the head of the snake. They'd all have to settle for that, but Garrett could tell by the empty look on Kinkaid's face that it hadn't been enough.

From experience, Garrett knew that revenge

didn't always come delivered with a nice tidy bow, just as Alexa had tried to tell him. And no matter how justified, vengeance wouldn't bring the only thing that Kinkaid would've wanted in return—his wife and child back. Their memory would always be tainted by the violence that had ended their lives, and Jackson would have to live with that.

Of all people, he understood Kinkaid's pain and his sacrifice. And Garrett knew the burden of guilt. He had more than his share of ghosts who would haunt him until the day he died. He only hoped that Kinkaid would eventually find peace and learn how to live with an ache that would never go away.

Jackson Kinkaid deserved better.

La Pointe, Wisconsin

Jessie had spent the rest of the morning into the late afternoon locating the few people who had actually reported seeing kids at the DeSalvo place during the week of Angela's murder. And after she'd exhausted those leads, she hit the ones she'd found in the newspaper archives—the colorful rumormongers of the town.

While Chief Cook and Sophia Tanner had been reluctant to talk about the old murder case, the people she'd tracked down were just the opposite. They all wanted to rehash it again, and they even embellished their original stories, probably fueled by the rumors they'd helped spread after things had died down. It was human nature. Everybody wanted their fifteen minutes of fame. And it had been in her best interests to keep them talking.

The few who had officially reported seeing the children to the police were consistent in their descriptions of a dark-haired little girl and a sandy-haired younger boy, while other townspeople ranted about DeSalvo running something illegal at her place. None of what they'd said ended up in Chief Cook's evidence box, and she could see why. It didn't take someone living in La Pointe to realize some folks loved having an audience. And a newcomer to town was gullible enough to listen to whatever they had to say without calling them on their bull.

So what had turned out to be a promising start to her day had ended in frustration by late afternoon. With food to go from Lotta's Lakeside Café on Main Street, near the ferry dock, she unlocked her motel-room door, and after she tossed stuff onto the table, she collapsed on her bed to stare at the ceiling.

She'd hit a dead end, but she still had Sophia Tanner in her sights. And the bastard who had tailed her the other day had gotten better. Earlier, she'd felt him but never actually seen him. If she was going to catch him in the act, she had to get cagey.

But just as she was figuring out how to do that, she got a call on her cell. She got up and grabbed her phone off the table and answered on the third ring.

"Hey there, Harper. What's going on? Great timing, by the way." She ran a hand through her dark hair and paced the room.

"Hey, Jessie. I've got you on speaker because I'm here with Sam," Seth said. "Say hi, Sam."

"Hey, Jess."

"Sam has something you need to hear," he said.

"Shoot, Sammie."

Jessie chewed a hangnail on her thumb. She was so wired, waiting to hear what they had to say, that she stared down at the carpet as she paced, unable to look in any of the mirrors. She was afraid what she might see in her eyes.

"Millstone isn't your father, Jessie. You hear me? I got my lab guys to confirm that. We had to search through evidence, but we found what we needed to make sure. It just never got digitized for the database, but that's fixed now."

Sam's voice got muddled in her head. After her friend had said that the son of a bitch who had tortured her wasn't her father, tears filled her eyes, and she had a hard time breathing. She sank onto her mattress when her legs felt wobbly.

"Oh, my God. Just give me a minute." She sucked air into her lungs like a drowning woman. And when she could finally speak, she said, "Thank you, guys. Not knowing has been killing me. That's good news."

"Yeah, it is. Ruling that bastard out means the odds of your having a brother are pretty good, Jessie." Seth came onto the line and told her what he'd found out. "You'd asked me to look for names and pictures of any boys Millstone might have abducted or killed. Well, I didn't find any. There were names like Cameron and Jamie that I had to chase down, but those were girls."

"Guess that's another good thing," Jessie said. "It means that my brother didn't end up with that scumbag."

"Yeah. I thought that was good news, too, but after I went over my dad's file for the third time, it got me thinking that the copy I had was something Dad had made when he left the force. Whatever I had wasn't what Sam would have if anything got updated after Max retired."

"Oh, my God. I never thought of that, Seth. I just figured after Millstone was killed, the case was done."

"And that would've been possible if the case had been a single homicide, Jessie." This time, it was Sam's voice that broke in. "But with the Millstone case being high-profile, other investigators contributed to the evidence after Seth's father quit the force. And, of course, the news media chased down leads on who Millstone was."

"So the two of you decided to compare notes and look through the updated evidence Sam had? Is that what I'm hearing?"

"Yeah," they said in unison.

"Gosh, I love you guys." Jessie couldn't help it. Even with all the runaround she'd gotten in La Pointe, it was nice to know she had real friends watching her back. "So talk to me. What'd you find out? I'm assuming you didn't call just to say hello."

When she only heard silence on the phone, Jessie couldn't sit anymore. She got off the mattress and paced the floor again. If they were both stalling, she figured it was for good reason.

"Spill it, guys. You're making me nervous."

"Someone had done a more thorough background check on Millstone after he'd been killed. I got this from other detectives who were around back then, working the case. They told me that folks came forward after the news broke. A lot of the calls were phony leads CPD had to chase. It took time to wade through it all, but in the evidence downtown at headquarters, we found a reference to Millstone that we thought you should know. You ready to hear it?"

Jessie didn't answer at first. She took in a deep breath and felt a wave of nausea. She had blocked out so much of that time period from her mind. As a kid, all she wanted to do was be left alone. And for her own sake, the foster-care folks had purposefully kept her isolated from the headline news during that time.

And after she'd gotten older, she had deliberately avoided anything having to do with Millstone, as if it had never happened. She still felt that way, but now she had to know how all this connected to any link she might still have to family.

"Go ahead. I'm ready. Tell me what you found out."

An hour later

After the lengthy call from Sam and Harper, Jessie had a hard time controlling her anger. She tossed her dinner without eating it. And her mind wrestled with the idea of what her next move should be, but all she had on her mind was confronting Chief Cook once and for all.

How much of what Sam and Seth had told her did Cook already know? And why had he made contact with her, only to stonewall her once she got to La Pointe? She knew he'd deliberately lied about there being two DNA samples tested by his state crime lab. Sam had discovered that. Had he also lied about the Tanner interview? She still had missing pieces to the puzzle, but she had one last shot at finding out the truth.

Jessie grabbed her rental-car keys, checked her Colt Python, and put it back in the holster she carried at her waist under her windbreaker. By the time she got outside, the sun had just drifted below the horizon. It would be dark soon.

When she pulled out of the motel parking lot, she might've missed the headlights coming on as she turned toward the police station, but with her hinky radar switched to hyperdrive, she hadn't missed those headlights at all. She'd picked up a tail again. Someone had been following her since she got to the island, and that old hinky vibe had jump-started a whole new surge of adrenaline. With all that was going on, she'd had enough.

As she drove the speed limit, careful not to spook the sneaky bastard, she made a call on her cell.

"This is Jessie Beckett," she said as she looked in her rearview mirror. It was too dark to see a face, but a man was driving the truck that followed her.

"Where are you, Chief Cook?"

"None of your business. You still in town, Ms. Beckett?"

"I thought you'd know that . . . since this is your town, Tobias." Before he found a new way to insult her, she didn't give him a chance. "I have a pretty good idea who killed Angela DeSalvo. And if you have any curiosity at all, you'll meet me in thirty minutes."

She eyed the mirror one more time as she made a turn, with the truck still with her and not far behind.

"Where?"

When she told him, the chief schooled her in how to cuss, but he didn't say no.

"I'll be there in thirty. And you better be on the level, or I'm locking you up and throwing away the key."

With a smile on her face, Jessie ended the call without saying anything more. And when she shifted her gaze to the rearview mirror, the truck was still with her.

If she was going to meet the chief in thirty minutes, she had to move quick.

Thirty minutes later

Right on time, Chief Cook pulled his squad car into Sophia Tanner's driveway. Jessie had parked on the road, not wanting to frighten the woman. Living alone on the island couldn't be easy for a woman. When the chief saw Jessie, he shut his patrol-car door and walked over to where she stood.

"Thought you'd be inside, scaring that poor woman. Are you blowing smoke . . . or do you really know who killed Angela DeSalvo?"

"I have a pretty good idea, but before we go inside, I've got a question for you."

The chief didn't bother to give her the go-ahead. He crossed his arms and cocked his head, waiting for the bullshit to flow, like he was expecting it to. And Jessie sure hoped she wouldn't disappoint him.

She stepped back toward her sedan, twirling her car keys on her finger. "Why did you have someone following me ever since I got to the island? What was *that* about?"

"Following you? What are you talking about?"

When Jessie popped her trunk, she and Chief Cook stared down at a man, tied up hands and feet in Flexicuffs with a gag in his mouth. He was bawling like a baby and was red-faced as a beet. And he didn't have a stitch of clothes on, except for some seriously neon red plaid boxers.

"Now you see, I would've figured this guy for briefs. He one of yours?"

"Jesus, Tyrell, what the hell are you doin' in

there?" Chief Cook glared at the man once his initial shock wore off.

"Yeah, that's his name. Tyrell Hinman. You see? I knew you could help me with this." Jessie fished the man's ID out of her windbreaker pocket. "He's one of your deputies, isn't he? I saw him the day I was at your station. He got me coffee, the sneaky, arrogant, son of a bitch."

"Is that so, Tyrell? Were you following her?" Cook leaned into the trunk and asked the man directly. When the guy only shrugged and had a hard time staring him in the eye, the chief turned to her. "I swear, Jessie. I have no idea why Tyrell would do such a thing, but I'm getting to the bottom of this, so help me God."

Jessie wanted to believe him, but there was still so much more he needed to explain.

"Until you find out what's going on, Tobias, I think I'd leave God out of this."

Once Jessie had gotten a good look at who'd been following her, she recognized him. But the night she'd chased him on foot, he was in civilian clothes, and she hadn't seen his face. Nothing fit until she saw him tonight, after she'd pulled a fast one on him.

She'd run a red light and left Tyrell pinned between two cars. And after she turned a corner and flipped off her headlights, she played cat and

mouse with him in the dark. It didn't take much
for her to lose him and flip the tables, tailing *him*
for a change. After he gave up, he pulled into a
parking lot to use his cell phone. That was when
she walked up to his car and showed him the
business end of her Colt Python.

When she aimed the muzzle square between
his eyes, she had one question.

"What are you . . . a boxers or briefs kind of guy?"

Now she had Chief Cook's full attention, even
with one of his deputies half-naked in the trunk
of her car, all bug-eyed and whining.

"Like I said, I have a pretty good idea who
killed Angela, but you and me gotta talk before
we go inside. I figure if I give you what you want,
maybe you'll give me what I need."

After the chief nodded, she asked, "What do we
do with him?"

Chief Cook grimaced and looked down at his
deputy, saying, "Tyrell? You're an idiot."

He slammed the trunk closed, with Tyrell yelling and pounding his fists as they talked.

"Why did you lie about there being two DNA
samples? Mine wasn't the only one."

The chief's face was dimly lit from Sophia Tanner's porch light, but even in the dark, she saw
that she'd surprised him.

"And that other sample had a 95 percent prob-

ability of matching mine. Do you have any idea
how scared I was that the sample belonged to
Danny Ray Millstone? After all he did to me, the
idea that he could have been my father tore me up.
And you kept your mouth shut even after you admitted checking into the Millstone investigation.
Why did you lie about all that?"

"Look . . . you don't understand."

"Apparently, I don't. Explain it to me."

Tyrell had been banging on the trunk until they
started talking. When he got quiet, Jessie knew he
was listening, too. *The jerk!*

"I *did* look into the Millstone case. And when I
made the connection to you, I wanted . . ." Cook
stalled and avoided her eyes.

"Wanted what, Tobias?"

"I wanted to be sure before I said anything. I
knew that wasn't something you'd want to hear.
And speculating about something like that would
give you some sleepless nights. I didn't want that
for you, but I guess that happened anyway." Cook
heaved a sigh. "I reran that unidentified sample
through CODIS and NCIC again, but came up dry.
That's when I went back to the source. The Chicago PD had the case files, so I put in a request to
search for Millstone's DNA the day you got here.
I haven't heard back yet, but wait a minute." Cook
narrowed his eyes. "You used the word 'scared,'

as in past tense. You said you were scared that DNA belonged to Millstone. Do you know something about that DNA I don't?"

"Well, yeah. When I had the same hunch you did, I had Detective Cooper pull the records and check Millstone's DNA, compare it to mine. I found out about that today."

"Guess I don't have your clout with the Chicago PD. I'm still waiting for word." Cook shook his head. "I knew that detective was a friend of yours."

"Okay, I pushed to get that done. And I may have some influence with CPD, but why did you lie about that interview being missing from your murder book? What were you covering up? And why are you protecting that woman in there?"

Jessie pointed toward the Tanner house. With their voices carrying in the night, she saw Sophia Tanner at her window, peeking through the drapes. And when Chief Cook saw her, too, he raised his hands and tried to calm Jessie down.

"Keep your voice down. Please." He shook his head and glanced back at the Tanner house. "I don't know how that interview got misplaced, I swear. I didn't lie when I said I'd seen it. And I wouldn't have marked it on my case map unless we had that interview in hand."

"You'll forgive me if I don't believe you. You

don't exactly have the best track record when it comes to telling me the truth."

"Guess I can understand why you'd think that, but what I've told you is the honest-to-God truth," he said. "And if that unidentified DNA wasn't a match to Millstone, then you've got a brother to find."

"Yeah, I guess I do, but where do I start looking?"

"Let's see if Sophia can help us with that. Maybe all she needs is the right motivation."

When Cook turned toward the house, Jessie stopped him. "Aren't you forgetting something?"

She nudged her head toward the trunk of her car and dangled her keys in front of him. Without a word to her, he grabbed them and liberated Tyrell Hinman. He pulled his half-naked deputy from the trunk and cut him loose with a pocket-knife.

"Get in my squad car and stay there until we're done with Sophia."

"Yes, sir." Tyrell had his head down and didn't look up at either of them. He headed for the passenger seat in the front.

"Oh, hell no. You're ridin' in the back. That's where criminals go, Tyrell."

Jessie couldn't help it. A smile tugged at her lips when she got a glimpse of Tyrell tiptoeing toward the chief's patrol car in his bare feet, but Tobias didn't see any humor in it. He walked with her in silence to the front door of Sophia Tanner's place.

She had a pretty good notion that Chief Cook would finally be honest with her. And if he did that, she might clue him in on who killed Angela DeSalvo.

CHAPTER 19

"What's this about, Tobias? It's kinda late. Can we do this tomorrow at a more civilized hour? I'm having my dinner."

Sophia Tanner stood in her front door, blocking the way into her home. And she was hurling every reason she could think of to avoid what was coming. Tomorrow morning might be more civil, Jessie thought, but nothing about this case would even remotely resemble civilized.

"Sorry, Sophia. This can't wait. May we come in?" Chief Cook didn't wait for her answer but took a step into her home, and she backed away.

"But I . . . I'd really rather not . . ."

When Cook didn't take no for an answer, Jessie was close on his heels and stood by him in the living room as the police chief took charge.

"Do you know any reason why Tyrell Hinman was following Ms. Beckett?"

"Tyrell? I don't know. Why would he? And why are you asking me?" The woman's face looked all pious and indignant, but she had a nervous twitch to her eyes that contradicted everything out of her mouth.

"I'm just gonna say this, so we can cut to the chase." Cook pointed Sophia Tanner to a chair, and said, "You better sit."

"Tobias, you're scaring me. What's this about?" Her voice cracked, and she fanned her face like she was about to faint.

"I asked you this before, but now I've got to know the truth."

"Are you insinuating that I . . ."

"Stop this, Sophia." Cook raised his voice and glared at her. When her eyes grew wide, Jessie knew the chief had her attention. "Just so you know, Tyrell has told me everything. But I told him I wanted to hear your side of it before I pressed charges against the two of you."

Jessie had to admit that Cook had a real folksy way of interrogating that reminded her of old *Columbo* reruns. He laid on a liberal dose of small-town cop and mixed it with street smarts that came from years of experience. He pretended that he knew more than he did to get her to open up. And from what she saw on Sophia Tanner's face, his tactic was working.

"Charges? What charges?" Mrs. Tanner slumped back in her chair and heaved a sigh. "Please don't arrest Tyrell. He only did what I asked him to do."

"I'm listening," Cook said.

"I only wanted to know what she was up to, that's all." Mrs. Tanner finally turned her attention on Jessie. "You're not an investigator helping with an old case. You've got a personal stake in this, don't you?" Mrs. Tanner raised her chin in defiance. "I asked Tyrell to do me a favor. He really didn't do any harm."

"But how did you know I was coming to La Pointe?" Before the woman answered, Jessie cocked her head. "Maybe I should rephrase that. The fact that I was coming here wasn't the important thing. You knew *why* I was coming, didn't you? Tyrell told you about the DNA report from the crime lab. That's what triggered all this, but why was I such a threat to you?"

Jessie had made a leap in logic about the DNA analysis, but it made sense. And when Sophia Tanner didn't correct her, she knew she'd guessed right about how she'd found out about the lab results. But the woman was hiding something more than getting a deputy and former coworker to do her a favor.

"Threat? You're no threat to me. I was just curious, that's all," the woman protested, but Jessie had a hard time believing her. And so did Chief Cook.

"Tyrell tampered with evidence when he took that interview of yours," the chief said, making a leap of his own that surprised Jessie. "I'd seen that original report years ago, but it's gone now. Why did you have him take it from evidence, Sophia?"

"Tyrell had nothing to do with that. I'd taken it years ago, when I worked at the station. I don't want him charged for something I did."

"But why? I mean, you gave that interview. Why hide it now? What was in it that you were so afraid of?" Jessie had to ask the question, but after thinking about Sophia's part in all this, she played a hunch. "You saw the kids at the DeSalvo place. You saw me, didn't you? You were the closest neighbor. What did you see, Mrs. Tanner?"

"My interview didn't have anything in it. I only said what everyone else did. With me living so close, I figured that's what folks would expect. And not saying anything about the children would've raised suspicion."

"I don't believe you. You're hiding something." Jessie had to work hard at keeping her voice calm and steady. All she really wanted to do was yell.

When the woman couldn't look her in the eye and kept her mouth shut, Jessie took a deep breath and tried talking to her another way. She knelt at the woman's feet and touched her hand.

"I had my childhood taken from me . . . by a man who tortured and abused helpless little girls." Jessie's voice cracked. "That man took me from my family, a family I've never known. And all I have left is proof that I have a brother. And I think you know something about what happened to us. Why won't you help me?"

Sophia Tanner put a trembling hand to her lips. And tears rolled down her cheeks.

"I want to help. Believe me, I do. But I just can't."

"You're protecting someone. Why?" Jessie pressed her for more. "You know something about what happened to Angela, don't you?"

"No"—the woman shook her head—"not really."

She'd pushed Sophia Tanner as far as she would go. Jessie saw it in her eyes. The woman was protecting someone very important to her. And no matter what happened because of her meddling, she didn't look as if she'd say anything more unless she was given no choice.

Chief Cook must have realized that, too.

"I know what you're hiding, Sophia." His expression softened, and so did his voice. "You may as well tell us what you know. All I need is a court order, compelling you to provide me a DNA sample. Is that how you want him to find out?"

Sophia Tanner's eyes watered as she gasped. She crossed her arms and rocked where she sat, muttering things Jessie didn't understand.

"Him? Can someone clue me in?" Jessie asked.

Cook didn't answer her. He stared at Sophia, waiting for her to break the strained silence. It didn't take long for that to happen.

"You were right about Tyrell telling me about that DNA. He was just passing the time, thought I'd be interested since I used to be Angela's neighbor. But when he told me, I lost it. I just knew someone would put two and two together. And I couldn't let that happen. I told him what . . . what I did. He was only trying to help me . . . protect someone. It wasn't his fault."

Sophia grasped Jessie's hand and squeezed it. "I'm just so tired. This has been such a burden. I was only trying to . . . do the right thing."

"I can see that, but please . . ." Jessie begged. "I have to know what happened."

"You have to promise me that you'll listen to everything I have to say. Please."

"I promise."

Jessie could've backed off and sat on the sofa, but she didn't want to sever the tie she had to the only woman who might know anything about her brother. She was so close to knowing something real that she felt a mounting ache in her belly when Mrs. Tanner opened her mouth to speak again.

"Angela had always been a little standoffish. Like I'd said before, we were never close. I'd talk to her, but she hardly ever offered anything personal back. It was like she was hiding from something . . . or someone," Mrs. Tanner began. "But one day, a man showed up. I saw him from my bedroom window. He had two children with him. And when he showed, Angela argued with him. They yelled so loud that I almost heard what they said, but they were too far away."

Jessie could have accused her of not reporting vital evidence, but instead of pointing the finger, she focused on the one thing she thought Mrs. Tanner would respond to.

"I bet those kids were scared, seeing them argue like that." Jessie tightened her grip on the woman's hand. "Was I scared, Mrs. Tanner? Was my little brother scared, too?"

"Yes, you were, at first. But when Angela let him into her house, I figured it was a lovers' quarrel, and everything had blown over. She took you kids in, and everything seemed all right."

"But it wasn't all right, was it?"

"No, it wasn't. And I was afraid for you kids. I began to watch that house. Angela's visitor scared me. He never acted like any father I ever saw. He ignored the little boy, but he never let you out of his sight. I thought that was strange."

Jessie shut her eyes, blocking out the images that were flooding her mind, dark memories of Millstone. She had to strain to hear Mrs. Tanner go on.

"Then one day that man's car was gone. I watched and waited to see Angela, but when I saw that precious boy wandering in the field between our two houses without Angela or that man around, I rushed to get him." When she shook her head and dropped her chin, a tear made a glistening trail down her face. "His little pajamas were covered in blood . . . so much blood. And he was hysterical, crying real hard. I knew something terrible had happened."

"Did you call the police?" Jessie turned to Chief Cook. "I thought a yardman had found her and called it in."

Before the chief could speak, Mrs. Tanner broke in.

"I grabbed that boy and held him in my arms until he calmed down. All I could think about was you. I had to know you were all right." She clenched her jaw and took a deep breath before she went on. "But by the time I got to Angela's property, the police were already there, and it looked real bad. I don't know why I did it, but I clung to that little boy. We hid in the bushes, with me rocking him to sleep in my arms. I hid and watched what the police were doing. I swear, I figured you were all right . . . that they had you, but when I read about the murder in the papers, they never mentioned finding a little girl."

"The police were right there. You could've told them what you saw." Although questions flooded Jessie's head, one weighed heavier on her mind. "What happened to the boy?"

It took Mrs. Tanner a long time to answer. She sobbed and looked at Chief Cook, who looked miserable with sympathy for her. Cook knew something about what she was about to say. That was why he'd bluffed her into talking.

"That boy is grown up now. His name is Ethan and he lives in Alaska. He's got a good job, and he's happy." Sophia Tanner's eyes watered again. "I never told him what happened. I just couldn't."

"Why? He had a right to know."

"That boy had a right to a normal life." The woman raised her voice and glared with a newfound fire in her eyes.

When Jessie glanced at Chief Cook with a puzzled look on her face, he obliged her with an answer.

"Ethan Tanner. He's her son," he said.

Jessie collapsed back on her haunches and

pulled her hand from Sophia Tanner's. And without thinking, she stood and looked at every photo the woman had displayed in her living room—seeing her brother's face for the first time.

In one, he had a white communion suit on. In another, he had cap and gown. Every photo told the story of his life as he grew up. He looked happy, and healthy, and whole. Jessie grabbed the most recent photo and held it in her hands. Her tears splashed onto the glass as she memorized his face and traced a finger down his cheek. He did look happy, and normal, and he was everything a little brother should be in a perfect world.

She clutched the framed photo to her chest and shut her eyes, feeling the sting of tears. If Sophia Tanner had gone to the police right away, Jessie might not have become one of Millstone's victims. The police could've followed his trail sooner, but that would have meant Ethan would have grown up in the foster-care system like she had. And he would've suffered through years of therapy like she did, trying to erase the nightmare of witnessing a brutal murder. Sophia Tanner had done the wrong thing, but Ethan looked happy and normal—and loved.

Deep regrets found a dark corner in Jessie's

heart and made the tears come faster, but she had a hard time blaming someone who had raised her brother as if he were her own.

"I'm so sorry, honey. I wish I could have found you, too." Mrs. Tanner's voice broke through Jessie's profound sense of grief.

"I couldn't have children of my own. My husband had left me for someone who could. I felt like such a failure as a woman, but that day I had a little boy in my arms. A beautiful little boy. And it felt so good to hold him and smell his hair and feel his warm skin as he slept. I couldn't give him up. I just couldn't."

"I knew Ethan wasn't your son, Sophia," Chief Cook said. "But you told everyone that a sister you had out of state had died and left him with you. Guess that was a lie."

"I made up a story about having to leave town quickly. One of my sisters had been in a car accident. I told everyone that I stayed to get her affairs in order. So when I came back with Ethan, no one questioned that. And when I adopted him, no one questioned that either."

Jessie kept her back to the woman, holding on to the photo of Ethan as Mrs. Tanner told the rest of her story. When the woman was done, Jessie turned to face her.

"I'd like his address."

This time Sophia stood and shook her head.

"No. That's not a good idea. I don't want him to know who you are."

"What?" Jessie wiped the tears off her face, glaring at the woman who had stolen her family. "He's my brother. I have a right to see him."

"You have to understand. It took years for his nightmares to stop. He'd cry himself to sleep and didn't know why, but he was so little, I figured he'd forget. And eventually he did."

"Trust me, he didn't forget," Jessie argued. "You can't forget something like that. When I went into that house, I knew I'd been there before because I remembered. Flashes hit me, and I knew I'd been there. You don't forget."

"But don't you see, you wouldn't have known that if you hadn't stepped foot into that house again. All that nasty business can become so . . . fresh, like an open sore that won't heal. I'm asking you . . . no, I'm begging you. Forget you ever had a brother. I've been a good mother to him. I'm all the family he needs. He needs to forget more than he needs a sister like . . . you."

Her words hung between them like a toxic cloud. By Sophia Tanner's admission and a 95 percent DNA match, Jessie had a brother. She had finally found her family, but if she showed up on his doorstep, she could ruin his life. That was what it came down to.

Making any attempt to see Ethan Tanner would be a purely self-serving act. Sophia was right. Ethan didn't need to find out he'd witnessed a murder and dredge up the nightmares she knew were only lying beneath the surface.

And he sure didn't need a sister as messed up as she was.

Jessie left Sophia Tanner's house feeling lower and in more emotional turmoil than when she'd walked in. And Chief Cook kept quiet, sensing her frustration. The only concession Mrs. Tanner made was letting Jessie keep the photo of Ethan. She carried it in her hands, held tight to her chest.

"If you want to talk to that boy, you let me know. He's a grown man, old enough to make up his mind if he wants to see his own sister. Just say the word."

Jessie hadn't thought of Ethan's being old enough, but Mrs. Tanner had made a good point. If Jessie cared what happened to her brother, making the decision to see him would take a lot more thought—and a damned good reason.

"Thanks, Tobias. I really appreciate your offer. And what you did in there, I'm grateful for that, too." She sighed and stared up at the night sky. "But if I need to track down my brother, I can do that on my own. That's what I do for a living, remember?"

"You promised to let me know who killed Angela, but I have a pretty good idea."

"Yeah, thought you would." Jessie forced a smile and turned toward him when she got to her car. "When Sophia talked about a man coming to see Angela, I figured you'd do the math. My friend Sam Cooper told me that she dug through the case. And in the updated records, they'd found that Millstone had a sister. And her first name was Angela."

"Well, I'll be."

"They found that out sometime after the case went national, but it never made headline news. Danny Ray stole every bit of limelight the media had. His atrocities were more important than any convoluted family tree with no follow-up interviews when she couldn't be found. Angela had run from her family, but she didn't get away, apparently."

"But if you weren't related to him, how did you and your brother wind up in his car?"

"Sam has a lead on something that happened in Detroit a few days before Angela was murdered, but I don't have my hopes up. She said that when a vagrant woman was arrested for drug possession, she made a claim that someone took her kids. CPD thought she was blowing smoke to distract from her possession charge, but she described the kids. And what she said matched our descriptions, but nothing ever came of it. She never pressed charges, which says it all."

"And since I never got a missing-persons hit on Ethan's DNA through NCIC, I doubt you'll find anything now," Cook said. "But you don't remember anything about where you came from? I can see Ethan not remembering, but you were older."

"No. The only way I survived Millstone was to zone out. It took me years to remember things. And I get flashes from time to time, nightmares mostly."

"I hate to say this, but maybe Ethan can recall something you can't."

"Yeah, maybe. But I can't see using him to find my answers. If there's a chance I could trigger a lifetime of bad memories for him, that would kill me."

"I'm sorry, Jessie. Wish things had turned out better for you, but I appreciate your help on my case. And at least now you know you *have* a brother. That's got to count in the win column."

"Yeah, it does." She nodded and filled her lungs with cool night air. "You're a good man, Tobias, but I've gotta tell ya. I'd never play poker with you." She forced a smile. "See you around."

Jessie got in her car, knowing Chief Cook was right. Finding out she now had a brother living in Alaska counted for a lot. She had ties to the Alaska State Troopers, through retired trooper, Joe Tanu. If she wanted to locate her brother, she could call Joe and find Ethan in a New York minute, but would that be the right thing to do?

Nothing in Jessie's life had *ever* been easy. Easy was for sissies.

Next day

The drive back from Wisconsin would have dragged on forever except that she filled her thoughts with the images of Ethan growing up. She pictured herself at his graduation and imagined whole scenarios in her head where she played the part of his big sister, giving him advice that he'd roll his eyes at.

Filling her mind with those kinds of memories were better than the ones she had—the gaps, the nightmares, and the flashes of new horrors that she knew were coming from Angela DeSalvo's house. Angela had been the only memory she had of a mother, but after she'd learned the truth, those memories would be tainted. The woman had tried to take care of them, but she never got the chance. And Jessie had to remind herself that Angela hadn't done the one thing she should have.

She should have called the police.

By the time Jessie got to Chicago and pulled into the underground parking of Seth's building, she couldn't wait to see Harper. She found her heart racing, just thinking about him. And when she got out of her rental car, she didn't even take her bag. She left it in the car and ran to Seth.

When he answered the door, with Floyd grinning at his feet, she flung herself into his arms and breathed him in.

"Ah, Jessie, I missed you, too. I'm glad you're home." He nuzzled her neck, and she felt his sweet breath on her skin. In his arms, she felt warm and safe—and loved.

"Home." She said the word, getting used to it. "Yeah, I'm home."

When Seth said the word "home," it sounded damned good coming from his lips. It gave her the courage to say what she'd come to tell him.

"I'm moving back to Chicago. And if the offer is still good, I want to make a home . . . with you. I love you, Seth."

He grinned and wrapped her in his arms. "Yeah, the offer's good. Are you kidding? I love you, too, Jess."

Jessie hadn't grasped before how much it meant for her to have a family, but on her drive down to Chicago, she realized she already had one.

"You're all the family I need, Harper."

Flashes of her brother's face melded into the many memories she'd already built with Harper, with more to come. And for the first time in a long while, Jessie was truly happy.

CHAPTER 20

Garrett had taken his time getting back to New York. He had justified the time by thinking he needed to clear his head, but in truth, he wasn't sure how to do that. Getting over a woman like Alexa Marlowe wasn't intended to be easy.

Riding in the back of a cab, he watched the blur of neon pass his window and barely paid attention to the streets as they went by. Seeing her as a brunette had surprised him. And she'd been fearless going in for Kinkaid, risking her life to save his. Garrett still hadn't gotten used to wrapping up a mission and having her walk out of his life until the next time. Coming back to New York wasn't the same, especially knowing she had taken a few days off to help Kinkaid heal.

The taxi pulled to the curb at the private entrance to his building. With a travel bag over his shoulder, Garrett paid the driver and headed inside. Before he got out his keycard to unlock the door, two men stopped him on the street as the cab pulled away.

"Donovan Cross wants to see you." The man nudged his head toward the curb as a black sedan pulled up. "Now."

One man stood in front of him, the other was at his back. And a third man emerged from the shadows to join them. From what he could tell, all of the men had weapons. And he knew the look. They were ex-military or covert ops. Cross had sent an invitation he wouldn't be able to refuse.

"Lead the way, gentlemen."

Before he got into the vehicle, they searched him for weapons and confiscated a Beretta that he carried in a holster under his suit jacket and the .380 Walther PPK/S that he had strapped to his ankle. Cross's men were quick and efficient. After they'd tossed his bag in the trunk, they opened the back door of the sedan and got in both sides, leaving him in the middle.

Garrett had let his guard down. Alexa had warned him about Cross. He knew something was off, yet he did nothing about it. He thought he'd have time once he got back to home turf, but that wasn't going to happen. For Cross to get this aggressive, he had to have a lot of confidence someone was backing his play. Whatever Donovan Cross was up to, Garrett was about to find out—and no one would have his back.

Forty minutes later

Garrett sat on a wooden chair under a harsh light. He hadn't been blindfolded, and his hands hadn't been tied. He was merely . . . waiting. He sat center stage in an empty warehouse that must have been near the docks. He smelled the faint odor of fuel that mixed with a heady stench coming off the East River.

The men who had taken him stood in the shadows beyond the light, making it hard for him to see them. Only the echo of their footsteps gave them away. And being good operatives, they hadn't talked to him.

"I thought you said Cross would be here," he called out.

When no one answered him, he squinted into the dark, looking for any means of escape, but before he found one, a door creaked open. He saw the shadow of a man in an overcoat eclipse a security light near a side entrance. And he heard the low murmurs of two men talking before one of them walked toward him. When the man came into the light, Garrett recognized him.

"Donovan Cross. I hear you've got ambitions and a touch of job envy," he said.

When he tried to stand, Cross shook his head, and said, "Please . . . sit down." And to the rest of his men, he yelled an order. "Give us privacy, gentlemen. I can take it from here."

Without a word, the three men left them alone in the warehouse. The move for privacy really stumped Garrett. He had no idea what Donovan Cross was up to.

"Why all the secrecy? A little melodramatic, even for you. What do you want, Cross?"

"I don't want anything from you, but I can't speak for everyone. You've made enemies, Garrett. And unfortunately, I'm the messenger."

"Ever hear of e-mail?"

Cross smiled. "You can't walk away from this, I'm afraid."

He looked at his watch and held it up to the light.

"It's almost time." Cross looked at Garrett. "For the record, I didn't want it to come to this, but I don't see any other way. I'm sorry."

Minutes later

Donovan Cross walked out of the warehouse just in time. The blast nearly knocked him off his feet. He'd cut it close. A fireball mushroomed into the night sky, and a series of explosions rumbled through the old warehouse, grinding metal and toppling steel as it went.

Garrett Wheeler hadn't been ready for his exit, but for the sake of the Sentinels, Cross had no other choice. While the building burned and sirens of emergency crews coming to the scene blared in the distance, Cross made a phone call.

"It's done. You see it?"

He knew the man was watching from a safe distance, a bird's-eye view.

"Yes, I do. And after you take over Wheeler's job permanently, you can thank me later."

The man ended the call, leaving Cross to watch the aftermath of what he had done. Now it was his turn to make his own enemies. And he had no doubt that Alexa Marlowe would top that list.

Somewhere in the Caribbean

Instead of going back to New York after Mexico, Alexa traveled with Jackson to the place

he called home. Years ago, he'd bought a small
private island in the Caribbean, using the money
he had stolen from the cartels over the years.
Most of his cash had wound up in the hands of
charities, like the missionary school in Haiti run
by his good friend, Sister Kate, the woman he'd
rescued in Cuba. Kate hadn't known about his
Robin Hood gig either. And as far as Alexa knew,
the nun *still* didn't.

Drug cartels made for dangerous victims, but
they never reported Kinkaid's outlandish and resourceful thefts because he was too good to get
caught. And Kinkaid definitely knew how to keep
a secret.

That's what he'd been doing before she hooked
up with him in Cuba. Back then, Alexa had
thought he was only a mercenary who sold his
services to the highest bidder, and he'd never told
her the truth until he'd brought her to his home
and shared his life with her for the first time.

Maybe Kinkaid's coming clean meant he cared
what she thought of him. She hoped she was right
about that.

Jackson lived modestly. He had a dock with
a boat to get around. And his home was a small
place on the beach. He had all the basic ameni-
ties, but he didn't live in a lavish style, considering
what he did for a living. But as simple and beauti-

ful as his home was, Kinkaid had secret storage under his floorboards and in walls where he kept his stash of weapons, money, fake IDs, and anything else he'd need to disappear in a hurry.

Some things never changed.

"We should change your dressing and check out your shoulder. How does it feel?" she asked. When he gestured for her to sit next to him in the sand, she did.

"I'm good." He nodded. "It feels better."

Kinkaid had been sitting alone on the beach in cutoff jeans, staring out toward the ocean. His long dark hair looked finger combed by the warm sea breeze. And even though his face was still bruised, the sun had colored his skin to a rich brown, masking the torture he had endured in Mexico. When Jackson had gotten up that morning, he had gone off alone without saying a word. After Alexa had awakened to an empty bed, she'd gone searching for him, to find out why.

"You're awfully quiet this morning," she said. Forcing a faint smile, she braced for the worst. "You want to talk about anything?"

When he didn't answer right away, she replayed every moment she'd spent with him, alone on his island. The days they'd spent together, while he healed, had been quiet, peaceful ones, filled with the sounds of lapping waves, exotic birds flitting from branch to branch in the lush green canopy overhead, and moonlit walks on the beach.

The first time they'd made love, it had been filled with urgent need that they both shared. Flashes of that memory would always be with her. And she remembered crying when it was over. The rush of emotion had overwhelmed her. Her being together with him, finally and completely, had been the culmination of years of her intense, one-sided attraction.

And last night they had made love on a blanket under the stars. Even though a bottle of chilled white wine had played a part in their loss of inhibition, the moon shining down on their bare skin had been magic. Jackson had undressed her. And his strong hands and warm mouth had stirred a passion she'd never felt before.

She never felt closer to him than she had last night, and she'd been certain that he felt the same, until this morning, after she'd awakened alone.

"There's something I want you to do with me," he told her. "You may not want to. And I'll understand if you can't . . ."

Before he finished, she let him off the hook and stroked his windswept hair. He'd become her addiction, and she couldn't resist touching him.

"What is it?" she asked.

He swallowed hard as he stared at the ocean,

but eventually he turned toward her, giving her his full attention with his intense green eyes.

"I have the ashes of my wife and child here on the island with me. I've kept them here. And I haven't been able to let them go." When his words caught in his throat, and his eyes filled with tears, he reached for her hands and held them in his. "But I think with you here, I can do that now. Will you . . . help me?"

Alexa had no words. She pulled him into her arms with tears of her own rolling down her cheeks. She knew how hard it would be for him to finally let go. And since she'd never been the type who wore rose-colored glasses, she also knew Jackson Kinkaid was far from whole.

But he'd asked her to help him deal with his grief. And that had to count for something.

Alexa woke up the next morning, listening to the sounds of Kinkaid's heart beating in the quiet. It was a sound she could get used to. Feeling his warm bare skin next to hers was addictive.

She ran a finger through the curly hairs of his chest. And when she saw his strong hands lying across his stomach, she remembered how gentle they had been when he spread the ashes of his wife and child in the ocean at dusk last night. The ebb and flow of the salt water at their bare feet had reflected the brilliant orange of the sunset. That memory would stay with her forever. He said his good-byes, as he spoke aloud to them, making her a part of his ceremony. And when it was over, she felt as if she'd lost her family, too.

They didn't make love last night. Without saying a word, they held each other and listened to the waves edging the shore until it lulled them both to sleep.

By morning, she could have stayed in bed forever, but when her cell phone rang, she felt compelled to answer it. Being with Kinkaid felt like she'd dropped off the planet. That was a good thing. She'd never felt so relaxed, but when her phone rang, she had to answer it.

"Hello."

"Alexa, it's me."

She recognized Jessie's voice. She wasn't used to having a partner as aloof as Jessie was. So for her to call out of the blue, it took Alexa by surprise.

"You still on your trip?" Alexa kept her voice low as she left the bedroom, trying not to wake Jackson. She slipped into a light robe and went outside to walk the beach.

"No, I'm heading back now. Harper says hello."

Alexa grinned. "I knew he had something to do with your great escape. You get things taken care of? Is everything okay?"

With a strange silence on the phone, Alexa waited for Jessie to answer.

"Yeah, I guess. But I've got something to tell you."

"Oh?"

"I made a decision, and it feels right."

"What did you decide, Jess?"

Alexa braced herself. She had no idea what Jessie would say.

"I decided to move back to Chicago. Seth asked me to move in with him, and I'm gonna do it."

"That's . . . great, I think. You still gonna be my partner?"

"Yeah, sure. Of course." Jessie cleared her throat. "Who's gonna watch your ass if it's not me?"

"Good point." Alexa grinned. "Well, I'm happy for you."

"What do you think Garrett will say? Both of you recruited me. And I think he wanted me to like New York more than I did. What can I say? I'm a Midwest girl."

Alexa hated to think about Jessie moving back to Chicago just as they were becoming closer as partners, but she heard the joy in her voice and knew she was doing the right thing.

"You leave Garrett to me. I got you into this. And I'm glad you're still my partner. When will you get back to New York?"

"Tomorrow. I'll call you. We've got catching up to do."

"Uh, I won't be there. I took a personal trip of my own, but I'll see you soon, okay?"

"Yeah, sure." Before Jessie ended the call, she said, "Hey, Alexa? I just wanted you to know that I'm happy you recruited me. Working a real job for Garrett and having Seth in my life, I feel like I've turned a corner, you know?"

Alexa knew about turning corners. "Yeah, I do. And I'm glad you're happy, Jessie. See you soon."

As she walked along the shore, Alexa turned toward Jackson's house, feeling the ocean breeze on her face. Hearing Jessie sounding so happy had been contagious. When her phone rang again, so soon after her partner's call, she had a grin on her face when she answered.

"What did you forget now, partner?"

She heard a soft sniffle on the phone, and a woman came on the line, "Honey, is that you, Alexa?"

She recognized the voice of Tanya Spencer.

"Yeah, Tanya, it's me. What's up?"

"I've got some bad news, baby girl. And this time, it's for real." From the sounds of it, Tanya was crying. And it took a lot to make that woman break down. "You've got to come home, honey. I can't do this without you."

"Talk to me, Tanya. Tell me what happened."

New York City
Upper East Side
The next night

Garrett's memorial service was in three days, but Alexa had come back early to help Tanya with the arrangements. Because of the severity of the explosion, his body had never been found. They'd only found enough DNA to make ID, but that was all they had.

Alexa thought about the lie Donovan Cross had once told her about Garrett being dead. Had Donovan Cross been predicting an outcome he would have something to do with, or had his lie been a coincidental guess? In the covert world she lived in, coincidences were always suspicious. And that left her raging against the man who had taken Garrett's job—and most probably, his life.

Jackson had come back to New York with her. He was sleeping in her bed, still weak from his ordeal. But when she couldn't sleep, she got up and slipped on a robe before she crept into her living room to pour a shot of single-malt scotch. Sitting in the dark, she drank and lost count of how many she'd had as she stared out her window to the park across the street.

She couldn't get her head wrapped around Garrett being dead. His smile, his face, his eyes were still fresh in her memory. How could his death be real? And yet this time she felt it was.

When her glass was empty, she went to refill it, but a shadow under her threshold caught her eye. And when she heard a soft swish and saw something slide under her front door, she went for her gun.

Armed, she kept the light off and reached for the door handle. Before she opened it, she listened for any sounds coming from the hallway. When she didn't hear anything, she flung open the door and aimed her weapon.

No one was in the hall, but someone had definitely been there.

She stepped back inside to find an envelope on her floor. After she flipped the dead bolt, she picked up the note, using her robe to hold it, not wanting to contaminate any evidence if it came to that. She dropped the note on her kitchen counter and used the end of a pencil to open it.

When she recognized the handwriting, she gasped and stared at the message, having trouble breathing. When she finally collapsed onto her sofa, she held the note in trembling fingers, careful to preserve the paper as much as she could.

From what she saw, the message was from Garrett.

Alexa—

I couldn't leave without telling you what happened. I'm alive,
Alexa. I didn't die in that blast,
no matter what proof they come up
with.

I don't know what role Cross
played in this but know that he had
a choice. He could've killed me, the
way he was probably ordered to do.
But if you say anything about getting this letter from me, or that
I'm still alive, they will hunt me
down and go after Cross, too.

There's still a lot I don't understand. And I don't fully appreciate what Cross did, but maybe
that will come in time. Thanks to
Donovan Cross, I have a chance to
make a new life for myself if I
want it.

Don't make the same mistake Jackson did, by clinging to the past.
Make a future that's worth holding
on to. You always deserved better
than I could ever give you.

```
   Know that I will always love you,
Alexa. Always.

   Garrett
```

When she'd finished reading, she felt the cool trail of tears on her cheeks. She hadn't realized she'd been crying. Garrett was alive? How was that possible? Her emotions ran the gamut from intense anger to relief that he might be all right— "might" being the operative word. She had no way to be sure.

It was comforting to believe Garrett had actually written the message, but she didn't trust Donovan Cross. The personal script in Garrett's handwriting, and delivered to her door in cryptic fashion, had been a nice touch. The words sounded like him, especially the personal part about Kinkaid, but she had no way of knowing for sure. Paranoia was a hazard of the job.

And not knowing the truth, one way or the other, hurt just as much as thinking he was dead.

Given the covert life she had made with the Sentinels—recruited by Garrett Wheeler himself— the truth was hard to recognize, even when it came in the form of a handwritten note from a man she would never forget.

Sentinels' Headquarters
Next morning

Alexa held her head high as she walked down the corridor to Garrett's . . . to Donovan Cross's office. She braced for the flood of emotion she knew she'd feel. Imagining someone else behind Garrett's desk would be a shock, especially now that she'd have to accept that Garrett was really gone from her life.

She'd wanted to believe that he hadn't died in that dock explosion. And the pain of her grief had been tempered by the hope that the message from him had been real, but she didn't want to play the part of a fool—*Donovan Cross's fool*.

If Garrett had a second chance at a normal life—knowing that returning to his covert world would be dangerous for him and the people he loved—would he take it? If he was alive, would he want his old life back, the one that had been stolen from him? Garrett had always been a fighter. She couldn't see him severing ties to a life he'd worked hard to build, not willingly.

The way she saw it, Donovan Cross and the men behind him had orchestrated a clever coup to eliminate Garrett. And the coup de grâce to put her out of her misery over his sudden departure had been that message. Maybe they thought it would shut her up and quell any curiosity she would have over what had happened to Garrett.

Alexa knew she had a choice to walk away and give up the life or stay put and keep an eye on Cross. With her partner Jessie so happy, the decision she'd made to stick hadn't been difficult. Someone had to watch Jessie's back, especially with the double-dealing Donovan Cross at the helm. If Alexa believed what was in Garrett's note, Cross might have saved his life, but the man was also working for the faction within the Sentinels that had ordered a hit on him.

How could she trust someone who played both ends to his advantage without a semblance of guilt or bad conscience?

She barged into his office to see Cross was on the phone, dressed in a sharp pin-striped navy suit with red power tie, looking impressively dapper. When he saw her, he ended the call in a hurry.

From the look on his face, Donovan Cross had been waiting for her.

"Ah, Marlowe. It's good to see you. How was Mexico?" The man didn't smile. He wanted her to know that nothing had escaped him. "Please . . . sit."

"Aren't you going to tell me how sorry you are about Garrett?" Alexa ignored his invitation to make herself comfortable. She'd never feel comfortable with this man.

"Yes, of course. That goes without saying," Cross said. A corner of his lip curved into a faint show of smugness. "Sorry for your loss."

"I'm having a serious déjà vu moment, hearing you say that. If this whole spy game thing falls through, you could always make a living as a gypsy, telling fortunes." She crossed her arms and glared at him. "Your ability is uncanny. When you first told me about Garrett dying, had that been a prediction . . . or a promise?"

"Neither, but I doubt you'll believe me."

"Now you're a mind reader. Truly amazing." She raised her chin and locked her gaze on the man behind the desk, Garrett's desk. "If I find out you had anything to do with what happened to him, there won't be a place you can hide."

Alexa didn't wait for his clever comeback. She wouldn't give him the satisfaction. She'd delivered the message she'd come to say. And she'd had her fill of smug.

"Are you quitting, Marlowe?" he asked, calling after her. "Because if you are, that would be a pity. I was really hoping we could work together."

"Quitting? Not hardly." She glared at him over her shoulder as she left. "Over your dead body. And I mean that."

Walking out of Cross's office, Alexa had a sly smile on her face. The word "quit" wasn't in her vocabulary—not today. She had no idea what Cross's agenda was, but she had every intention of finding out.

She'd do it for Garrett.